Closer to Fine

Closer to Fine

A Novel

Jodi S. Rosenfeld

SHE WRITES PRESS

Published 2021
Printed in the United States of America
Print ISBN: 978-1-64742-059-8
E-ISBN: 978-1-64742-060-4
Library of Congress Control Number: 2020921434

For information, address:
She Writes Press
1569 Solano Ave #546
Berkeley, CA 94707

She Writes Press is a division of SparkPoint Studio, LLC.

Closer To Fine
Words and Music by Emily Saliers and Amy Ray
Copyright © 1989 GODHAP MUSIC
All Rights Controlled and Administered by SONGS OF UNIVERSAL, INC.
All Rights Reserved   Used by Permission
Reprinted by Permission of Hal Leonard LCC

Seasons Of Love
from RENT
Words and Music by Jonathan Larson
Copyright © 1989 FINSTER & LUCY MUSIC LTD. CO.
All Rights Controlled and Administered by UNIVERSAL MUSIC CORP.
All Rights Reserved   Used by Permission
Reprinted by Permission of Hal Leonard LCC

For my grandfather,
Lazarus Ribak z"l
אליעזר בן יצחק ז״ל
1912–2006

There's more than one answer to these questions,
pointing me in a crooked line.
The less I seek my source for some definitive,
The closer I am to fine.

—Indigo Girls

2019

"I want you to close your eyes and think of someone you love."

The fourteen graduate students in my Art of Clinical Psychotherapy seminar gently close their eyes like a class of practiced meditators. I wait several seconds, letting them conjure up the face of a close friend or family member.

"Now open your eyes. Is this person you thought of alive right now?" I ask this with a certain innocent indifference, almost a shrug of my shoulders.

They all nod, looking around the long rectangle table at one another.

"Yeah."

"Sure."

Their eyes meet mine with a hint of collective confusion. The question always throws people, just slightly.

"How do you know?" I ask.

They are quick to the defense. One young woman, slouched low with tightly crossed arms over an oversized wool cardigan, says without raising her hand, "I thought of my sister. I just texted with her before this class started."

"Okay," I say. "But do you know with 100-percent certainty that she is alive *now*?"

Two students on the left side of the seminar table are nodding and glancing at each other as if to say they know where I am going with this.

The woman with the sister continues. "So you're asking if it's possible that something tragic could have suddenly happened to her in the half-hour since we've spoken?"

"I am," I say, holding her gaze.

"Fine," she continues. "No. I don't know with *certainty* that she is alive."

1

A well-dressed male student speaks up from across the long table, sitting where a husband would sit at the opposite head of a large family meal. "Professor Levine, I hear what you're challenging us to think about, but I'd like to think that I can base my answer on statistical probability. It is highly unlikely that anything has happened to my son since I last checked in with my wife about him, so I feel pretty confident in saying that he is alive right now."

A palpable wave of relief washes over the room as they say silent prayers of gratitude to statistics.

"So you're suggesting," I say to the man with the living son, "that *probability* helps you mitigate the anxiety you might otherwise feel about the well-being of your loved one?"

"Sure. I mean, the world is unpredictable . . . but we need a way of dealing with that without it overwhelming us. So, yes, I think we use probability all the time to keep us from being overcome with worry. We probably couldn't function if we allowed ourselves to really acknowledge all the risk, the uncertainty, that's all around us. When my son was born last year, my wife and I found ourselves wanting to stand at the side of his crib all night long just to make sure he was still breathing."

"And did you?"

"Did we stand at his crib all night? Well, no, of course not. We needed to get a little sleep."

"So, in order to keep living, yourselves—to function, as you put it—you needed to accept the uncertainty about whether or not your baby would keep breathing. Is that right?"

"Yeah, I suppose so." Then he adds with a hint of jest, "Or perhaps we just live in denial that anything bad could happen to *us*."

The others let out a sound—part exhalation, part laugh. It is the sound of comic relief.

"It's true," I say, smiling myself as I let go of the worried thought I've planted in my own head that *my* loves—my children, my spouse—might simply be gone. "The majority of us function in this uncertain world because we hold on to some amount of healthy denial. We ignore what we stand to lose in a moment's notice. But this kind of coping doesn't work for everyone. In your careers as psychologists, you are going to encounter client after client for whom denial simply doesn't work. They will come to you anxious, sometimes frozen with panic. Your job will be to help them learn to live in a world of uncertainties. How will you do that?"

After what feels like minutes, one young woman raises her hand. "Maybe I'd try to help the client look at the likelihood of something going wrong, like we were just saying. I'd try to help them see that, yes, anything can happen, but that chances are very good that everything will be fine."

A middle-aged woman across the table from her jumps in. "Yes, but for really anxious people, I don't think probability helps. They're always the ones who say, 'Sure but I'll be the one in a million who *does* get struck by lightning this year.'"

"That's right," I say. "Reassurance about the odds *does* calm some people's anxiety, but for those of us who are genetically loaded to be worriers, who come into this world with an acute awareness of all that we don't control, probability does not offer much solace. So what are we left with to offer our clients?"

My oldest student, a retired financial planner starting a late-life second career, lifts his head from his binder of notes. "Acceptance?" he asks.

"Acceptance," I repeat, nodding. "But before we can ask our clients to really accept the uncertainties of their lives, what must we do?"

This time no one is looking at me.

"Write this down," I say. "It is a prerequisite to your becoming therapists. We cannot ask our clients to accept the uncertainty of *their* lives until we've accepted the uncertainty of *ours*."

As I start my minivan in the parking lot after class, there is a light rap on my window. It's the student with the sister.

"Professor Levine," she says, holding up her cell phone, the screen catching the sunlight. "I texted my sister as soon as class was over. I had to make sure she was okay—I couldn't stand the anxiety."

I grin, somewhat sadly, hoping she has a good therapist herself.

"Honestly," she continues, "I'm feeling a little triggered by the whole exercise. I mean, just how long does it take to do this work of acceptance? I can't imagine ever really being done with it."

Now I smile for real. "I think perhaps it is our life's work." I glance at the clock on my dashboard. "I'm sorry, I have to run. Let's pick up this conversation next class?"

As I put the van into reverse, I glimpse myself in the rearview mirror. My dark curls are shot through with silver, my beaded earrings dangle almost to my shoulders. I think of my graduate school days in Boston and how we used to laugh about how all our professors had that psychologist look—"quasi-ethnic" we called it. I look down at my long skirt and flowy blouse, bemused. I have been a psychologist for two decades, and I have learned to dress and speak the part. But this work of accepting the uncertainties of my life?

Practice, practice, practice.

1995

Chapter 1

I know Zayde is watching me. I can feel his gaze from behind his yellowed curtains, and it's fine—cute even—that he is waiting for my arrival, but now I have to parallel park and that is *not* fine. I'm just pulling up next to the front car and already I'm sweating.

"Come on, Essie, we can do this." Yes, I'm talking to the car—Essie, my Ford Escort. We've been together seven years, Essie and I, and we are a power duo when it comes to suburban and rural roads, but this is the real test. We are city girls now, and we will show that peeking grandfather that we can handle parallel parking. We'll show him, and those teenagers sitting on the stoop next door, and the hundreds of pairs of eyes that are surely watching from every window on this block of Sandal Street. No sweat. Except there is so much sweat.

I startle at the sound of my hubcap scraping the curb and there's Zayde, on the sidewalk, his eighty-six-year-old arms gesticulating wildly, knotty fingers pointing circles in the air.

"You can still go back a few inches! A little to the left . . . now turn the wheel haahd," he yells, his Boston accent thick. His throat sounds all scraped up like the hubcap, the way elderly people's voices sometimes do when they try to project.

And now I'm inching, forward, back, forward, back, and I'm really in. Essie is wedged between two cars right in front of Zayde's house. I may never move her again.

"Rachel, my *shayna meydeleh*, you made it."

"Shayna meydeleh," Yiddish for beautiful girl, has been my zayde's nickname for me for as long as I can recall. I hug him and feel the familiar prickles of his whiskers on my cheek.

"Let me help you with your things," he says with an extra squeeze of my shoulders.

I haven't brought much with me from my parents' house in Bryn Mawr, not nearly as much as I stuffed Essie with to bring up to Wesleyan each fall. The plan is for me to stay in my mother's old bedroom, which is pretty cluttered already. I give Zayde my small suitcase with wheels and, slinging my large, worn duffle over my shoulder, follow him up the front steps and into the kitchen.

Zayde's kitchen—well, his whole home—seems frozen in time. He and Bubbe bought this little house in Somerville, just outside of Boston, in the 1940s, and it looks like it still belongs there. Most of the kitchen appliances are the originals—white, porcelain-enameled steel models with impossibly heavy doors. For as long as I can remember, the small rectangular family room has been wallpapered in something akin to burlap, sort of a straw-colored, ropey texture. I ran my knuckles across it once as a kid and got little burns, then scabs. Each doorknob and hinge in this house is the original, which is evident from the chips and spots of rust. I suppose it smells old, too, but to me it just smells like Bubbe and Zayde's house.

Zayde has a can of Streit's Chunky Chicken Noodle Soup boiling on the stove and a loaf of freezer-burned challah defrosting on the counter.

"Are you hungry?" he asks, pulling out a chair for me. And, before I can answer, "I hope you stopped in Montvale and Vernon." Zayde knows the trip well as he's been coming for visits ever since my mother decided to move to the Philadelphia suburbs when she married my father. He never varies from his two favorite pit stops—one a kosher-style deli just outside of Hartford, and one a particularly bright rest stop on the Garden State—though, since my bubbe's death, he's started taking the train.

"Of course I did, and I have the knishes to prove it." I reach into the courier bag I use as a purse for the takeout container of the doughy potato treats. "And, yes, I *am* hungry, and that soup looks perfect." I sit at the table, knowing he will want to play host and serve me on this, my first day.

My zayde's kitchen table is one of the most familiar places I know—without even looking, I know that the side against the wall is lined with prescription bottles, days-of-the-week pill boxes, and powdered fiber supplements. There is always a large box of tissues; Zayde uses these instead of paper napkins. Once, when I was about eight years old, I asked my grandfather why he used tissues this way. In a sudden show of frustration, he snapped, "Because we just do, okay?" I remember my mother pulling me aside as tears stung my eyes. She explained that my grandparents were "children of the Great Depression" and that there were certain kinds of savings that they would just always do and that perhaps asking about those things reminded Zayde of hard times.

Zayde can still be like that—silly and playful one minute, then snappy and brusque the next. My little brother Zeke and I had a code for this when we were little. We referred to Zayde's jolly side as Big Bird (the perpetually cheerful Sesame Street character) and to his grouchy self as Oscar (the trashcan-dwelling character from the same show).

As I wait for my soup to cool, I decide to test him.

"Zayde, I would know your table anywhere, because you use tissues and not napkins!" I keep a smile on my face and in my voice, yet it feels a little risky. I want to know if he'll scold me again, now that I'm twenty-three and starting graduate school. I wonder where his lines are—now that I am an adult, can we have honest conversations about the things he's lived through? Will he talk to me about the Depression? Losing four Polish cousins in the Holocaust? His relationship with my bubbe after her illness took hold? My mother has always implied that these topics are off limits, that they would upset my unpredictable Zayde.

He doesn't respond to my tissue comment. I'm not sure his hearing aid is on.

There are strict rules about what *I* can't tell *him*. My mother made it perfectly clear last night, appearing in my bedroom doorway as I packed my last few things for Boston.

"Rachel, I think it's lovely that you want to live with Zayde while you're in your graduate program. I, I mean, I think it will mean a great deal to him," she stammered, a deep crease between her eyebrows, her cheeks red. "I don't know what it is you're calling yourself these days, 'gay,' 'bisexual,' I don't know." She used air quotes as if to make clear that these words weren't hers. "But what I do know is that you cannot let your grandfather know about any of it. It would *kill* him, Rachel."

She said "kill" like I might truly be a murderer. Like I might murder her father. Like I might still be slowly murdering her.

When I came out to my parents at the end of my first year of college, crazy in love with my college girlfriend, I was naïve about the consequences. I gave them books to read, pamphlets from PFLAG (Parents and Friends of Lesbians and Gays), the go-to source for struggling family members. Only after giving them the PFLAG information did I realize that the word "bisexuals" was not in the title. It just served to reinforce their either/or thinking.

I tried explaining to them how I had come out to myself, thinking that, if I could bring them into my *process* they might feel less threatened. I told them how, in human sexual behavior class my first semester at Wesleyan, a panel of students from the lesbian, gay, and bisexual community came to speak to the class about their coming out experiences. The second student from the left on the panel, a junior with a long blond braid over her shoulder, explained what it meant that she was bi.

"As a teenager," she said, "I didn't even know the words. All I knew was what I felt. If I liked a boy, I just liked him and didn't question whether that was normal. And if I liked a girl, it was just the same—it felt completely right."

I'll never forget it; it was like all those years of crushes on boys and girls finally made sense.

It wasn't like I hadn't heard of bisexuals, of course. My eighth-grade science teacher, an enormous man with a greasy comb-over, used to tell us jokes like, "What is a bisexual?" Then, after an uncomfortable beat, "Someone who can't get sex, so they have to buy it!" He would snort-laugh while running his fingers over his bald spot, making sure those sweaty strands were in place.

So yes, I knew the word. But this was different. This person was saying there was a name for what I had always felt to be true about myself, that I could fall in love with a person for whoever they were. I'm not saying I was gender-blind. The girls I'd had crushes on, I chose *because* they were girls—soft and intuitive and emotional. I was attracted to boys *for* their masculinity—they were strong and their arms around me made me feel protected. It wasn't that gender didn't matter; it was that it didn't stop me.

Nora, the girl (we said *woman*, sometimes *womyn*) on the panel, eventually became my girlfriend. We took women's studies classes together and went to Indigo Girls concerts and wrote love poems on the insides of each other's arms.

My father, ever faithful to his role of keeping the peace and calming my agitated mother, said all the right things—that he loved me no matter what, that he wanted me to be happy. Meanwhile, my mother's eyes seemed permanently brimming with tears, her nose always red as if she might be drunk with grief. Zeke, who I thought of as my little hero that summer, was unflinchingly loyal. One time, when I was lying on my bed listening to my Discman to drown out the sound of my mother's audible keening down the hall, then-sixteen-year-old Zeke came into my room and sat on my bed. He put his hand on top of mine and said, "Sis, I have two things to say to you: You are awesome, and our mother is behaving like a child."

As it turns out though, Zeke didn't get bisexuality either at first. A year or so later, he asked, "Rach, don't you have to choose eventually?"

I had become used to explaining myself. "Zeke, you consider yourself to be a straight man, right?"

"Duh," he said, totally deadpan.

"Seriously, Zeke, do you identify as a heterosexual person?"

"Yes," he said, seeing that I meant business. I was determined that someone in my family really understand.

"So, that means that you feel attracted to women but not to men—and not all women, but some women you meet, some you see on TV or pass on the street, right?"

"Right so far."

"So, you base your chosen label, 'straight,' on the fact that you have these attractions to women whether these feelings are toward a woman you are in a relationship with, or toward a stranger, or in a dream."

"Okay . . ."

"So now, let's assume that one day you meet one woman with whom you choose to live your life. You marry her and you are monogamous. Are you still a straight man?"

"Yeah, I guess I'll always be a straight man."

"Right? Your identity doesn't change just because you are with one person! So, if I identify as bisexual because I experience attraction to some men and some women, that means that, even if I choose to live my life with one person—male or female—I will still retain my sexual identity. I'll still be bisexual."

"I think I get it. But, do you *want* to settle down with one person?"

"Yeah, I mean I'd like to have a family with someone eventually. I just don't know who that person is yet."

He winked at me. "Duh."

༄

I can't imagine my mother sleeping in this bedroom. Of course, when she was a girl, I'm sure it wasn't the storage space it has become in recent years. There are two tall filing cabinets opposite the twin bed that seem to be full of receipts and old tax forms, china tchotchkes on the dark bureau, a pile of photo albums on a chair. The small black-and-white TV stopped working long ago, though the antennae are still stretched open in a wide V, like arms lifted toward the heavens, waiting for a signal. Before he retired, Zayde owned a liquor store a few blocks from the house (he called it "the bottle store"), and there are two large boxes in the corner full of who knows what, stamped with "Veresk Vodka" and "J&B Rare Scotch Whisky."

To the right of the bureau (my mother would say, "burah" betraying her New England upbringing) stands a heavy, oval, full-length mirror on a pedestal. I stand in front of it, as I imagine my mother must have often done. I look at my slightly chubby upper arms peeking out from under my cap-sleeve T-shirt. My mother calls these "Hadassah arms" and makes no secret of the fact that she considers them unsightly. I wonder, too, about my long unruly curls cascading over my shoulders. I can almost see my mother standing behind me, looking over my shoulder in the mirror.

"It really should be several inches shorter, Rachel. You aren't in college anymore. If you want people to recognize you as a professional, you need to look groomed. And please don't go to graduate school with your hair in a ponytail!"

I pull my hair off my shoulders, trying to appease this

mirror-dwelling version of my mother. Do I look older? More professional? I wouldn't give her the satisfaction of cutting it while I was home in Bryn Mawr, but now that I am in Somerville, maybe I will go to one of those walk-in haircut places tomorrow. Maybe just for a trim.

When I go downstairs, I find Zayde in his usual spot—his recliner in the small family room off the kitchen with the *Wall Street Journal* splayed across his lap and the TV on whatever cable channel scrolls the stock ticker across the bottom of the screen. He alternates between reading, watching, and snoozing. I startle him. I am a little afraid that he's forgotten I am here, but he quickly snaps awake.

"Oh, hello my dear! I was wondering if you'd like to go out to dinner to celebrate your first night in town."

I know this means the diner with the pot roast and mashed potatoes. "That would be lovely, Zayde." I remember they have good pie.

As it turns out, Zayde is somewhat of a local celebrity at the Union Diner. As he takes off his signature woolen flat cap, he is greeted by several of the wait staff ("Hello, Mr. Kessler!") and, from the owner, "Good evening, Mr. Kessler. This must be the beautiful granddaughter you've been telling us so much about!"

"Zayde, how often do you eat here?" I whisper after we've been seated in a booth in the back.

"Oh, your bubbe and I used to come here two, three times a week. I don't come so often now. Maybe one time a week. Or two."

Just then our waitress, an older Black woman with a wide smile, comes over. "Is this the psychiatrist?" she asks, giving Zayde a squeeze on the shoulder and looking at me.

"Oh," I say, realizing that she means me. "Psychologist actually. Well, actually I haven't even started school yet, so um, just granddaughter."

"That's my girl!" says Zayde. He is beaming. I feel my chest swell. His pride in me feels like the best kind of love.

Lying in my mother's old bed that night, a wave of anxiety rolls over me that takes my breath. The smell. Not just of the house, but of oldness. Only this time I feel like I'm suffocating, like I'm trapped. *I don't want to live here.* My brain floods with images of peeling paint, rusty radiators, the worn carpet on the stairs. My heart races and I am overcome with the sensation that I am not really in my body. *What if I can't sustain making my zayde proud of me? Would he love me if he really knew me? Clearly, my living here will make Zayde happy . . . but will I be happy?*

He cannot know about me. It would kill him.

Then I remind myself, *Living with Zayde is a mitzvah, and a mitzvah means more when it's hard.*

Chapter 2

Zayde's synagogue, Beth El, is a beautiful, old brick building just a few streets away in the Winter Hill section of the city. The building's cornerstone, just outside of the main entrance, says "Erected 1925" but the congregation is actually over a hundred years old, having been formed by a small group of families who emigrated from Eastern Europe in the 1890s. For years, Zeke and I couldn't help but giggle and elbow each other every time we walked past the word "Erected" engraved in that stone.

The seats in Beth El's small sanctuary aren't individual theater seats like at our synagogue on the Main Line; they are long benches like church pews and have been covered with the same thread-bare upholstery for decades. This *shul*, like my grandparents' house, seems always in need of renovation, and, like their house, I can identify the building by smell alone.

When Zayde and I walk in through the back of the sanctuary that first Saturday morning, I stop short. On the raised *bimah* in the front of the room stands not the elderly, bearded rabbi I've come to know over the years of visiting, but a middle-aged woman. She wears a prayer shawl of bright colors and a matching, woven yarmulke. She is singing a Hebrew tune I've only ever heard in a much lower register. "Zayde," I whisper into his hairy ear. "Who *is* that?"

"That is Rabbi Lorel Stein," he says through clenched teeth. And suddenly, he is Oscar the Grouch.

I sometimes regret that I wasn't born a quarter of a century earlier so that I might have been a college student in the 1960s, burning my bra and marching on Washington. I didn't know that Conservative synagogues even allowed women to be rabbis. Maybe this is Conservative Judaism's moment for women's liberation. Maybe I've arrived just in time.

Back at the house, Zayde slams his hat down on the counter. "I don't know what the selection committee was thinking when they offered her the position! She doesn't even look like a rabbi. She sings in a lady's voice—it drives me nuts!"

"Zayde," I protest, "What does that even mean, 'look like a rabbi'? She's brilliant and I think she has a *beautiful* voice." I try to steer away from his blatant sexism as if doing so will make it untrue.

"Rabbis need to be wise and experienced!" His voice is beginning to take on that raspy, shaky quality it always does when he is upset. "Rabbi Jacobs was a *learned man*. I just don't think it's a role for a woman."

There it is.

"Zayde, didn't we *all* stand at Sinai?" I am pulling out the big guns, trying to speak his language. "What if *I* wanted to become a rabbi? Would you support me?"

His eyes widen, considering this. "You, my Rachel, could do anything you pleased but, a rabbi? How would you raise your babies?"

"I'm going to become a psychologist, aren't I? Can I do that and still have children?"

He shakes his head. "Honestly, I don't know how you will do it. Fathers today stay home with their children! This world is turning upside down. Is that your plan? To marry a man who is a mother?"

I pause at the irony of his question. "Maybe, Zayde, just maybe."

When I was a child, I thought Zayde was the smartest person I knew. That started to change when I was at Wesleyan; I couldn't be silent in the face of what was quite literally the patriarchy. My mother found this unnerving. At a Passover Seder at our house during my junior year in college, I introduced the idea of an orange on our Seder plate. The orange was a new, feminist addition to the traditional mix of symbolic items on the plate. I explained the story of the orange like this:

Long ago a young woman went to her rabbi and said, "Rabbi, what is the place of a woman in Judaism?" The rabbi scoffed and said, "A woman belongs in Judaism like an orange belongs on the Seder plate!" Dejected, the young woman went home to her parents and told them what the rabbi had said. At Passover that year, they placed an orange on the Seder plate and said that it would stay there until the rabbi said differently.

"Well how about that!" exclaimed my father, ever the peace-maker, slapping his hand down on the table. My mother busied herself with the brisket. Zeke snickered. Bubbe, her dementia advancing, didn't react at all. Zayde, always animated in his responses, was quick to challenge me.

"Shayna meydeleh, how could you possibly think that anyone believes women don't have a place in Judaism? Who raises our Jewish children? Who runs the Sisterhood?"

I felt the heat rising in my cheeks. I was not used to talking back to my grandfather, but I was also no longer able to keep quiet.

"Zayde—that's just the thing. I mean where do women belong in religious *practice*? It is only recently that women counted in the *minyan* at your shul! When my mom became a Bat Mitzvah, she couldn't even read from the Torah! Women's real involvement in Judaism is in its infancy."

Next to me, Zeke began to sing, "Papa can you hear me?" under his breath, and I kicked him hard.

"When Esther was president of the Sisterhood," Zayde continued motioning toward my bubbe, his voice rising, "she was very involved, very active!"

We all became quiet then, reminded of how vibrant a woman Esther Kessler had once been. We looked at Bubbe, her eyes far away. Continuing to argue felt all wrong.

∾

I didn't expect that attending Saturday services with Zayde would become routine for me this year, but it has. I find Rabbi Stein intoxicating. She reminds me of some of my college professors—grounded in knowledge and history but leading a new generation of us forward. Her sermons are provocative; she tells of women being arrested at the Western Wall in Jerusalem for daring to pray publicly with a prayer shawl; she speaks of current events and quotes op-eds from the *New York Times*. Beth El's familiar comfort always makes it feel like home, but Rabbi Stein makes Judaism relevant to my life. Relevant enough to get me out of bed on Saturday mornings.

After services each week, we gather in the social hall for a buffet Kiddush luncheon. Zayde talks with his friends, the *altacockers* he's known for decades, in hushed and sometimes not-so-hushed tones about their disapproval of Rabbi Stein.

"Did you hear her take on the Torah portion today? Honest to God! I don't think she has any understanding of what the laws of marriage even mean!" This from Sophia Goldblatt, too loudly. I nibble at my bagel with tuna salad, trying not to speak.

Sophia's husband, Murray, chimes in, "If I hear one more modern interpretation of the laws of Deuteronomy! How about the *original* intent of those laws?"

I can't help myself. "But isn't the beauty of Judaism that we are always re-interpreting the original text?"

Five pairs of elderly eyes fixate on me. The silence is like ice. It is broken by Murray, shifting into a smile. "You must be so proud of her, Lew, going for her PhD."

"It's actually called a PsyD," I interject. "It's a clinical doctorate."

"What?" asks another friend, Bess. "I've never heard of that. Is that some sort of new degree?"

"It's been around for a while," I explain. "For a PhD in psychology there is more emphasis on research and teaching. This degree focuses solely on clinical practice and, since what I really want to be is a therapist, it makes more sense for me."

"Will you still be called 'Doctor'?" asks Murray, even louder than his wife had been.

"Oh she'll be called 'Doctor,' all right," says Zayde, winking at me. "Even *you,* Dr. Goldblatt, will have to address her as 'Doctor'!" Zayde's eyes twinkle and his friends beam at us.

We have become a duo, a pair, and after several months together, we have a rhythm. I am often in the kitchen already when Zayde comes down the stairs for breakfast in the morning. He has a habit of calling out, "Good morning Esther!" when he reaches the third stair from the bottom. I am guessing that he started greeting my bubbe this way when she was moved into a hospital bed in the living room some months before her death. There is a cadence to how he says it, almost a tune, and I imagine that his calling out to her might have been the one thing he could count on when he came down the worn staircase each morning of those final months. It has never struck me as worrisome. It feels like a way of honoring her soul's presence in the house; it feels like his morning prayer.

After our brief overlap in the kitchen each morning, I head out for the day, either to my practicum placement (a public middle school where I run groups with students), to the library or to classes at the Boston School of Clinical Psychology. In the evenings, I cook dinner for Zayde, and we eat off of TV trays in the family room with *Wheel of Fortune* on or, on special occasions, at the small kitchen table.

As I drive Essie downtown to the old brownstone that houses BSCP, I sometimes smile at my own reflection in the rearview mirror. I am proud to be in graduate school; I am proud of the routine I've created with Zayde—the balancing act of grad student/granddaughter.

My mother is concerned.

"Rachel, I worry. You should be going out with your peers. What about your classmates?"

"Mom, I *am* going out with my classmates." The truth is, I'm not. I like the people in my program, and we sit in the student lounge at school, drinking coffee and commiserating about our long practicum hours. You could say we've formed a support group of sorts. But except for the occasional happy hour organized by the student activities committee, we don't see much of one another outside of school.

But dinner with Zayde feels sacred, like the other geographical touchstones of each week—the classroom, the library, the student lounge, Zayde's table, Beth El. Everything is predictable, and I like the way it feels.

Chapter 3

When the phone rings after nine, I know something is wrong. In the year I've lived with Zayde, the phone has never rung this late. As Zayde answers an extension upstairs, I gently lift the receiver of the kitchen phone and cover the mouthpiece with my hand, listening in.

"Good evening, this is Lew Kessler."

"Lew, it's Gil Margolis. I'm sorry to call you so late, but I have some bad news. Ivan Resnick passed just a few hours ago."

Zayde makes a sound, part grumble, part sigh. "Ah, I'd heard he wasn't doing well. That's a shame."

"It sure is. He was a good man. I'm actually calling on behalf of the Chevra Kadisha. We're trying to fill slots at O'Donnahue's between now and Sunday morning. I know you prefer early morning shifts."

"Of course. What do you need?"

"Could you do four hours tomorrow morning, from five to nine?"

"Sure thing, Gil. I appreciate your call."

I wait until Zayde hangs up before I do. "Zayde?" I call out, running up the stairs to his bedroom, "Who was that?"

"Oh, there's been a death in the community. I don't think you knew Ivan Resnick. He's been too ill to come to synagogue for some time. Was living in a nursing home. I'm going to sit with his body tomorrow." He's putting away newly folded laundry and doesn't stop when I sit on the edge of his bed.

"I'm so sorry. Was he a friend of yours?" Zayde stops for just a moment, as if to consider this. He doesn't make eye contact with me. "Yes," he says holding a small pile of folded white undershirts to his chest, "Ivan was a friend." He quickly returns to his chore, saying nothing more about how this might feel to him. I know he has lost several friends. I know he reads the obituary section every day. But in this moment, all he seems to care about is laundry.

I'm embarrassed not to know about what seems like some obvious Jewish practice, but I'm also too curious to care. "Zayde, what do you mean that you will be sitting with his body?"

"The Chevra Kadisha? Oh, think of it like a volunteer burial society. You know, in Jewish tradition, a person is made up of a body and a soul, right?"

I nod and watch him moving between dresser drawer and bed and closet.

"We believe that the soul leaves the body at the moment of death, but that it stays near the body, some say in a confused state, until burial. You know we bury the body as soon as possible, within a day or two."

"Yes, of course." I do know this.

"We don't embalm or view the body. We cover it in a white, linen shroud and bury it in a simple wooden coffin."

"Right. And isn't there something about not using metal hinges or screws on the coffin?" I am letting him know that I do know *some* things about Jewish funerals.

"That's right. We don't want anything to slow down the decomposition process. Now, during the hours between death and burial, there are rituals to be performed." He is all business.

I stand up, following him back and forth. "Like what rituals?"

"There's *tahara*—washing the body—and *shmira*—watching over the body and comforting the soul. These are the things the Chevra Kadisha does."

"Zayde, when did you join this group?"

"Oh, I've been doing it all my adult life, certainly since we moved to Somerville."

"But why have I never heard about this?"

"I think it's unusual for a small synagogue to do these things themselves. Most of the pre-burial rituals happen at a Jewish funeral home. The nearest one to us is in Brookline, so Beth El has an arrangement with O'Donnahue's—a local funeral home just down the street. While the body waits there, members of Beth El's Chevra Kadisha take shifts sitting with body so that it's never alone. We are the *shomrim*—the guards—and it's our job to calm the soul while it hovers near the body, waiting to be buried."

"But how do you know how to do this, Zayde? How do you comfort a hovering soul?"

"The tradition teaches us to keep a focused vigil, almost like meditation. We are not to eat, talk, or even think mundane thoughts while we sit."

"How is that even possible? How do you keep mundane thoughts from coming?"

"You read Psalms," he answers, look up from his sock drawer with a proud smirk. He clearly knew I didn't expect a real answer. I should have known; in Judaism, every question has not only one answer, but multiple ones.

"Psalms? All of them?" I make a mental note to look up the Psalms and see what about them is so special that they can keep mundane thoughts away.

"Yes. You start at the beginning, and, when you finish, you start over again. Out loud," he adds. Then he comes over to the edge of the bed and sits, patting the spot next to him for me. I sit next to him and he turns and looks squarely at me, punctuating his words with his index finger. "Rachel, watching over a body is the highest mitzvah you can do, because the dead can never repay the favor. When your bubbe died, it was a great comfort to me knowing that our friends were with her around the clock until we could return her to the earth." My breath catches in my throat when he says this—*Bubbe's body, returned to the earth*. I think of her funeral on that cold, February day a few short years ago. The way the light snow fell as we gathered around that gaping hole in the ground, mumbling the Hebrew of the Kaddish prayer. I remember Zeke whispering something to me about the white sheet the snow was making over us all being like the white shroud our grandmother lay beneath in the plain, pine coffin. I thought he was making some sort of joke, the way Zeke might do as a way of avoiding what he didn't want to feel. When I looked at his face, though, I saw that he wasn't joking after all. He was looking up at the snow descending on us, tears rolling down his red cheeks. I looked up too, letting the little white stars of ice blanket my cheekbones and eyelashes. When I think about my bubbe's burial, my face still stings.

At the end of the burial service, the rabbi explained that we would all be able to shovel earth into my grandmother's grave. I hadn't remembered this from the burials of my father's parents, having been so much younger when they died, and I must have looked shocked because the rabbi went on to explain this ritual, looking at me as he did.

"We help to bury Esther," he said, "because this is the final kind-ness we can give to her—to see that her body, her soul's vessel, is returned properly to the earth. It is our last gift to her." He motioned then to the long-handled shovel stuck into the large pile of just-dug dirt and rock. "You may do so with this shovel or with your hands if you prefer," he added.

Zayde went first. He walked over to the hill of earth, my aunt holding his arm to steady him, and seemed to stare at the shovel for a moment. Then he bent over, gathered a scoop in his two hands, and turned to face the hole in which my bubbe's casket had been lowered. He raised his arms out so that his hands were above the casket and let his hands fall away from each other. The hard thunk of rock and earth landing on the wooden box in which my grandmother lay was the most terrible sound I'd ever heard—hard and dark and final.

Everyone after Zayde used the shovel, as if there were an unspoken understanding among us that we should let the use of hands be his alone. Again and again, the thunk of earth on wood. I can't remember what it felt like to hold that cold shovel in my hands; I only remember the sound.

I turn my attention back to Zayde, sitting with me on the edge of this bed, and kiss his scratchy cheek. "Let's get some sleep. We have to be up early if we're to get to O'Donnahue's at five."

His eyebrows arch high as he watches me walk toward the door.

"I want to go with you."

◆

The sun has not yet risen, and Zayde and I are in his white Mercury Grand Marquis headed to the funeral home to sit with Ivan Resnik's body. Zayde is not a very safe driver anymore but he does feel confident driving the short distance between his house, Beth El, and his local Star Market. Since O'Donnahue's is within this radius, he's behind the wheel. Whenever we are going to one of these nearby spots I make sure to ask him to drive, in hopes that it preserves a sense of autonomy for him. As for the Mercury, it seems to me to be the same car he's driven all my life. He's always had some enormous, white boat of a car, and I can never tell the difference between any of them.

The front seat of Zayde's car is always littered with yarmulkes.

Sometimes he remembers to take one to wear into shul; sometimes he gets a new one inside and forgets to put it back until he's back in the car. The collection is forever rotating, each one stamped on the inside with the Bar Mitzvah or wedding of someone I don't know. This morning, he takes a bright orange one and puts it over his bald spot. I am holding Zayde's worn copy of the Tanakh, the title page of which reads, "The Holy Scriptures—A New Translation." It is copyrighted 1917.

In every Jewish writing I have ever encountered—from the Torah to the prayer books used during services—not only has God been male, but every last pronoun has been male. During Saturday morning services, I change "mankind" to "humankind" and "forefathers" to "ancestors" in my head. I replace every He and Him in reference to God with the Hebrew "Adonai" or simply "God." I am sure Zayde has heard me do this when we read aloud during responsive readings, but he has never said a thing to me about it. The Reform movement just published a new gender-neutral prayer book, and I have heard that my synagogue in Bryn Mawr is planning to replace their old ones with this new edition. There is no such revision of the Conservative prayer book and no doubt Zayde's 1917 Tanakh has nothing to say about women.

Still, the worn book feels heavy and ancient in my hands, and I find myself excited about reading from it in this most sacred of rituals. We enter the funeral home. I recognize the man who greets us as a Saturday morning regular. He leads us into a side room off of the chapel where Ivan Resnik's body is lying face-up on a special table with wheels. His body is draped in a white sheet; I wonder about his soul.

Is Ivan's soul in the room with us now? Is it relieved to see his old friend, Lew? It? Is Ivan's soul a "he" or does it lose gender when freed from the body? Are you here, Ivan?

I *am* concerned about my mundane thoughts, which I know I am sure to have. I took a meditation class as an undergraduate, and I remember learning that even the great Buddhist monks who sit in silent meditation for months at a time say that the mind always wanders, that even with all the practice in the world, we cannot stop thoughts from coming. This thought comforts me as I settle in on one of the plush chairs set up near the table. When I turn to Zayde to tell him that it is okay if we can't keep totally focused on Psalms for the entire four hours, his eyes are closed, his face alert but still. I remember that he's done this many times before.

He opens his eyes and nods to me. I take the first psalm, clearing the early-morning grogginess from my throat:

> Happy is the man that hath
> > not walked in the counsel of the
> > wicked,
> Nor stood in the way of sinners,
> Nor sat in the seat of the scornful.
> But his delight is in the law of the
> > Lord;
> And in His law doth he meditate
> > day and night.
> And he shall be like a tree planted
> > by streams of water,
> That bringeth forth its fruit in its
> > season,
> And whose leaf doth not wither;
> And in whatsoever he doeth he
> > shall prosper.
>
> Not so the wicked;
> But they are like the chaff which the
> > wind driveth away.

Therefore the wicked shall not stand
in the judgment,
Nor sinners in the congregation of
the righteous;
For the Lord regardeth the way of
the righteous;
But the way of the wicked shall
perish.

My thoughts are not mundane after all. My heart has started to pound. *This* is supposed to sooth poor Ivan Resnik's confused soul? I feel as if I am saying, *Listen, Ivan. If you prayed day and night and never sinned, you're in luck! If not, it's all downhill from here.* It feels so un-Jewish to me, this angry, judgmental Lord. This is certainly not *my* higher power. My mouth agape, I turn to my grandfather. His face is full of peace, a light smile on his lips, a hint of tears collecting in the corners of his again closed eyes. *This* is soothing to him? And then it occurs to me, that this God—this male, spiteful God—*is* in fact the God of the Torah.

I feel clobbered.

"Are you okay, shayna meydeleh?"

"Yes, of course, sorry Zayde. It's just a little overwhelming."

He pats my hand. I can tell he thinks it's the situation that's getting to me. He would be shocked to know how much deeper this goes. What would Zayde think if he knew how much I hate the traditional view—*his* view—of our God? I feel myself starting to panic, like there isn't enough air. Then I remind myself that the Psalms are a sort of meditation, to keep me present with Zayde and Ivan's soul, to partake in the centuries-old practice of shmira. I breathe and re-focus.

We continue to read aloud, stopping after every 150-psalm cycle to rest and be silent. I want to love shmira, to feel like I am doing something profoundly sacred. But after hours of repetition, I am bored. And I mean, wildly, shatteringly bored. I think that, at any moment, I might impulsively break into Pig Latin or worse, peek under that white sheet.

Chapter 4

Despite the fact that I put on extra deodorant this morning, I am acutely aware of having wet pits. They are first-day-wet-pits, the kind that say, "She may look all calm and confident, but under here we know the truth."

It is the first day of my second-year practicum at the counseling center at Concord College, a small liberal arts school just west on Route 2. I am waiting in the group room for the other trainees and for our supervisor, Dr. Maria Vargas. I met her once, at the interview last spring, and was immediately intimidated. As she enters the group room, I remember why: She is a *presence*. She is one of those women who commands the space around her, who makes you look up, then sit a bit straighter. She is a large woman with broad hips and deep, olive Latina skin. Today her black, thick hair is in a low bun at the nape of her neck. My mother would say she "dresses smart" with her crisply pressed pants and linen blazer.

Dr. Vargas's eyes are steady as she comes in and takes a seat at the rectangle table where we have all gathered. Her eyes meet each of ours, holding our gaze for just a second, just long enough to say, "I see you."

She starts by going over the details of the practicum. We are expected to see ten clients in weekly individual sessions; we will have two hours of weekly supervision, a one-on-one with her and one as part of a group.

"I understand that some of you are very green," she says in her smooth, deep voice, again making eye contact with each of us so as not to betray who in particular she might be thinking of. I am sure it is me. "You have much to learn. Nevertheless, I expect you to conduct yourselves as full-fledged psychologists both ethically and professionally, and I will treat you as such. The students at Concord come to the counseling center expecting and deserving the highest quality treatment. I will supervise you, but they are *your* clients. It is your job to provide that treatment."

"Dr. Vargas?" A trainee from a graduate program at Boston University raises her hand. "I notice you said 'client.' I'm used to saying 'patient.' Does it matter?"

"I use the word 'client,' because I don't adhere to the medical model," says Dr. Vargas coolly. "The young women and men who are seeking your guidance are college students. They very well may come to you with serious mental illness, but your job is to partner with them on a journey, not to administer treatment to a passive recipient."

"But don't you think that, at its best, this is what the medical model also aspires to?" This from my Harvard colleague and the only male in our training cohort. He continues, "I mean, patients in a hospital setting or a doctor's office shouldn't be passive recipients either. All healing should ideally come from a place of partnership between sufferer and healer, right?"

I want to roll my eyes. I expect Dr. Vargas to come back with something dismissive; instead, she pauses, reflecting on the question.

"Everything you say in a session," she says, "or on the phone with a client, or in the waiting room matters. Every word you choose conveys meaning, just as every word chosen by the client conveys meaning. In our current culture, whether we agree or not, the word 'patient' has a connotation of disempowerment and we *never* want to disempower our clients. One of the things we will be listening for in your audio-taped recordings is word choice—why the client has said something in a particular way, but also why you have responded in the way that you have."

Tape recordings?!

I am suddenly doubting my choice of training sites. I admire and want to learn from Dr. Vargas, but the idea of that tape rolling through every session, the thought of her hearing my quavering voice caught in the act of pretending to be a psychologist—I think I might throw up.

∽

"Tell me about Charlie," Dr. Vargas says during our second individual supervision meeting. We are sitting across from one another, her low coffee table in between us. I rifle through my stack of manila folders for the one marked "C.L.": Charlie Lindon. Inside the folder are the scratchy notes I took after my first session with Charlie earlier this week.

"Charlie Lindon," I read from my notes, "is a nineteen-year-old, Caucasian, transfer student from Virginia. He left his reason for seeking treatment on the intake form blank."

"Shall we listen to the beginning of your tape?" asks Dr. Vargas.

It isn't a question, of course. I find the recording in my locked box of cassette tapes. These, as well as our written notes, are locked in the office at all times to protect client confidentiality, but I go this extra step to keep them, or perhaps myself, secure. I pop "C.L." in the player and focus on my breathing.

"Welcome Charlie, you can have a seat right there. Um, before we get started, I'd like to do a few house-cleaning . . .

uh, I mean a few house-keeping things . . . to get them out of the way."

The sound of my anxiety blares from the tape player. Dr. Vargas is watching me. I close my eyes and listen to myself review the consent for treatment form.

"As it says here on the form, what you say in this room will remain confidential between you, me, and my supervisor. Because I am in training, I will be sharing these tape recordings with her. But whatever you say will stay between the three of us. Oh, except for a few important exceptions. Um, if my notes are subpoenaed by a judge, if, um, you are to tell me of a situation where a child or elderly person is being abused—then I'll have an obligation to report that. Uh, and finally, if I believe that you are going to hurt yourself or someone else, then I would have to break confidentiality for your safety—or for that person's safety."

Still no sound from Charlie. I sound like a freak.

"So, why don't you tell me what brought you in here today?"

I have been trying this on as my opening line. Sometimes I use, "Tell me how I can help you today," but that feels too retail, like I might follow it up with, "Can I start a dressing room for you?" I know there are some therapists, analysts mostly, who sit down after the client (in this case definitely "patient") and say nothing at all, letting the silence be there until the client breaks it. I knew well before I started graduate school that this would *not* be my style. I had seen two different therapists in the years leading up to my move to Boston. One of the things I valued about both of them was their authenticity.

They didn't pretend to be non-judgmental blank slates; rather, they met me where I was—which was needing to talk to someone real.

"I'm not sure where to start really—"

"How about at the beginning?"

Shit. Did I cut him off?

"Well, the beginning was a long time ago. As long as I can remember ago maybe—"

"So maybe it makes sense for us to start with your childhood?"

"Okay, stop the tape," says Dr. Vargas. "Rachel, what are you feeling right now, as you listen to the recording?"

I don't look her in the eye right away. "Well," I begin, "I'm just feeling embarrassed, I guess. It's so clear from how much I'm talking that I'm anxious with him."

"And why do you think you were anxious?" she asks.

"Um, I'm not sure?" I start, then stop because I am lying. Several seconds pass before I start again. "I'm anxious with him because his anxiety is so palpable and because it reminds me of mine—at his age I mean."

What I really felt is that, in those brief opening moments with Charlie, I had picked up on so many signals that he was gay. I don't normally espouse judging people according to stereotypes, especially not so quickly, but when it comes to gaydar, mine is razor-sharp. Though I don't say this to Dr. Vargas, I could read Charlie, with his physique, his clothes, his voice, his mannerisms, as one very gay adolescent boy who, if I had to guess, was not yet out of the closet.

But why should that have made me anxious? If I have come to this work with any expertise, it is working with gay youth. I spent several summers teaching at a progressive summer camp where I served as a sort of advisor to the teen Gay/Lesbian/Bisexual Alliance. I, myself, along with so many friends went through the coming out process in college. So why should Charlie's presentation in my office throw me? Then I remember: on Charlie's intake form he had written "evangelical Christian" as his religious affiliation. The school in Virginia from which he'd transferred was a Christian college. I am no longer on familiar ground.

Dr. Vargas waits a few seconds, looks over at the clock on the wall then says, "Rachel, it's time to stop supervision for today. You can leave your tapes with me."

⤳

When Zayde and I go to services each Saturday, we sit six rows back, on the left side of the aisle, me on the end and he just to my left. When I'd come to visit my grandparents as a teenager (several times I was allowed to take the Amtrak up by myself, feeling smug and grown up as I handed the conductor my ticket), I would join them for Saturday services, and we sat in this very same place. Bubbe sat between Zayde and me then, and I'd hold Bubbe's hand throughout the service.

I had been a student of my grandparents' hands my whole life. I can't explain why the landscape of their hands fascinated me so much, but, from a very young age, I'd committed them to memory. The skin on Bubbe's hands was paper-thin and soft like woven silk. Her fingernails had deep ridges and were always filed to a point. I'd loved to hold my zayde's hand too. I would run my finger along the branching, green rivers of his veins, pressing and releasing the soft tubing that ran under his skin. Unlike my bubbe's curved, ridged nails, his fingernails were flat and smooth. Zayde's hands were the biggest I'd ever seen. When I'd put my little hand in his, I'd curl my fingers into a fist so that his hand would cover mine completely, making me feel kept and safe. I find myself noticing Zayde's hands as they hold open his prayer book. They are the hands of an old man now. Someday, Zayde's body—his wide, warm hands, his veins—will decompose and simply cease to exist, just as Bubbe's paper skin was now dust. But what about their souls? I hadn't felt anything like a soul hovering over Ivan Resnick's body. Surely there is a spark of divinity in each of us—an energy or a light or something—that doesn't get eaten by worms but that travels. Does it travel into the bodies of loved ones? Or back into some larger soup of energy? Is that what we mean by God?

I look up at the ark. The Torahs are hidden behind heavy gold curtains, with Hebrew letters embroidered on them. As a child, I asked Zayde during a Yom Kippur service what the Hebrew words meant. He looked at me reproachfully for being noisy during services, then leaned down and whispered, "Know Before Whom You Stand." Remembering this, I look at the congregants in the room around me and wonder if I am the only one who doesn't know before whom she stands.

I take my zayde's hand in mine, and he squeezes mine and winks at me. It is a lovely but short-lived moment between us, because Zayde's friend Bess is just arriving and sits in front of Zayde, nodding at him and giving him what seems to be a knowing look. I have known Bess all my life, since back when her husband Larry was alive and would sneak us hard candies during Rosh Hashanah services. As the service continues, other friends of Zayde's, several of whom we don't normally see on Saturday mornings, start to arrive and sit near us. They all seem to be flashing glances at one another as if something is up. I have that nervous feeling that happens when people around you start acting weird, and you think maybe they are about to throw you a surprise party, only it isn't your birthday so it doesn't make sense. I lean over to Zayde and whisper, "Is something going on?"

He whispers back, "The rabbi is planning to speak today about some changes she wants to make in the way she runs services. No one is happy about it."

I am struck by the notion that everyone but me seems to know what the rabbi is going to talk about. Then I remember that Beth El is a small community and that if something has been mentioned, say at a board meeting or something, word spreads like fire. I look around at the sea of white hair that surrounds me and wonder if "no one" being happy means that this particular demographic isn't happy. I might be sitting among a vocal faction of which I might not want to be a part. I hang onto Rabbi Stein's every word more than usual.

"In today's Torah portion," she is saying, "we read about Abraham and Sarah inviting three strangers into their tent. Abraham, sitting in the heat of the day, notices the three strangers approaching and doesn't just call to them. He runs to greet them. He bows to the ground before them and asks them to stay and wash their feet and eat bread with him and Sarah." She pauses. "A warm welcome."

All around me, grey eyebrows are knitted and tense.

"Jewish scholars have been interpreting this scene from Genesis for thousands of years, illuminating the Jewish virtue of welcoming strangers into our homes. In fact, the Torah reminds us of this edict over and over again, as in Exodus 23:9 where we read, 'You shall not oppress a stranger, for you know the feelings of the stranger, having yourselves been strangers in the land of Egypt.' The rabbis of the Talmud tell us that we can understand the word 'stranger' to mean the same as 'newcomer' or someone who has chosen to join the community. In other words, someone who feels unaffiliated, but wishes to belong."

She pauses as if thinking about this for the first time herself. "What fascinates me is the idea that the obligation to welcome the stranger goes deeper than mere hospitality. Our sages had much to say about the connection between welcoming the stranger and honoring God.

For example, in the Talmud, Rabbi Yehuda suggests that 'welcoming guests is greater than receiving the Divine Presence.' A later text by a medieval commentator, Rabbi Yehuda Loew of Prague, draws on the idea that all human beings are created in the image of God to conclude that 'when you welcome a guest it is tantamount to honoring God.'"

It is customary for the rabbi's talk, her D'var Torah, to be based on the week's Torah reading. So far, nothing seems out of the ordinary.

"You may be familiar with the idea that, in Conservative Judaism, only Jews, meaning those born to Jewish mothers or those who have converted to Judaism, are traditionally welcome on the bimah. For several generations in this country, this went unnoticed. It went unnoticed because observant Jews simply didn't marry out of the religion. Conservative synagogues were filled with Jewish people and occasions for non-Jews to come up on the bimah simply did not arise. But times have changed. Among our younger families at Beth El, those with children in the religious school for example, almost 20 percent are interfaith families."

A grumble seems to rip through my small section as Zayde, Bess and the others exchange disapproving looks and shake their heads.

"The parents of our religious school students are active, vital members of our Beth El community. Jewish or not, these parents are responsible for bringing their children to our school, for assuring that their children fulfill their service requirements, and for attending our holiday events with their families. Jewish or not, they are part of the fabric of our Beth El community."

This makes total sense to me, but I stop myself from nodding.

"So when a child in our community celebrates their Bar or Bat Mitzvah, how can we invite that child's Jewish parent up to the bimah to bless the Torah, to make a speech to the child, to participate in the ceremony, and ask the non-Jewish parent to stay seated among the congregants? How are we like Abraham and Sarah, welcoming the stranger into our tent, if we can't extend this most basic gesture of inclusion?"

At this, Zayde lets out an audible sound of disgust. I feel heads turn toward him. I am mortified.

The rabbi continues, "I have given this issue a great deal of thought and wanted to share with you all this morning that, from this point on, when a child from an interfaith family becomes a Bar or Bat Mitzvah, both parents will be welcome on the bimah. Both parents will be allowed to stand at the Torah, though only the Jewish parent will say the Hebrew blessing. This is in accordance with Halacha—Jewish law—which states that one must be Jewish to say this blessing. Halacha, however, does not say anything about non-Jews standing at the Torah or joining their family on the bimah. While doing so is a departure from tradition, it is not a departure from Jewish law. I am excited that our non-Jewish community members will be taking a more active role in their children's rite of passage. And I ask you to consider that as Abraham and Sarah honored God by welcoming others into their tent, we too are honoring God by making our rituals more welcoming to our non-Jewish family members. *Shabbat shalom.*"

We finish the service with concluding prayers. The tension in the sanctuary is palpable. I notice some younger families across the aisle smiling and looking pleased at what the rabbi has said. My section is characterized by pursed lips and tight shoulders. I want to escape.

As soon as everyone starts to move toward the social hall for the luncheon, Zayde fishes his keys out of his pocket and says, "Let's go, Rachel."

"But what about lunch?"

"There's plenty of soup at the house."

The silence on the short car ride home is painful. I wait until we are in the kitchen and Zayde is opening the can of Streit's Chunky Chicken Noodle with his old manual can opener. While reaching for two bowls, my back to Zayde at the stove, I say, "So I take it you disagree with what Rabbi Stein had to say this morning."

That is all it takes.

"Rabbi Stein," he says bitterly, like there is an actual bad taste in his mouth, "is a fool! She's a child! She has *no idea* what she's doing. If she thinks that we are going to stand by and let her turn our synagogue into a church, she is sorely mistaken. I've been part of this congregation for fifty years, and I will not have tradition tossed out by some upstart!"

This is far worse than Oscar the Grouch. Zayde is shaking, his finger pointing (at me?) with fury. I don't know that I've ever seen him this angry before.

I take a deep breath and say, "It sounds like it's her decision to make though. I mean, she's the religious leader of the congregation—"

"We'll see how long that lasts," he interrupts.

"What do you mean?" I'm suddenly feeling very protective of and scared for the rabbi.

"Her contract is up next fall and there is *no way* we are going to renew it!"

We are quiet for the rest of the meal, and I can barely stomach my soup.

Chapter 5

"**I** listened to the tape of your first session with Charlie," Dr. Vargas begins at our next supervision meeting. "I've cued it up to a place I'd like to review with you."

I nod tentatively. "Okay."

She presses play.

"Charlie, can you tell me a bit about your old school. What was your first year in college like?"

"Well, it was pretty bad actually. That's why I transferred. The college is the same one my brother went to. It's about forty minutes from my hometown. It's affiliated with the same church my family belongs to."

"And what church is that?"

"It's called the True Faith Evangelical Church. My uncle is a preacher, and, like, my whole family is really active there."

"And how about you?"

"Well, I've always loved church for the most part. I mean, I grew up there. Like, all of my friends are from my youth group. It's kind of all I know. It's just that . . . the college had all of these rules, you know, Christian codes of conduct and stuff, and I just didn't like it there."

Dr. Vargas pauses the tape player. "Rachel, I like that you are asking about his religious identity. Often, therapists—especially young therapists—are afraid to explore religious beliefs with their clients."

I become suddenly nervous about exploring religious beliefs with Dr. Vargas. I know that she wears a gold cross on her neck and that she is Latina, so I am guessing she might be Catholic. But I don't know how she feels about Evangelical Christians, Jews, or gay people.

I decide to be brave. "I think the anxiety you are hearing in my voice on the tape, and also in here when we talk about Charlie, is about me. You know I am Jewish, by my name if by nothing else, and I am aware of not knowing much about Christianity. But the truth is, I do come to my relationship with Charlie with some preconceptions about his particular, I don't know, *brand* of Christianity. I want to hear what it means to him without imposing my own biases—but I'm not sure I can do that."

Dr. Vargas waits. I inhale and decide to jump.

"I mean, I think that his church probably does not support gay people. And I'm pretty sure Charlie is gay—I mean, he hasn't told me that, so of course I don't really know yet. It's just, I think he is. And, if I had to guess, I'd say that is why he left his former college."

"We don't *guess* in therapy, Rachel," says Dr. Vargas. "You will have plenty of time to get to know Charlie and to find out why he transferred and why he is seeking your help."

"And also," I stammer, "I'm gay. I mean bisexual really, but you know, gay enough." *Ugh, did I really just say "gay enough"?*

Dr. Vargas looks at me with her serious eyes. "Then you have to be extra aware of your own possible tendencies to make assumptions about your client."

When the supervision hour ends, I go for a walk on campus to clear my head.

"You have to be extra aware?" What does that even mean? Does she think I'll try to convert him or something? Doesn't she know that gaydar is real? Maybe not a legitimate clinical assessment tool, but still—real?

I walk past the black box theater and the old stone building housing the history and English departments. I turn past a cluster of dorms and head toward the quad, leaves crunching under my low work heels.

Autumn on a New England college campus might be my idea of heaven. The colors of the trees are close to bursting, the breeze is steady but far from cold, and the students are sprawled in little groups on the quad, cupping hot drinks and laughing together. The moment makes me nostalgic for my undergraduate days, but the yearning feels more specific than that. Something in the weather or the late afternoon light brings to mind a particular scene.

I was sitting on the front steps of my dorm with my girlfriend and two other friends. One was playing a guitar, and I was playing with Nora's thick, long hair, braiding and twisting it. I was wearing a long-sleeved, white, cotton pullover shirt that I loved, one I bought at the Gay Pride march in Boston the previous spring. The image on the shirt looked like a European license plate, a long rectangle of black uniform numbers and letters that read "2QT2BSTR8"—too cute to be straight.

Now, as I settle on an empty bench along a brick pathway, I realize that what I am feeling is invisible. In college, we were all so busy defining ourselves, then wearing those definitions on buttons on our backpacks. In my post-college life, I am who I am depending on *where* I am: a good granddaughter and unmarried Jewish girl at Beth El, a student in the classroom, a trainee at the counseling center. It has been several years since I've been in a relationship with a woman.

Does the world see me as straight? The thought makes my stomach sink. *Who in my life really knows me?* As I head back to the counseling center, I feel a new resolve rising up in me. I will not let myself disappear.

~

My two best college friends, Kara and Doreen, come up to Boston to visit. Since I don't want to inconvenience Zayde—and seriously need to get out of the house—we find a last-minute discounted hotel room in Copley Square. Kara, Doreen, and I know how to have sleepovers—a perfect mix of eighth-grade slumber party and late-night dorm life that makes me fantasize about spending my life living in a commune of women. I pick up Chinese takeout on the way to meeting them at the hotel, and by 6:30, we are in our flannel pajamas, chopsticks in hand.

"So," I say, "do you ever just feel like it was so much easier in college to feel *seen*? I mean, if you were a vegetarian, you lived in the vegetarian house. If you were musical theater geeks like us, you hung out in the box office and your room was covered in show posters. It was just easier to say to the world, 'This is who I am.'" I steer clear of the bisexual stuff since both Kara and Doreen identify as straight.

"I don't know," says Doreen, who has recently started singing the Star-Spangled Banner at minor league sporting events. "I guess I feel like I have different outlets for expressing myself post-college. It's why I do the National Anthem thing I think. It's either going to be that or bad community theater."

"No, I totally get what you're saying," says Kara. "I spend every workday in the corporate world—which is *so* different from Wesleyan—and I think that no one there really knows me. They know me as, like, efficient and organized, but they don't know what I wear on weekends. They don't know what music I listen to or which political candidates I support."

"Right!" I say, my chopsticks punctuating the air. "It's like, remember when we were in tech week for *West Side Story*, and Julie made that last-minute decision to light the intro to 'Something's Coming' with that stationary spotlight? Tony had to walk into the light out of darkness—"

"Oh yeah, and he kept not being able to find his light?" asks Doreen with a laugh and shake of her red curls.

"Yeah, and Julie kept yelling, 'We can't see you, Tony! Feel the fucking light on your face!'" Julie had been the biggest diva when she directed that play.

"Okay, what does this have to do with identity though?" asks Kara.

"I just think it's a great metaphor," I say. "I mean, there was Tony, ready to start the number, but he couldn't find his light and so the audience couldn't see him."

"Not catching your drift," says Doreen shaking her head.

"It's like, you know how sometimes the spotlight operator follows the actor? It's the operator's job to make sure the actor is seen. But with 'Something's Coming,' the spotlight was shining first, and then it was the actor's job to walk into the circle of light. It felt like when we were in college, there were spotlights shining on us everywhere we went because, I don't know, college is just lit that way, but now we have to *find* our light if we want to be seen."

"Feel the light on our *fucking faces*," Kara says in an imitation of Julie's director voice.

"No, I think it was feel the *fucking light* on our faces," corrects Doreen, even more shrill.

"*Fucking feel the fucking light on our fucking faces!*" I screech, and we crack up because we are still just young enough.

It is a Saturday in early January and I am sitting next to Zayde in the Torah service part of Shabbat morning. I often drift during the Torah service. Truth be told, I don't read along in the English. I just like the sound of the chanting, the rhythmic trope of Torah reading that I've known all my life. It doesn't much matter to me what it says; it's the melody that feels spiritual. During this part of the service, it is customary for individuals to be honored by being called up to the Torah for an *alliyah*, during which one says a blessing before and after the reading of a section of Torah. My attention is snapped back to the bimah when the rabbi calls up a woman I've never seen before. She looks about my age but tiny, having the compact body of an athlete, and wears a trendy pants suit and chunky shoes. The rabbi pauses a moment between Torah readings to publicly greet her, something usually reserved for special occasions or special visitors.

Putting her arm around this small, chunky-shoed woman, Rabbi Stein looks out at the congregation and says, "It is an honor this Shabbat to welcome back one of our own, Elizabeth Abraham. Liz has been living and working abroad for several years. Just last year, we said goodbye to her parents, Fran and Arnold, when they relocated to Florida, and now Liz has moved back to the Boston area." She turns to her, "*Brucha Haba'a*. We welcome you home."

Liz chants the Torah blessing in a clear, assertive voice, occasionally looking up at the congregation as if she is summoning our participation. Her eyes are like nothing I have ever seen—they are a deep green that contrast against her short, black hair like jewels and shine even to those of us many rows from the front of the sanctuary. When she returns to her seat, I watch her out of the corner of my eye as she sits a few rows behind me, on the right side of the aisle. I am careful not to turn around.

At the luncheon, though I never talk to her, I am aware of this Liz's whereabouts at all times. She is greeted with hugs from many long-time congregants and seems to be answering question after question about her time away. She holds her small frame as if it is made of pure strength. I look at her shoes, which I then recognize as Doc Martins.

Later that afternoon, I ask Zayde, "So who is this Liz Abraham anyway?"

"Hm?" he says, not lifting his eyes from the *Wall Street Journal* he's reading. "Arnie and Fran's daughter? Oh she's a world traveler I suppose. She grew up at Beth El."

"And her parents moved to Florida?" I ask, hoping for something more. Anything.

Zayde looks up from the *Journal*. "They were snowbirds for years, but then they decided to move down there permanently. Arnie was an ophthalmologist. They had Elizabeth very late in life."

"So she's an only child?" I ask, leaning forward.

"No, no they have two older children, a son and a daughter. Probably fifteen years older than Elizabeth. The daughter married an Orthodox man, lives in Baltimore—a bushel of kids."

"And the son?"

"Oh, I don't know where he is." His head is bent over the paper again. "Never married. Strange fellow."

Chapter 6

L iz comes by herself to Saturday morning services every week
for the next several weeks. I observe everything—her walk, her
clothes, when she gets her hair cut. We never speak.

Though I am preoccupied with spying on Liz during these cold
January weeks, I can't help but notice that the buzz about Rabbi
Stein's announcement a couple of months back has gathered energy
and seems to be all Zayde and his friends talk about. When I notice
the monthly synagogue newsletter sitting open on the kitchen table,
I understand why. There in black and white is a copy of the rabbi's
talk from the fall, with a bold message in a box at the top of the
page. "Please join us at our monthly board meeting on January 23rd
where we will discuss your reactions to this policy change. Everyone
welcome."

"Zayde? Are you planning to go to the board meeting this week?"

"You better believe it! I suspect it will be a very crowded meeting,"
he answers while puttering around the kitchen.

I sit and flip through the newsletter, keeping off of the page I'd
first seen. "I think I'd like to go too."

The Beth El library is packed. When Zayde and I arrive, just a few
minutes before the meeting is scheduled to start, people are already

bringing in extra folding chairs and trying to make sure the older congregants have seats. The building's dry heat feels oppressive as we pack in; I help Zayde find a seat, and I stand against the back wall, wanting to observe the action from the outskirts as much as possible. My heart does a little leap when Liz, in jeans and boots and a puffy winter parka, appears in the doorway. She surveys the crowded room and then finds a space to stand against a side wall. I can watch her using my peripheral vision, and I can't believe my luck.

The president, a serious man who looks as if he's just come from his office job, begins the meeting. He moves quickly through the initial things on the agenda—the financial report, announcements of upcoming programs, and then puts his pen and agenda sheet down and sits back in his chair.

"Well," he says, looking around the room, "I don't know that we've ever had this many people show up to a board meeting. I would say that I'm flattered, but I don't think your being here has anything to do with me." An awkward chuckle runs through the room. "It seems that several of you have strong feelings about some recent changes the rabbi has made. Many of you have contacted me personally to talk about these changes, so I thought it best to offer some time at this meeting for us to air our feelings. Usually, the rabbi attends board meetings. However, I asked her if we might meet privately tonight so that people would feel free to express themselves. She understood, but asked that she have the opportunity to talk further about her proposed changes at a later time."

"It was my impression that she wasn't making a proposal. It sounded to me like she'd made a decision, and it was a done deal!" interrupts Zayde's friend Murray Greenblatt in a loud and abrasive voice.

"Murray, yes—the rabbi did make a decision. I didn't mean to imply that she was asking permission from the board—"

"And what about that?" This from Zayde, matching Murray's

volume and tenor. "Since when does she get to act unilaterally without the consent of those of us who've built this synagogue?" A murmur of grumbles runs through the library. Zayde's face is red and pinched. "Okay, one thing at a time," says the president, taking back the reins. "The truth is, Lew, that the rabbi does have the authority, as our religious leader, to determine how services run. As she explained in her talk back in November, including non-Jews in certain aspects of a religious service does not violate Jewish law. So the question of whether or not she is within her rights to make such a change is a moot point. She is. Now, I understand that people have different opinions about this change, and I am hoping that we can use this time to—respectfully—share with one another our reactions and feelings. If you want to speak, I ask that you please raise your hand."

Hands shoot up.

The president calls on a middle-aged woman sitting toward the front of the room.

"I'm sorry," says the woman, a little too quietly. I have to lean forward to hear her. "I just don't understand what all the commotion is about. The rabbi is simply assuring that all members of our community, Jewish by birth, Jewish by conversion, and *not* Jewish all feel welcome here. She is acknowledging that Jewish families are made up of many different combinations of individuals and that each of those individuals play an important role in a family's life cycle events."

More hands shoot up.

This time Sophia Goldblatt speaks. "The commotion is because this is a *synagogue*. In order to participate in the religious activities here you have to be a Jew. Period. The rabbi is watering down our Jewishness with her liberal agenda of making everyone feel good. It's not right."

I watch as Zayde, Murray, and Bess nod at Sophia. She grins, proud of her own bravery and articulateness. They are like their own octogenarian debate team.

Then the president calls on a man standing against the wall near Liz. At first I am thrilled to be able to cast my eyes in her direction without being obvious. But then his story pulls my attention, and I, like the rest of the room, become very quiet and focused on his words. "Listen, let me be clear about my role here," he begins. "My name is Michael DeMatteo and this is my wife, Karen." He motions to the woman standing to his left, her eyes fixated on the floor. "We are the reason this has all come to a head right now. I am not Jewish; Karen is. We are raising our two children, Sara and Alexander, as Jews. They have come to religious school here all their lives; they are in the youth group. We celebrate Jewish holidays at home and identify as a Jewish family." He pauses and takes a deep breath. "Sara's Bat Mitzvah is coming up in the spring. After attending the Bar and Bat Mitzvahs of her friends over the past year, Karen and I have become very disillusioned. I have always been treated as a full-fledged member of this community. I have served on committees and been an active participant here. But when we realized that I would essentially be cut out of our daughter's Bat Mitzvah because I myself was not Jewish, I became upset. Frankly, I felt made a fool of—believing all these years that we were respected as a Jewish family here. Sara was very upset. So we brought our concerns to the rabbi. I feel honored and included because of the changes she is making. I am hoping that maybe knowing our personal story might give this discussion some context."

The room stays quiet. Bess speaks then, without raising her hand. Her tone is soft and genuinely curious. "Michael, do you mind if I ask you a question?" she asks, then continues without waiting for an answer. "Why did you never convert?"

Michael takes a slow breath and seems to consider this, but the president speaks.

"Bess, Michael, I am going to ask you to pause," he says. "We've shared a lot here tonight, and it's clear to me that there are many differing, strong opinions in the room. I am going to suggest that we hold our discussions until next month when I will schedule a town hall-style meeting specifically dedicated to this issue. We will advertise the meeting to the entire congregation so that everyone has the opportunity for their voices to be heard.

"It is important that the board understand the majority feeling of the entire community on these changes. As many of you are aware, the rabbi's contract is up for renewal after the High Holidays next fall, which means the board must start the negotiation process with her this spring. Before we do so, we need to know how the community as a whole is feeling about the direction she is leading us. Let's adjourn for tonight and I will be setting a date for that meeting shortly."

I don't go over to Zayde right away. He is grumbling with his friends. I look over to where Michael and Karen are standing, thinking that I'd like to go thank Michael for sharing their story. Liz and a few others are already engaging in conversation with them. I chicken out and just watch as she slips her arms into the sleeves of her jacket, that puffy parka swallowing her little body whole.

∽

On the first Saturday morning in February, his "Good morning Esther!" sounding scratchier than usual, Zayde comes into the kitchen in his robe.

"I'm going to stay home this morning dear," he says. "I'm coming down with something."

I fix him some breakfast and tell him to go back to bed, that I will bring him home a bagel with whitefish salad after shul.

When I enter the back of the sanctuary, I see that Liz is sitting in her usual spot on the right. Without allowing myself the time to change my mind, I walk with purpose down the aisle and take the seat next to her. I smile a quick "hi," grab a prayer book from the back of the pew in front of us, and busy myself with finding the right page.

After several minutes pass, Liz leans over to me and whispers, "I wondered if you were ever going to stop watching and actually approach me."

My heart is pounding, and I have the irrational fear that she can hear it. I have no idea how to respond. I look at her, and our eyes meet for the first time. Simultaneously, we break into smiles, almost laugh. I think I might be having a heart attack.

I don't hear a thing the rabbi says for the rest of the service. I am completely in my head, lulled by my own perseveration, *Oh my God, Oh my God, Oh my God*, over and over. It is as if my own awareness of my right arm next to her left is enough to create a magnetic force field between us. I pray that she can't see me shaking, but then realize that of course she can. All she has to do is notice my hand each time I go to turn a page of my prayer book. I am a mess.

When the service ends, as is customary, we wish each other a "Shabbat Shalom." Then Liz asks, "So where's your grandfather?"

"He has a cold—decided to stay home." I shrug, trying to be convincingly casual.

"Want to grab some lunch?" she asks, and there is just a split second where I think she has said, "Want to grab me?" I am dizzy. She continues, "I mean out, not here."

"Yeah!" I say, way too enthusiastically. Shit. "Um, where do you want to go?"

"It's a nice day. Let's walk into Davis Square."

"Okay! Um, I'm just going to run to the bathroom first." I exit the sanctuary, slip into the ladies room, and into a stall where I stand with my back against the wall just breathing. I don't even have to go to the bathroom, I just breathe. *I cannot believe this is happening.* After I collect myself, fix my hair in the mirror, and check my makeup, I find Liz waiting for me outside of the coat closet, wearing her coat and holding mine.

"Thanks," I say, surprised. "How did you know this was my coat?"

She looks at me, with a kind of sly expression of confusion, eyebrows cocked. "Do you think you're the only one who's been watching?" She heads toward the door.

Oh my God she's flirting with me, Oh my God she's flirting with me. I follow, putting on my gloves.

As soon as we are on the sidewalk, a cold wind smacks against my face. I can't believe that this is her idea of a "nice day." In a matter of minutes my nose will be bright red and running. I am not so attractive in the cold.

"So, Rachel Levine," she says, glancing sideways at me as we walk, "who are you?"

"Well," I begin, so impressed with her directness that I almost forget to be nervous. "Uh, I'm twenty-four. I'm a doctoral student in clinical psychology. I'm from Philly—"

Liz makes the sound of a buzzer and crosses her index fingers into an X. "Nope," she says. "I know those things. I mean who are you *really*?"

I'm not sure if I should be offended, but I'm not. I love her question. I take a deep breath and slowly, carefully let myself unfurl. "Okay." Then thoughtfully, "I love seeing indie films at the Somerville Theatre. I'm a little bit homesick. I love my grandfather, but I don't always love living with him. And," I pause then decide to beat her at her own game, "I'm fascinated by you."

She smiles a huge, luminous smile. "What's your favorite recent film?"

"*Antonia's Line*," I say without hesitation. "It's Dutch."

"Saw it in France," she replies with an assured nod. "Loved it. What are you homesick for?"

"Not for my parents really. Not Pennsylvania. Maybe for college—Wesleyan—for a place where I was really known."

"When did you graduate from Wesleyan?"

"'94."

She nods again. "I graduated from Yale in '90. I had some friends at Wesleyan, but they were probably there before your time." I feel a little defensive at this, at both her superior age and her Ivy League status. "How come you live with your grandfather?"

"Complicated," I say. I am proud of my ability to keep up with her clip. I don't stammer or hesitate. I refuse to let her rattle me. "The most obvious reason is that I can live there for free while I'm in school. Also, though, I feel a certain—I don't know—responsibility for him. It's like taking care of him is this mitzvah I feel compelled to do. The question is though, if I'm compelled, is it really a mitzvah?"

"Interesting question. I bet you're a really good therapist."

At this I smile despite myself. She doesn't ask why I find her fascinating.

We walk for a few more blocks, discussing where we should eat. We pick a newish café in Ball Square, not quite to Davis, and I am relieved because, as predicted, my nose is running, and my one tissue has become a tattered shred of fibers in my pocket. As we are seated, I mention that I should find a pay phone to call Zayde and let him know that I would be running late.

"No worries," says Liz, as she pulls a mobile phone from her pocket—smaller than my clunky car phone. "Remember, I've been in Europe. Everyone has one of these there."

"I should call right from the table?" I ask, certain that this would be perceived as shockingly inappropriate by everyone around us.

"If you're uncomfortable, you can go outside, but I think it's fine to call from here."

I'm not so sure, so I step into the foyer of the café and call from there. "Zayde?" I say when he answers, feeling awkward and conspicuous as a young couple enters. "Hey, I just wanted to let you know that I decided to grab lunch with a friend I made at shul. I'm not sure how long I'll be out. Will you be okay for lunch? I can bring you home something later—"

"No, no, I'm just fine. I have a can of soup here. I'm glad you made a new friend. You girls enjoy yourselves!"

"Thanks, Zayde. I love you. Shabbat shalom." I go back to the table and hand the phone back over to Liz. "Thanks," I say. I am suddenly aware that she's been asking all the questions. "So, tell me about France. Were you studying there?"

"After I graduated," she says, cupping her hands around her mug of coffee, which arrived while I was on the phone, "I got a Fulbright to study the history of feminism in France for a year. I was also a research assistant at a French feminist think tank that year, and then I got really lucky and they offered me a full-time position with them. So, I was able to get a work visa and I worked there from the fall of '90 until this past fall." She pauses, looking into her coffee. "It's good to be back."

"That's amazing," I say, feeling pitifully mono-linguistic. "What was the job like?"

"At first, it felt really exciting, you know, living and working in Paris. But my work there actually ended up being a little boring. I was sort of a glorified office assistant. Also, I realized that I hated politics."

"Huh. Well, why did you stay six years at a job you didn't like?" I am fishing.

She knows it and waits, deciding. "Her name was Helen," she says as if admitting defeat. "She was a lawyer in the organization." She pronounces it like the French, no H-sound and accenting the second syllable. "It was great until . . . it wasn't. Then I came home." Her green eyes seem suddenly far away and sad.

"I'm sorry." I'm not sure what to say. There is an awkward pause. "So, what are you doing now?"

"Right now," she says, leaning forward, meeting my eyes, "I'm having lunch with someone who apparently finds me fascinating, and who, I must say, I find fascinating as well."

We both smile. My cheeks hurt from smiling this much.

"But for my day job," she adds sitting back in her chair, "I just started as a training coordinator at a new, local non-profit. It's called Makom and works for the inclusion of LGBT Jews in Jewish life."

"That sounds like an amazing position." *Ugh, I'm saying "amazing" too much.* "I mean, how cool is it that we live in an age when Jews can even acknowledge that the tribe is made up of all different kinds of people." *The tribe?*

"Sure, but it really depends on which groups of Jews you're talking about. The Orthodox don't want to hear a thing about inclusion of queer Jews. The Conservative movement? They're coming around."

"Speaking of inclusion, what did you think of that board meeting last week?" I ask, relieved to have something concrete and shared that we could talk about.

Liz thinks for a minute. "I thought it was sad," she finally says. "I get that change is hard for everyone, and I also get that the older folks in any synagogue have an experience of Judaism that is very different from our own."

"What do you mean?" I ask, a little worried about coming off as ignorant or simple or something.

"They are part of the last generation of Holocaust survivors, right? So, for them, the idea of expanding our Jewish circles to be more inclusive of outsiders is threatening. They are all about preservation and safety. Then, this progressive, young, *female*—don't forget that— rabbi comes in and wants to open the doors wider. They are incredibly afraid that this is the beginning of the death of their community. But the irony," she continues, "is that what Rabbi Stein is doing is actually preserving and growing the community. Each successive generation of American Jews is more intermarried, and this trend will only continue. If the Conservative movement is not willing to become more open to interfaith families, then *that* will be the death of the community. Reform Jews totally get this."

"So what made you come back to Beth El, you know, since it's a

Conservative synagogue, instead of joining a Reform one?" I am so drawn to her intellect.

She laughs. "I suppose I chose familiarity over change—so that I could work to push the community toward change over familiarity, maybe." She shrugs at herself. "How about you?"

"I grew up in a Reform synagogue. I'm used to a very egalitarian community. I'm at Beth El because of my grandfather. But you know what? I love Rabbi Stein and I might be there even if it weren't for Zayde."

She smiles. "I totally get that. Actually, Beth El has always been on the cutting edge of Conservative shuls. In the early 1980s, we were one of the only Conservative congregations in Boston to count women in the minyan. The others still defined it as a quorum of ten or more Jewish *men*. I remember because I had just had my Bat Mitzvah, and I was one of the first girls to be able to make a minyan. It was pretty cool. I also know, because my dad was on the board with your grandfather at the time, that your grandfather didn't approve of allowing women to count at first. I think he's come a long way. My guess is that he'll eventually come around on this issue, too."

I sit shocked for a minute. Liz knows this piece of information about Zayde that I don't know. He was against women counting as legitimate Jewish adults in a minyan? It strikes me that this is the most basic of human rights—to count. "I don't know if he'll come around," is all I can think of to say.

I change the subject then, not wanting to talk about Zayde. I tell her about my practicum training at the college counseling center, about Zeke and my parents.

"What was coming out to them like?" she asks.

I hesitate, not because I am choosing my words but because it is still hard to talk about. "I was naïve," I say nodding slowly. "I thought it would be easy, I suppose because coming out to myself was so easy.

I mean, it just never occurred to me that anyone could feel anything but happy for me, right?"

Liz purses her lips as if to say, "Oh, I wish it were that simple."

"I know," I continue. "I mean my dad, he was fine. But really, I think he thinks it's just a phase. My mom, she spent a lot of time crying. I actually think she may have cried every day for a year. She asked all of those bad textbook questions. 'Where did I go wrong?' and 'How could you hurt your family like this?'" I shrug. "It sucked, you know."

"What's it like with them now?"

"We don't really talk about it now. It helps that I'm living here and, frankly, that I've been single. Actually, the last person I dated—when I was living at home the year after college—was a guy. I'm not sure if that made it better or worse. I mean, if I start dating a woman, I might have to come out to them all over again." I am nervous saying this, worried that I am being too presumptuous about what woman I might be dating.

"So, you're bi?" asks Liz, pushing the last bits of salad around on her plate.

"Yeah," I answer, then raise my eyebrows. "That okay?" I am partly being sarcastic but partly not.

"Of course, it's okay," she says. "I mean what kind of training coordinator for LGBT inclusion would I be if it weren't okay?"

"So, you identify as lesbian?" I ask, trying to throw the focus back on her.

"Yes," she says. It feels formal and I wonder why we've stopped smiling.

∽

That night, I hold my breath at the squealing sound of the dial-up internet connection. When I see her name in my email inbox, I burst into one of those cheek-hurting smiles.

From: eabraham@alumni.yale.edu
To: rlevine@bscp.edu
Sent: Saturday 2/1/97 6:04 PM
Subject: Two apologies and an invitation

Dear Rachel,

It was great to hang out with you. Something you should know about me: If I think I've screwed something up, I say so. I drilled you with a lot of questions about "who you are" today. I fear I was more than a little overbearing. I get like that when I'm nervous. ;) Also, I know I got weird when you said you were bi. That's my baggage and henceforth, I fully intend to leave it at the door. I'm actually a much nicer person than the one you met today.

I just read that Dar Williams is playing at Club Passim in Harvard Square next Saturday night. Do you want to go with me?

Liz

I reread the email fifteen times.

From: rlevine@bscp.edu
To: eabraham@alumni.yale.edu
Sent: Saturday 2/1/97 9:13 PM
Subject: Re: Two apologies and an invitation

Liz,

I LOVE Dar Williams! (Did you know she is a Wesleyan alum?) I would love to see her with you. Dinner first?

No need to apologize. I like your no-bullshit questions.

So . . . I make you nervous?

Rachel

That night, I hardly sleep at all.

Chapter 7

When I meet with Dr. Vargas, I am lighter—more confident and less concerned about screwing up with Charlie. Everything feels more vibrant and more alive, even in the gloom of a New England February. I don't cringe internally when she plays my tape.

"How has your week been, Charlie?"

"Okay . . . good actually. I mean, I've been doing some pretty cool stuff. I ended up getting a chorus part in *Anything Goes* and we started rehearsals last night. I think it's going to be fun."

"That's great! Did you do musical theater in high school and at your previous college?"

"A little. Not in high school. Last year, I worked on the stage crew for one show."

"How was that?"

"It was fun. But I think this show is going to be better. Just a cooler group of people I think."

"Good. I did musical theater in college, too. It was the best experience."

"Oh. Cool."

Click. Dr. Vargas stops the tape player right there. "Rachel, tell me about that choice."

"The choice to tell him that I also did musical theater?" I ask, suddenly a little queasy.

"Yes." She looks inquisitively at me, eyebrows raised.

"I feel like I'm still trying to build rapport with Charlie. I was thinking that it might make him feel more connected to me if he knew we had something in common." I pause. "And, also, I was fishing." Even over seven sessions, he still hadn't come out to me.

"Okay. So let's look at the pros and cons of your choice."

I'm not sure if I understand what she means, but I try. "The pros are that, having something in common with me might make him feel safer—more understood? It's good for rapport. The cons? I guess maybe he'll think I'm competing with him? I'm really not sure."

It is hard to tell Dr. Vargas that I don't know the answer to her question. One of the things I've always prided myself on is knowing the answers to questions. I was "good at school" as a kid and knew how to tell grownups what they wanted to hear. Admitting *not* knowing is something I usually avoid at all costs, but I can't fake it with Dr. Vargas.

"I'm not suggesting that you made the *wrong* choice, Rachel," she starts. "I'm just interested in knowing whether it was an informed decision. Whenever we make a choice with a client, we need to know why we've made it. Is it possible that, by telling Charlie you were also involved in musical theater in college, you were trying to tell him that you understand him?"

I think about this. "Yeah, I suppose so. Maybe it was my way of saying 'I get you'?"

"Okay. And what are the possible pitfalls of thinking that, just because you've experienced something similar to someone else, you understand what their experience of it was?"

"I think I get it. The potential danger is less in what I was communicating to Charlie and more in what I might be assuming about him. The reasons I chose to do theater might be very different from his reasons. What I got out of the experience may be very different from what he gets out of it."

"Right. We always have to be aware of that assumption in our work. Just because something in our background is the same as our clients' doesn't mean that we understand their experience."

I soak up Dr. Vargas's words like a dry sponge. She is the smartest woman I've ever known.

When Saturday comes, I am a nervous, excited wreck. At the luncheon after services, Liz comes right up to Zayde and me with her little plate of cheese and kugel.

"Shabbat shalom, Rachel, Mr. Kessler." She nods at each of us and shows just the slightest smirk.

"Oh, hi Liz!" I say, in a slightly too high pitch. "It's good to see you again. Um, Zayde, this is Liz Abraham."

Zayde reaches out his hand to shake hers. "Shabbat shalom, young lady. How are your parents doing?"

"They're just fine. Enjoying the Florida sun. I'll be sure to tell them you asked."

"Please do. And how is that sister of yours—is she still in Baltimore?"

"She is. She's very happy there."

Zayde nods. He doesn't ask about her brother.

I spend the afternoon making myself as irresistible as I possibly can. This includes a ridiculously long shower in which I remove every possible unwanted hair. I am made only slightly anxious by the thought that Zayde is downstairs, listening to the water in the pipes and worrying about the water bill. I cut my nails. I don't know what is going to happen on this date, but if it's sex, I intend to be very ready.

I try on several outfits before picking one and change my hair more than once. I might burst into "I Feel Pretty" at any moment. When I go downstairs, Zayde looks up with surprise from his chair.

"Don't you look lovely! Where are you off to tonight?"

"Thank you, Zayde." I go over and kiss his cheek. "I'm actually meeting up with Liz Abraham and a group of her friends for a concert. There's a possibility we'll all sleep over one of the girl's houses if it gets late." Just in case.

Liz and I meet at a Thai restaurant around the corner from the café where the concert is. I arrive a few minutes before her and wait in the cold foyer, practicing a casual smile. When she comes through the door wearing a red, knitted winter hat pulled down tight over her ears, I almost don't recognize her. With a big smile and "Hey, Rachel," she pulls off the hat, revealing that beautiful, shiny black hair. She doesn't even have hat-head. I opted for cold ears and no-risk hair.

I know what I will be ordering before we open our menus: pad thai. It is the same dish I have ordered the few times I've eaten Thai food and I know I like it—noodles with ground peanuts and bits of fried egg, not at all spicy. As Liz starts to look through her menu at the items with long Thai names, marked with little chili peppers denoting the level of spiciness, it occurs to me that Pad Thai might be the hamburger of Thai food. It is probably the thing most ordered by Americans with no palate for spice or, worse, no taste for adventure.

I am ordering vanilla ice cream at the Baskin-Robbins "31 Flavors" counter. I think of the words from the Ani DiFranco song, *"I am thirty-two flavors and then some."* Yes! I want Liz to think I am thirty-two flavors and then some—complex and nuanced and full of risk. Except I can't tolerate spicy food even a little.

I am reminded of a silly argument I got into at the Arts House my senior year in college. I'd been hanging out with some friends who lived there—theater friends mostly but of the more tattooed and blue-haired persuasion than Kara or Doreen. Somehow the term "vanilla sex" came up and before I knew what was happening, all eyes were on me. "Rachel Levine—you *totally* have vanilla sex!" declared Vincent, my most flaming of gay friends, pointing his long, manicured finger at me.

"What? I do *not!*" Though I was not at all sure what this accusation meant or if it were true.

Proclamations of, "Oh you sooo do!" and "I would bet money on that!" echoed Vincent's. There was laughter, loving and good-natured, but completely at my expense.

"Listen," I had said, my red cheeks and smirky grin betraying my humiliation, "You guys don't know what I can be like! I am an *animal* in bed!" I emphasized the word *animal* so as to conjure up the image of something fiercer than, say, a puppy.

"I'm sure you are, sweetheart," said Vincent, "what with that storage container under your bed full of all those whips and handcuffs!" More laughter. I laughed along because, of course, they were kind of right. I wondered if Vincent had ever really noticed the storage box under my bed in my dorm room and if he knew that all it held were turtlenecks.

"What are you going to order?" asks Liz, pulling me back to the unnecessarily open menu in front of me.

"I'm thinking about the Pad Thai," I say. "I love noodles." *I love noodles?*

"Oh that's always good here," she says. "I'm thinking of trying the Kaeng Pa Curry." I'm not sure what she sees in my face that makes her say, "You don't like spicy food, do you?"

I smile, in spite of myself, and answer, "I really don't. But I do love trying new foods—new, non-spicy foods that is." Read: *I'm not into leather but don't think that means I'm boring in bed.*

Liz smiles back as if sensing that I am self-conscious about my gustatory limitations. "No worries," she says. "Do you like Indian food?"

"Uh, I don't know."

"Next time I'll have to take you to my favorite Indian place. Everyone thinks that all Indian food is spicy but there are some really great dishes that aren't."

I love that she says "next time." When we've eaten and the check comes, she reaches for it and says, "This is on me."

"But you got the concert tickets," I protest.

"Okay, but I asked you out." Then she says it again. "You can get it *next time.*"

Club Passim is a little basement of a place across from the Harvard Coop. The room is crowded with people gathered around small tables in little semi-circles facing the low stage. We grab a table for two off to the side and pull our chairs not quite next to each other and slightly angled apart. I wonder what the couple behind us would guess if, perchance, they were playing that game where you guess the relationships of strangers based on their body language. *They're old friends. They've been together for years. They're on a first date.*

Then, Dar comes on stage. She is funny and real and makes me feel totally at home with her stories about Wesleyan and about love in her twenties. She sings a song about Iowa that makes me want to go there and one about being in love but not at peace that, I see, makes Liz tear up. I wonder if she is thinking of Helen, and I pretend not to notice.

Toward the middle of the concert, Liz pulls her chair closer to mine. *It's probably so she can see the stage better. She's so short, it must be hard to see.* But a moment later, I feel her hand on mine. She doesn't hold my hand in that clammy, gripping way boys do in movie theaters. Rather, she touches me so lightly—just the tips of her fingers interlacing with mine. My fingers respond without my even knowing it and we spend the rest of the concert with our fingers entwined in an almost imperceptible dance. Following each song, we need to let go to clap. After each round of applause, there is that little thrilling moment where our fingers come back together, not desperately like two lovers running to each other in an airport, but almost tentatively, like two children peeking around a corner to see if the other is still there.

When the concert ends, we notice through the little windows at the top of the basement walls that it has begun to snow. We wrap ourselves in our winter coats and scarves (and Liz in her hat) and follow the crowd up the steps to the cobblestone street outside.

"Oh my God, that concert was so amazing!" I say, looking up into the cascading flakes of snow. I stick out my tongue to catch them. *Wait—do only little kids catch snowflakes on their tongues?*

"It was really great." She sticks out her tongue as well, and I am flooded with relief. After a quiet minute, she says, "Let me walk you to your car." I am thinking that this is code for, *Let me walk you to your car so you can drive me home and we can spend the next twelve hours in my bed*, but when we get to my car, she says, "So, I'll see you soon, yes?" I think that she's spent too much time in France, ending her sentence that way.

"I could drive you home," I suggest, unsure how to play this game.

But Liz, not one to play games, says, "It's too soon. Let's not mess anything up by rushing."

Before I have a chance to feel disappointed, Liz walks in closer to me so that I am pushed back against my snowy car door. I realize that if I let myself lean against the car and slide down just a little, we can be the same height, face to face. Liz puts her thick red mittens against my cold ears, holding my face. *Oh my God, she's going to kiss me. Oh my God, oh my God, oh my God.* And then her soft lips are on mine. I feel my cheeks burning. *Is it the cold or the heat?* The snow falls on us, and we stay there kissing for what might be minutes but then is not nearly long enough. She pulls away and says slyly, "Hey, did you slide yourself down the car so you could be shorter?"

"Yup," I answer smugly as I open my car door. I slide into the driver's seat, start the engine and lower the window. "I'm either going to drive you to the entrance to the T or follow behind you at two miles per hour to make sure you get there safely."

"Two miles an hour?" she calls back to me as she starts to jog backwards toward the exit of the lot. "Don't you know I'm a runner?" She breaks into a full run toward the T entrance down the block.

I didn't know.

Chapter 8

The next Wednesday is particularly warm for February. I call Liz from between classes at school and ask her if she wants to go hunting for crocuses after she gets off work.

"I don't know what that means," she replies, very seriously.

"It means take a walk with me later!" I giggle, all nerves.

"I would like that," she says in her no-nonsense Liz voice. "Where and when?"

"I could drive over to your office after my classes get out at 4:30?" I know her office is near Kenmore Square and that she takes the T to work. "We could walk along the Charles—"

"I will be ready and waiting."

❧

The sun is just about to set as Liz and I start our walk together. She is wearing a different winter hat; it looks hand-knitted and has those thick, braided ties that little girls tie under their chins but that Liz wears dangling over her shoulders. I wonder if she is a snowboarder. "Tell me about your siblings," I ask, opting for a question I've rehearsed, in case of awkward silence.

"Well," she begins, "Michael is the oldest. He's sixteen years older than me. Alana is two years younger than him. I'm the accident." She says this as if it is a story she's told many times, or at least one to which she's memorized the essential lines. "So, by the time I was four, they were both out of the house. I never really lived with them. Anyway, Alana married David when she was twenty-four. I was ten—you should have seen the poufy kid-sized bridesmaid dress they made me wear. They live in Baltimore and have five children— Modern Orthodox. Michael has lived with his partner Barry in San Francisco for as long as I can remember." She inhales and exhales slowly, as if deciding what to say next. "My parents pretty much disowned Michael when he came out to them as a teenager. I was too young to remember any of this, but he told me all the gory details when I was old enough."

I have so many questions to ask, but Liz just keeps talking like it's a story she needs to tell and hasn't in a long time. Her hands are shoved tightly into the pockets of her parka like she is bracing for a blast of cold wind.

"I would always ask my parents why Michael never came home for Thanksgiving or for Chanukah and I always got some version of the same answer. 'Oh your brother is very busy with his life in California,' as if it were his fault that he didn't want to come home. I would talk to him on the phone from time to time, but I never felt like I really knew him. He didn't come to Alana's wedding or my Bat Mitzvah and I didn't know why. When I was almost fourteen, he came to visit. I hadn't seen him in years. Anyway, that was when he told me. He took me to the science museum for the day."

She pauses, grinning and shaking her head. "I remember that my mom was so weird about him and me spending the day alone together. I could tell she didn't like it. She must have known that we would talk about everything. So really we spent the majority of the day sitting in the food court at the museum. I had so many questions—I wanted to know what happened between Michael and my parents, but also I had a pretty good sense by then that I was gay, too. He told me how he had known since like elementary school and how my mom was always scolding him for things like wanting to play with girls and not liking sports. When he was sixteen, he told my parents that he had a boyfriend—this kid in school—it was all a huge secret. My mom basically flipped out. She slapped him and told him that he couldn't see his boyfriend anymore. They took him out of the public high school and put him in this Jewish day school in Brookline. Michael said that the next two years were hell. He went to college as far away as he could get, and he's stayed on the West Coast ever since."

I notice that Liz has taken her hands out of her pockets, and I take her hand, tentatively. I want to show support but also, I want intimacy. She grins at me as if to say, "I don't need your sympathy but thanks for the thought." She doesn't take her hand away though.

"So, how did *you* come out to them?" I ask. I am so scared of pushing too hard. It's like I am just learning to dance with Liz and I might betray my clumsiness by stepping forward when I should be stepping back.

"I didn't," she says. "I simply lived my life in secret until I could leave."

"Did you date anyone?" I ask, afraid that *she* is stepping back.

"Nope. I told them I wasn't interested in anyone—that the prom was for losers. I basically became a very angry teenager. I didn't really unleash my true self until Yale. That," she smiles, "was amazing."

"Tell me," I say, letting her smile relax me. I can imagine Liz ignited, lighting up her campus.

She laughs. "I joined Yale Lesbians before classes even started. I cut my hair. I slept around a lot."

"Is that when you got the nose-ring?" I ask.

"Oh yeah. I pierced my nose, got the tattoo . . ."

I raise my eyebrows.

"You haven't seen it—yet," she adds.

We lock eyes and hold each other's gaze for that extra second that moves it from one kind of looking to another. It is such a perfect moment that I want to preserve it just as it is. I catch my impulse to say something flirtatious, to try to hold on to that energy, knowing that if I do, it will be ruined. So I don't. Instead I say, "What is it like with your parents now?"

"Now, I'm the other distant child. I visited less and less throughout college, spending my summers working in New Haven. Then I left for Europe, and they moved to Florida. We talk on the phone every couple of weeks. I saw them when I first came back to the States. They don't ever ask about my personal life, and I don't ever volunteer information. They know, of course, but I don't think they know me at all."

I want to say that I am overcome with sadness for Liz. I want to say that I am feeling her pain, imagining her parents on their Florida lanai, not calling her. But I am thinking of my mother. I want to call her, to tell her about this beautiful dark-haired girl holding my hand in the dusk by the Charles. But all I would hear on the other end of the line are her tears.

༄

As I drive across the Mass Ave bridge, bringing Liz home to her apartment, I am thinking about my breath. I want to kiss her when I get there; I will, I will kiss her, but for this, I need perfect breath. For this, I need at least two of the Tic Tacs from the little box sitting in the dashboard ashtray. I start to reach toward it then think, *Ah! She will totally know I am getting ready to kiss her!* and instead I press the eject button on the cassette player and flip the tape, shoving it back in its slot with a sharp click. *But I need those Tic Tacs. Fuck it. It doesn't matter if it's awkward, I will be minty fresh for this moment.*

So I grab the little plastic box of green pill-shaped mints, flip the little top with my thumb and oh so coolly tip my head back while I shake it just above my mouth. I suddenly remember an episode of this new show *Animal Planet* I saw with Zayde where they said that an animal exposes its neck to show submission and I wonder if I am doing just this. The problem is, the Tic Tacs are somehow jammed in their box and as I casually shake shake, nothing comes out. I shake harder and swerve a little.

"Let me get that for you," says Liz, reaching out for the box and laughing. And suddenly I am being handed two mints by the girl I want to kiss so that I can kiss her. I am so embarrassed—until I see that she takes one as well. Now everything inside is flipping around like one of those little toy monkeys suspended between two sticks.

I pull into a loading zone at the side of Liz's building. I put on Essie's hazard lights and unclick my seat belt in one swift move before this moment of bravery can pass. I turn in my seat and reach with both hands for the hanging braided ties of Liz's hat, pulling her face toward me. I kiss her passionately, like I mean it. Like I want all of her. Like I have the best breath.

Moments later, she pulls back just enough to ask, "How about I make you dinner on Saturday?"

"In your apartment?" I reply, smiling slyly.

"In my apartment," she confirms, opening the passenger door. Then, turning back, "And tell your zayde not to wait up for you."

❧

The next three days pass like thick mud through an hourglass. I feel like an antsy child in the back seat of my parents' car whining, "Are we there yet?" I have never wanted someone as much as I want Liz Abraham, and every minute of waiting makes me fidget. Thursday after class finds me in Filene's Basement. (Filene's Basement! Like my mother in her stories about taking the bus to Downtown Crossing with her girlfriends to shop for prom dresses.) I have come in search of new sexy underwear and a matching bra. As I stealthily and oh-so-casually wander into the lingerie department, an older, slim woman with a tan pencil skirt and cowl neck sweater makes a beeline for me.

"Can I help you find anything?"

I am caught. *Yes, actually I'm a vanilla bi-girl wanting to seduce a hot, dykey woman who, though interested, seems a little aloof, you know? I want something subtle. It shouldn't scream Fuck Me but should make her want to nonetheless. Can you help me with that?* Instead, I grin and say, "No thanks, just looking," and duck away toward the cotton Jockey display.

A few minutes later, the woman safely assisting another shopper, I allow myself to wander back toward the flirtier options and, after lots of sifting through things too red, too lacey, and something that resembles dental floss for a tush, find a simple, silky set in very pale lavender. I try it on in the dressing room and, standing in front of the fluorescently lit tri-fold mirror, suck in my soft belly, wishing I could suck in these Hadassah arms, too.

Saturday afternoon's date prep is similar to the previous one. This time, when I come downstairs at 5:30, Zayde lets me have it about the water use.

"Rachel, your showers are *too* long. The water bill has been going up and up." He is angry, and I think about the Great Depression.

"I'm sorry Zayde," I say and kiss him on his scratchy cheek. "I will try harder to take quick showers." His crankiness scares me a little. "Um, I'm going out with some school friends. I'll probably stay over in Boston."

I remind myself that this is not a malicious lie. I am protecting Zayde. From me.

Liz's apartment is exactly what I've envisioned: small but classy, like Liz herself. There are no tapestries hanging on the walls like in the apartments of my just-out-of-college friends. Rather, there is real art—sketches and watercolors bought from street artists along the Seine and framed in simple black wooden frames. There is a cozy living room with a matching loveseat and arm chair, a combination TV/VCR, and bookshelves full of books. The eat-in kitchen is tiny, but as I watch her small frame moving about in it, it seems the perfect size for her. There are candles lit on the kitchen table; I have brought flowers from Star Market, and she arranges them in a vase next to the candles. The folk duo The Story plays softly on her CD player.

I say, "It smells amazing in here." And it does. Liz is cooking some incredible stir-fried vegetable dish. She pours me wine, something red that is definitely not the usual Manischewitz we have on Friday nights at Zayde's. I suddenly feel the difference in our ages. Liz is a grownup—she knows about wine and art and lives on her own. I am still such a child. I gulp the wine.

Liz must be picking up on my feelings because, when I ask if I can bring the bread over to the table, she says, "Yes, nervous Nellie," and kisses me quickly as if to say, "It's okay."

I put the bread down and sink into a chair. "I'm sorry. I am a nervous wreck, aren't I?"

Liz puts down the spatula she's been using and walks over to me. She puts her hands gently on the back of my neck and leans over and rests her forehead against mine, our noses touching. "I'm a nervous wreck, too, you know."

My first reaction is surprise; nothing about Liz's demeanor reveals anxiety. But then, she has told me that when she's nervous, she acts overly self-assured. I remember her question from that first lunch date, "No, who are you *really*?" I love that she is nervous, but I love even more that she is willing to tell me.

"Why are you nervous?" I ask, pulling my face away just enough to see her clearly. I want to know what it is about me that makes her feel this way.

She cocks her head slightly to the right as if considering me. "Because I haven't felt this way about someone new in a long time, and it terrifies me."

Someone new. Meaning someone who isn't Helen. That woman must have really broken her heart.

I am breathing faster and, for a moment, think that we might skip dinner altogether, that Liz will let that stir-fry burn for wanting me so uncontrollably. But then she turns back to her creation, snaps off the burner on the stove, and says, "Dinner's ready!"

"Oh good," I lie for the second time that night. "I'm starved."

We sit at her little wooden kitchen table for two, our kneecaps occasionally brushing. "Okay, I told you about Michael and Alana. Tell me about this baby brother of yours," she says.

I love to talk about Zeke because he is one of my favorite people on earth. "Zeke," I say between bites, "is probably the reason I'm becoming a psychologist. I mean—" I stop myself because I realize I am describing Zeke first by how he affects *me,* and I don't want to be caught being so self-absorbed. "Zeke is amazing. He'll probably always be my best friend. It wasn't always like that. When we were little, we definitely fought a lot. But then Zeke developed OCD when he was in middle school. It's been pretty severe at points in his life, and I think that being a part of his treatment and seeing him work so hard to overcome his compulsions gave me so much empathy for him. It's also what led me down this career path."

"OCD like hand washing and germ phobia?" she asks. Everyone always asks this.

"No. I mean, some OCD manifests that way, but Zeke's involved having bad thoughts—thoughts like terrible things happening to his loved ones, like our mom being in a car crash or our dad getting cancer. He would obsess about these worries and then do all these rituals to try to keep those things from happening."

"What kind of rituals?" she asks.

It makes me smile. I love that she really wants to understand this. "The tricky part was that his rituals were both active and then inside his head. His active ritual was usually checking. Like, if his OCD was flaring up and he had a thought that, say, I was hurt in an accident, he would ask my mom over and over when she'd last heard from me and if I was okay. His inner rituals included all sorts of patterns— counting certain numbers, thinking certain phrases over and over, that kind of thing."

"So, how do you treat that? And how were you a part of the treatment?"

"He worked with this great therapist who did something called exposure and response prevention with him. Basically, it meant exposing himself to what scared him—thoughts of bad things happening to us. They would write stories about all these terrible things, and Zeke would have to read them over and over. The response prevention part was that Zeke wasn't allowed to do his rituals—he couldn't check that we were okay, and he had to stop himself from doing all the mental counting and stuff. It was incredibly hard. My parents and I had to go to a bunch of sessions and learn how to help him do exposures at home. Like, if he asked us if we were okay, we weren't supposed to reassure him."

"That sounds so cruel! How did you do it?"

"I know. It sounds awful, but the truth is it really works. In the beginning, his fears got a little worse, but then, as we practiced the exposures with him every day, it started to get easier. Like, when I had a fever and Zeke got worried, I said, 'Zeke, I could have a life-threatening illness. I think the chances that I do are very slim, but we can't know for sure.' That's what it was all about—learning to live with not knowing anything for certain. Anyway, he worked really hard all through eighth grade and by the time he started high school, he was significantly better."

"Did it ever come back?" By this time Liz is so curious, she's stopped eating. Or maybe she just doesn't want to finish her meal ahead of me.

"OCD isn't really something you cure. It's more like, it comes and goes and can take different forms, and when it crops up, you just start doing exposures right away and kind of nip it in the butt."

Liz, looking very serious but suppressing a little smirk leans in. "Did you just say, 'nip it in the butt'?"

My heart might stop. I feel so dumb. "I did. Is it bud? It's bud, isn't it." I feel the heat rising in my cheeks; I hate saying the wrong thing. I especially hate it when it involves biting and butts. Fortunately, the warm look she gives me makes me feel cute rather than stupid.

"So Zeke's at Hopkins now?"

"Yes, and I can't believe he's graduating this May."

"I didn't realize he's almost done," she says. "Does he know what he'll do next?"

"Get this," I say, swallowing. "He's waiting to hear back from medical schools. Oh and his girlfriend will probably move with him wherever he goes. He really *is* going to be my parents' perfect child!"

"Nice," she says, with a nod of understanding.

"Seriously though, Zeke is really a gift in my life. He kept me sane when I came out to my parents." I pause and take a deep breath. "And speaking of coming out to family members, I need you to know that I'm not out to my zayde. My mother told me before I moved here that it would kill him. I'm just not sure I can take the risk right now."

Liz raises her wine glass. "To dysfunctional families."

"To dysfunctional families," I reply, clinking my glass with hers, exhaling my fear of her judgment. "And," I keep my glass raised, "to this amazing meal."

She smiles and adds, "And to you."

❧

After we've cleaned up the kitchen and shared a pint of Ben and Jerry's New York Super Fudge Chunk, I ask to see pictures of Paris. We sit down on her couch to look at her photo album, which is full of stunning photographs. It turns out that not only is Liz a scholar and an activist and a runner, but she is an artist with a camera as well. There are some pictures of Helen, who is blonder and thinner than I would have liked, but mostly her photos are of the Paris streets: cafes and churches and Parisians on bikes. They are exquisite.

"Why don't you have any of these on your walls?" I ask looking around the room.

"I do," she says. "In here . . ." and I follow her into the bedroom. It is noon on Sunday before we emerge.

❧

Let me be clear that "making love" is a term I *never* use. It is something my parents would say or something Captain and Tennille would sing about, and the phrase generally makes me cover my face and squirm with discomfort. But after that first night with Liz, it is the only phrase I can find to adequately describe what we do together. "Having sex" sounds pedestrian and, frankly, boring. "Fucking" sounds too aggressive—though we are sometimes very aggressive. Maybe it sounds too male. There is something that happens to me when Liz touches me that is unlike anything I've ever experienced. It is like every defense I have evaporates, like all of my armor falls clattering to the floor.

Chapter 9

February is also the month Charlie finally comes out to me. I listen to the tape with Dr. Vargas.

"Charlie, what I hear you saying is that the transition from being at home to being back at school was harder than you'd expected."

"Right, it was. But it's more like the transition between 'Charlie at home' and 'Charlie at college' is what's confusing."

"How do you mean?"

"It's like, at home, I'm expected to be this one person . . . you know, youth group organizer, church goer, that kind of thing, and when I'm here I'm sort of free to be someone else. Someone—I don't know, just someone different."

"Can you tell me more about the person you are here?"

"I'm just . . . like I'm more social. I can date here or hook up or whatever."

"Charlie, is this about who you feel free to hook up with or date here that you feel you can't at home?"

At this point, *I* stop the tape player. "Okay, I know I was trying to be patient and let him be ready to tell me, but I couldn't take it anymore. I feel like what he needed was for me—for *someone*—to just ask, to normalize the question."

"Rachel, I think you made a fine decision. Let me hear the rest."

"Really?" I press play again, suppressing the smile itching my lips.

"Yeah." [Here I remembered that he got teary and had to wait a moment before continuing.] "I mean I like guys. I've always liked guys and I can't be that person anywhere but here."

"Charlie, I'm sure it wasn't easy for you to tell me that, but I'm so glad that you did."

"Are you surprised?"

"No. I never make assumptions about anyone's sexual orientation."

Here, my eyes meet Dr. Vargas's for the briefest of seconds before I roll mine, indicating that I know I am full of shit.

"Really? I think everyone I've ever known has assumed I was straight since like the moment I was born."

"Charlie, they assumed that about me, too."

I press stop again and am so glad that our time is up.

In addition to daily emails, Liz and I speak every night on the phone. I learn to charge my clunky car phone each day so that I can crawl under the covers at night and use it as my secret communication device. I can't have Zayde noticing the nightly calls on his phone bill. Also, we end up having a lot of phone sex and, though Zayde is long asleep by that hour, it just isn't worth the risk of having him accidentally pick up an extension and hearing his granddaughter gasping that she is coming.

We spend the rest of the weekends and several stolen hours on weeknights that winter in her bed, where I let go of every last ounce of control I think I have. There is no question that Liz is the top and I am the bottom, though I loath these heterosexist distinctions. There is no getting around them though—she dominates me in every possible way. It's not that she teaches me new things per se. Nora and I had spent those college years exploring every position, contortion, and feat our bodies could manage. I half expected my college transcript to read, "Lesbian Sex—A" under electives. No, it is something altogether different that Liz is bringing out in me—the ability to inhabit and own every inch of my body, to experience the power of completely letting go of power. To have orgasms that make my blood pressure spike then drop so that my ears ring and I am dizzy as the blood drains from my head, washed in release.

"Unbelievable," I say, my eyes still closed in a post-orgasmic haze.

"Really?" says Liz, lying at my side, propped on her elbow, grinning.

"Really," I say. "Like I am drained of everything." I can barely speak.

"You know in French it's called 'La petite mort' right? The little death. Such linguists, those French."

I suddenly feel myself waking up. *Why is she speaking French? Is she thinking about Helen?* "Yeah, I don't get that. The little death? I mean, the little birth maybe, but the death analogy has never worked for me."

Liz kisses my shoulder. "I think it just means that the release afterwards, you know the letting go, is like dying a little. But if you are feeling reborn, my dear—" She pulls me on top of her and we giggle because we both know I've been caught being jealous.

In March, we go away together for a weekend. We find an adorable, rustic Vermont bed and breakfast in a guidebook of gay-friendly inns. It is sunny but still winter in Vermont, and we rent snowshoes, something neither of us has ever tried. We race each other across a small field behind the inn and laugh at our stumbling selves until icy tears roll down our cheeks. I even wear a hat.

That night, we build a fire in our room and make s'mores. As we sit on the floor in front of the fireplace, debating our opposing preferences for burnt marshmallows versus lightly toasted ones, Liz in her usual non-sequitur-hard-question way suddenly says, "So what's your take on God?"

I smile, sucking sticky marshmallow remains from my fingers. "What's my take on God like, do I *believe* in God?"

"No, more than that. Like, *what* do you believe in, and how do you imagine that thing? And do you even call that thing God?"

"You *do* know that I'm the one who asks probing questions for a living, right?"

She smiles at me, but her eyes stay serious. "I mean it."

I stare into the fire for a long moment, thinking. "I believe in something greater than us," I say. "Something we don't have any way of wrapping our heads around—like maybe it's some kind of force-field or even something we, as humans, can't conceive of. I think we personify this greater-than-usness because that is the only way we can have language about it—you know, like how we can only create narrative about things we know. But that's where I get stuck. I don't like how our religion personifies God—first because he's male, and that annoys me, but also because he's kind of mean, you know? I get that we need to have some kind of physical representation—a way to think about this amorphous idea—it's just not how I would represent it." I feel good about my answer and also kind of psyched that I've used the word amorphous.

"I hear you," she says nodding. "I've battled with the male God idea all my life. I've also struggled with how to imagine God as something else. It's like, after so many years of hearing the same language over and over it just becomes ingrained. So how do you personify God then?"

I do have a way that I personify God. I've never told anyone about it and I've certainly never been asked. I stop worrying about using big words and, with a rush of excitement, get up on my knees. "Okay, promise not to laugh?" It is just an expression; I don't really think she will laugh. "So when I need to talk with God—when I need to put an image to this thing that is bigger than me—I picture what I think of as the Shekhinah . . . do you know the Shekhinah?" My hands are flying around as I speak, the way my friends so often tease me about when I get all animated about something. "The feminine aspect of the divine—I think the Kabbalists talk about her a lot?"

"I do," she says nodding, urging me to continue.

"So, my Shekhinah? She's like this woman-angel who's very maternal and all-knowing. She has wings made out of flowing quilts and she is big—always just bigger than me, so that she can hover behind me and wrap me in her blanket-wings if I need protection or comfort, you know?" I am talking very fast. "And her quilt-wings—they are made up of squares of all of the things that have ever made me feel in touch with divinity." I stop sort of abruptly. *Am I making any sense?*

Liz seems to be considering this. She stares at the fire. "What kind of things are in these quilt-wings?"

"Some of the squares are visual images, but others are music or scents or tastes. Like, the sound of the Indigo Girls and acoustic guitar is a square, and the image of my favorite tree is a square, and the smell of a cookout . . ."

"And the sound of cicadas?"

"Yes! And the smell of a pine forest after rain, and the feel of warm sheets just out of the dryer."

She keeps nodding. "And a murmuration of starlings."

"A murmur-what?"

"You know, how huge flocks of starlings fly together and form patterns."

I stop. I had never thought of this, but suddenly I see them—thousands of little black wings morphing into formation in the sky. The shape of God. "Yes," I say. "Starlings, of course."

"Does she speak?"

"Very little," I say. "She only makes a few sounds, like 'Shhh' when I need soothing or 'It's okay.' The simple words a mother might say to an infant."

Then, looking more thoughtful, Liz asks, "Does she judge you?"

"Never."

Liz stares into the fire with a quizzical expression, like she isn't sure she buys it. "You're lucky."

"How so?"

She looks away from the fire and into my eyes. "You're lucky to be able to believe in a God you can't disappoint."

I think for a minute. "I guess I've never really understood why anyone would choose to believe in a judgmental God."

Liz shrugs. "I don't know that it's a choice for most people. I think most major world religions teach that their God or gods reward humans for certain behaviors and punish them for others. I think that model of a higher power, like the idea of God's maleness, is foisted upon most people from the time of birth. It makes choosing otherwise pretty difficult."

I am not sure how I am able to think about God differently, or if I really do at all. Perhaps unconsciously, I do believe in a judgmental, male universe and have just created my quilt-winged, maternal Goddess in defiance. All I know is that I do feel lucky.

A moment later, Liz stretches out on the floor and puts her head in my lap and closes her eyes. We are silent for a long time, and I run my fingers through her hair and listen to the sound of the fire crackling. Then, with just the lightest possible touch of my finger, I trace her face in my lap—the curve of her cheekbone, her eyebrows, her long straight nose, the depression just above her upper lip.

When she finally opens her eyes and smiles up at me, I say, "Liz, I don't think I have ever been this happy." What I mean is "I love you." I am so afraid to say it because, while things between us seem so great and solid, Liz has these faraway moments sometimes where I know she is scared. I don't know if she is thinking about Helen, but I know that she isn't fully present either. I am terrified of scaring her away.

She reaches up and touches my face. "I love making you happy."

This is as close as she will dare.

Chapter 10

I have not met one-on-one again with Dr. Vargas when we gather in the group room for team supervision the week after the coming out session with Charlie. That's what we call group supervision, "team." It has a connotation of coordinated treatment providers working together to tackle a case, but what it feels like this morning is anything but team-like. I have decided that I will talk in team supervision about my decision to come out to Charlie, even though (or maybe because?) I haven't yet spoken with Dr. Vargas about it. I feel very anxious about the possibility that she disapproves of my decision, but I also feel confident in my reasoning and want to get feedback from the group. Or maybe I hope it will be a safer place, knowing that my fellow trainees are of my generation and will be more likely to support my choice.

So that I won't change my mind, I begin as soon as we are all seated. "I'd like to discuss a case today."

"Go ahead, Rachel," says Dr. Vargas.

"Well, my client, 'Tyler,' came out to me in our last session." We don't use real names to protect confidentiality. "And then—I came out to him."

I look around to gauge the faces in the room. Harvard raises a critical eyebrow. BU doesn't seem to feel one way or another. The other trainee from my program, a friend, winks at me in support. Dr. Vargas just waits.

"I put a lot of thought into the decision to self-disclose and, while I feel good about that process, I am curious to know everyone's feedback."

Harvard is the first to challenge me. "Why would you choose to disclose something so personal?" I don't think he knew I wasn't straight before this moment.

"First, I believe that the personal is political. And this client comes from a place—politically, religiously, geographically, culturally—that tells him he is bad. I think that my job is to help him become comfortable with who he is, and part of that means providing him with a role model where he hasn't had any."

"So you're his role model?" asks Harvard with a hint of disgust. "I don't think that's your job at all."

Dr. Vargas interjects, "What do the rest of you think?"

My friend speaks up. "I'm not sure what I think about the role model piece—I need to think more about that. But I do think that we *all* come out to our clients. We wear our identities with wedding bands on our fingers or pictures of our children in our offices." Considering that Dr. Vargas is the only married person in the room, I think this comment takes serious *chutzpah*.

"I don't know," says BU. "I mean, it's a really significant self-disclosure and I think it changes the therapeutic relationship."

"I don't disagree that this changes the therapeutic relationship," I say. "But I think the relationship—like all relationships—is dynamic and that everything we choose to say or not say changes it."

"Rachel," says Dr. Vargas, "maybe you could tell us more about your process, how you came to the decision to self-disclose."

I still can't read her. "Sure. As I've discussed in here before, I've been working with Tyler for several months, and I've been pretty sure about his sexual orientation for most of—well, for all of—that time. I've watched him being so careful not to trust me with this information. I've been especially listening for all of the ways in which his world tells him that he can't possibly be this person—and there are lots of ways. It occurred to me that, if I could be one of the people in his life who says, 'Who you are is great,' that would matter more than any amount of listening I could do. And then I realized that I couldn't possibly support who he is without being honest about who I am as well. It would be hypocritical."

I can see Harvard shaking his head in my peripheral vision.

"And about being a role model," I hear my voice getting a little edgier. "I think the role of therapist is always multifaceted. Different clients need different things from us—and they usually make it very clear what it is they need. I think Cha—Shit! 'Tyler,' sorry—I think Tyler needs gay role models in his life. If I can provide him that, just by being out, then I owe him that."

"Or," Harvard jumps in, "what he needed was to have a moment that was *his*. It sounds like no one has seen him for who he really is and that he waited a long time to have this moment with you, to take the risk of showing you who he really is. And the first thing you did was make it about you."

At this, everyone is quiet. I let what he said sink in. *Is Harvard right? Have I done that forbidden therapist thing and made it about me?* I think about how invisible I've been feeling, how closeted. Maybe he has me pegged.

Dr. Vargas takes the reins. "It sounds like we have a very interesting discussion point on the table. I'd like to take a minute and look at the issue of self-disclosure in general rather than at Rachel's particular case."

I exhale, relieved to have the spotlight turned for a moment.

"When we make the choice to self-disclose to a client," she continues, "we must first always weigh the pros and cons, and to do this, we need to have clarity about our own needs and about who is being served by the disclosure. We must always ask ourselves the question, 'Is my sharing of this information in the client's best interest or in mine?'"

Harvard jumps in, "Right, and if the motivation to disclose is about our own—"

I cut him off. "But why is that an either/or question? Isn't it similar to trying to discern if something is completely altruistic? I mean, I can think of things I've done—charitable things for example—that seem altruistic, but if I'm being honest with myself, doing that thing also makes me feel good." My mind flickers with images of Zayde and me in his kitchen, me cooking at the stove, asking if he's taken his medication. "In the case of self-disclosure, can't something be in the client's best interest but also fill a need for the therapist?"

"I agree," says my friend, nodding. "I don't think the two are always mutually exclusive."

"Nice point," says Dr. Vargas. "So then what do we do when a disclosure serves both the client and the therapist?"

"I think it's sort of a cost/benefit analysis," says BU. "First, the benefit to the client must outweigh any possible cost. Also, though, I think the benefit to the client has to be greater than the benefit to the therapist."

"I totally agree." I can feel the heat hitting my cheeks. "So with my client, if I am to weigh the pros and cons, which I did, it seems to me that any possible cost to him—my putting the focus on myself, whatever—is insignificant compared to the comfort my coming out to him could offer. Is there something in it for me? Sure. I get to be seen in a relationship where I am usually a mirror. It allows me to be present in a way that, I admit, feels good to me."

"Let's talk about *that*," says Dr. Vargas. "What does it feel like to each of you to be in these intense relationships where there is *not* mutuality—where you do all the holding and, in return, do not get held?"

There is a long moment of silence.

"It's the hardest thing about this work," I say.

∾

Team supervision is not the only contentious meeting of the week. The town hall meeting at Beth El has been advertised to congregants for weeks as an opportunity to discuss the direction the synagogue is heading in. On Sunday morning, while Hebrew school is going on upstairs, about seventy members come together in the social hall. This time there is a chair for everyone. I sit next to Zayde, Bess, Murray, and Sophia on my right. Liz sits to my left.

I am surprised to see the rabbi here. As it turns out, she has asked to speak at the beginning of the meeting before leaving to let the assembled discuss what she clearly knows is the future of her contract as Beth El's religious leader. She addresses the group without an ounce of defensiveness. She is warm and articulate as always.

"I am so glad that so many of you came out this morning. I asked the board if I might open the meeting with a short *d'rash* based on a poem I love. Perhaps you know it. It is by a great American poet named Robert Frost and it is called, 'The Road Not Taken.'"

A murmur of recognition goes through the room. It seems we've all had to memorize this poem at one time or another. I find myself testing my memory and reciting all the lines in my head in the quick, rhythmic cadence of my eleven-year-old self.

"I'm not going to read you the entire poem," continues the rabbi. "Rather, I'd like to take a close look at the first few lines: 'Two roads diverged in a yellow wood / And sorry I could not travel both / And be one traveler . . .'" She pauses and then repeats the selection, slowly. "Frost is talking about the challenge of choosing. And it is a challenge.

Choosing is a challenge for many reasons—perhaps it is because we don't know what lies ahead, where one path or the other might lead. Perhaps it is also because, as I think Frost suggests, when we choose, we have to take all of ourselves down the chosen path. We can't split ourselves in two—sending one half to check out one way of being and the other half to check out the other—we have to be *one* traveler. In the chosen path we gain the experience of *that* road, but don't we also lose something? In choosing, don't we lose the opportunity to experience the road *not* taken?"

I feel tears gather behind my eyes. Zayde shifts in his seat to my right.

"When I announced in the fall that I would be conducting Bar and Bat Mitzvah services differently, that I would be making a change that moved away from tradition and toward a more inclusive way of *davening*, of coming together in prayer, I chose a path. I think it only fair to tell you that that path will likely include other, newer ways of including non-Jews in our community. For example, while the Conservative movement prohibits me from officiating at an interfaith wedding, it does not prohibit me from honoring an interfaith couple on the bimah for an *aufruf* ceremony on the Shabbat before their wedding day. There are certain lines that the Conservative movement will not permit me to cross. I will, however, move in the direction of those lines to the extent that I can, because I feel it is the right path for this congregation.

"I am asking the congregation to come with me on this journey. I acknowledge that there is another path to choose and that that is the path of preserving the way things have traditionally been done. It is my belief that, if we are to thrive as a Jewish community, we need to be on a more progressive path."

In my peripheral vision, I can see Liz nodding. I want to nod. I want to stand up and clap.

"I realize that the community may decide that it prefers the path of adherence to tradition. As Frost notes, we would not be able to travel together were that to be the case. We could not be one traveler if we differ in this choice. I would be saddened not to continue to lead you, as I have come to love this community very much. Having said that, I respect and honor whatever path you choose and hope that you can come to some consensus as a group today and in the discussions that follow."

I look at Liz, letting our eyes meet for just one knowing instant.

The rabbi leaves, and the room is quiet for a moment. The president stands up to address us. "I'd like to get a sense of where the majority of you stand—whether you agree with the rabbi's push to be more inclusive of non-Jews than the average Conservative synagogue—or whether you reject this change. This will help the board know whether or not to renew the rabbi's contract with the congregation." He is asking each of us to pick a road.

The father from the prior meeting is the first to raise his hand. "For those of you who weren't at the board meeting last month, or who don't know me, my name is Michael. DeMatteo," he adds after a beat as if deciding at the last second to include his Italian surname. "I spoke at the last board meeting about how my family, my Jewish family, is made up of my wife Karen, who is Jewish, myself who is not, and our children Sara and Alexander. In preparing for Sara's Bat Mitzvah, which is coming up, Karen and I realized that, under traditional Conservative Jewish practice, I would not be welcomed on the bimah to participate in Sara's day. This has been very distressing and is what I assume has prompted this discussion. I was asked at that board meeting why I never converted to Judaism, and I want to take this opportunity to answer that question. I didn't choose to convert for several reasons—because my Catholic parents wouldn't understand and I didn't want to hurt them, because I am agnostic at heart and didn't really know if I wanted to personally identify with any organized religion. I think there are lots of reasons why someone might choose to participate in the raising of a Jewish family but not themselves convert to Judaism. I can only tell my story and just wanted to share that piece with you."

Michael sits down next to Karen, and then several others speak, most seeming to support both Michael and the rabbi's proposed changes. Then Zayde's hand goes up.

The president calls on him, and he slowly rises, making his way to the front of the room. I covertly press my knee against Liz's and hold my breath.

"My name is Lew Kessler, and I am eighty-seven years old," he begins in his raspy, Oscar the Grouch tone. He looks at no one in particular and his voice sounds booming to me. "I think this group is making a terrible mistake. This is a *synagogue*! You have to be *Jewish* to be a member of this congregation!" He is shaking with anger. "This is not about a choice! This is about doing the right thing! Thank you."

After a few more people speak, Liz raises her hand and goes to the podium.

"My name is Liz Abraham, and I grew up here at Beth El."

She is such a steady speaker—so focused and self-assured. I swell inside.

"When I was a child, my father used to come to daily minyan here at the shul. He explained to me that, when one loses someone in their immediate family, that person is commanded to say the Kaddish prayer in honor of the deceased every day for up to a year. There was a catch though. Kaddish could only be said in the presence of a minyan—a quorum of at least ten Jewish adults. I thought that was a lovely idea, that mourners could only say this prayer in the presence of a group so that they were supported and didn't have to mourn alone. My father went to minyan each day, not because he was in mourning, but because he felt an obligation to help 'make the minyan' so that those who needed to mourn would have enough people to do so. What a beautiful idea."

She pauses for effect. I cheer on the inside.

"And then one day, I asked my mother why she never went to help make the daily minyan. That was when I found out that women didn't count. Oh, they *did* count at my friend's synagogue in Newton—the Reform synagogue—but at Beth El, only male adults counted. That was when I first told my parents that I wanted to change shuls. They explained that I could make my own choices when I grew up but that we were staying, and besides, my Bat Mitzvah was coming up. As it turns out though, the Conservative Movement had changed its stance on only men counting in Conservative minyans and it was just months before my Bat Mitzvah that Beth El adopted this change. Suddenly I was to become a Jewish adult who counted.

"This was a hard change for many, I assume. It wasn't the traditional way things had been done. It was a new road. But I will tell you without hesitation that, if we as a congregation hadn't taken that road, I *would* have, and would have changed communities as an adult. I would not have traveled with this one.

"What we're *not* talking about today is that we are a dying breed. Jews now make up only 0.2 percent of the world population—less than *half of a half* of a percent. And while we have survived plagues, the Inquisition, pogroms, and the Holocaust, we have survived only just barely. The numbers of Jews in the United States who affiliate with synagogues and practice their religion is declining with each generation."

Where has she gotten all of these statistics? The room is rapt.

"We have an opportunity here. We can choose to do what we've always done, interfaith families can go elsewhere or nowhere, and our already small shul can fold. Or, we can change with the times. We can become more inclusive, just as we did when we allowed women to be counted in the minyan. And perhaps we will continue to survive. I am glad I stayed. But, if we don't make this change and we turn away this dynamic, progressive rabbi, I think I, among many others, will move on as well."

She returns to her seat. Zayde shakes his head. I feel like a frayed rope in a tug of war.

Chapter 11

A month later, I drive Zayde to Bryn Mawr for our annual family Passover Seder. We are six around the dining room table again this year, as we were for so long before Bubbe died. Zeke has brought his girlfriend, Becca, home with him from Baltimore.

"Rebecca, it's lovely that you could join us," says Zayde, as my father collects everyone's Haggadah (the paper book retelling the Exodus and containing all the rituals of the Seder.)

"It's lovely to be here with you all, Mr. Kessler," she says to Zayde all straight white teeth and good manners.

"Oh, call me Zayde," he says with a coy, playful smile. My head jerks up at him, seemingly of its own accord. *Since when is Becca his granddaughter?*

"Rachel, can you help me in here with the matzo ball soup?" my mother calls from the kitchen. I haven't even eaten my gefilte fish, but knowing my mother likes to keep the courses running smoothly and suddenly wanting out of the dining room, I slip into the kitchen to help.

"Mom, don't you think it's time we replaced these old Haggadahs with something more contemporary?" I ask as I ladle soup into bowls.

"What? These are the ones I grew up with. Your Zayde's finally letting me keep them here rather than bringing them back and forth every year."

"I know, but there are so many innovative ones out there now—you know, ones that feel more relevant to the issues of today."

My mother laughs out loud and shakes her head as she heads back toward the dining room with a bowl of hot matzo ball soup in each hand. "Oh, I don't think your Zayde would like that very much."

As we sit eating a dessert of spongy Passover cake and coffee, Zeke says, "So I have some news I want to share with everybody."

Everyone stops what they are doing to look at Zeke. Spoons freeze mid-stir, creamer seems to suspend in the air between carafe and coffee cup. I stop chewing, the cake dry in my mouth. *They can't be engaged—they're still in college. Besides, Zeke and I just had a long phone conversation last week. Granted most of the conversation was me blabbering on about Liz, but we talked about him and Becca too. He would have told me this.*

"Yesterday, I received an acceptance letter from Georgetown Medical School," he says bursting with excitement and a hint of relief. "It's my first choice and I plan to accept and move to D.C. this June!"

My mother claps her hands together with joy and gets up to hug Zeke. My father's eyes are brimming.

"Haha!" Zayde yells, slapping his hand down on the table. "I always knew we'd have a doctor in the family!"

Zeke is quick to say, "Rachel is going to be a doctor too, you know."

I smile at him and say, "It's different. I understand," and hug my baby brother.

When all the commotion settles, my father looks to Becca who is holding Zeke's hand. "Becca, do you know your plans yet for after graduation?"

"Well," she says, smiling sideways at Zeke, "I'm planning on going to Washington as well. I'm going to live with a group of friends and work while I apply to graduate programs in biology for the following year." I am surprised to hear they won't be living together.

Zeke again pulls me back into the conversation. "Hey Rach," and for a moment I am afraid he is going to ask about Liz. In our phone conversation last week, I made him promise he wouldn't mention her to Mom and Dad. Not yet. "You're definitely going to have to come visit us in D.C."

I exhale. "Definitely."

When all the dishes have been cleared, I sneak up to my father's office and rush to boot up the computer. Liz is in Baltimore this week, spending Passover with her sister's family. We are communicating by email, and I miss the sound of her voice. I see her email to me first thing.

From: eabraham@alumni.yale.edu
To: rlevine@bscp.edu
Sent: Wednesday 4/23/97 11:22 AM
Subject: Miss you

Hey beautiful. How is Passover in Bryn Mawr? I am writing from the Pikesville Public Library as my sister doesn't have a modem at home (she wouldn't let me use it even if she did, as it is "yontif.") It's nice to get out by myself. It's very loud there.

So get this, I get to Alana's on Monday afternoon and my parents are there! They weren't supposed to be coming up but then they called her on the weekend and said they'd decided to come. They are being weird—nervous or something. My mom said something to Alana like, "We can all talk later in the week once the Seders are over." I wonder if they are splitting up or something. I'm leaving Friday morning so they'd better hurry up.

I hope you are sleeping well in your old room with the Duran Duran poster (ha!) I miss your smile and the smell of your hair.

L

I write back right away:

From: rlevine@bscp.edu
To: eabraham@alumni.yale.edu
Sent: Wednesday 4/23/97 8:42 PM
Subject: Re: Miss you

Oh, do I miss you! I am making a list of all the things I want to talk to you about this weekend (we'll be back on Friday, too . . . you're all mine on Saturday). Here is my list:
- Zeke's med school
- Becca
- Feeling lost at my family's Seder
- The wildly sexy dream I had about you last night
- An idea I have for a trip for us this summer
- Your parents
- Your loud nieces and nephews (I only know Levi and Shoshana's names, who are the other three?)

I'll check my email before I leave on Friday but I understand if you can't get back to the library before then. Talk Friday night (and we are totally having Shabbat phone sex that night. Does it count as a mitzvah if it's over the phone?).

xoxo,

R

It is so hard not to say "I love you" to Liz. I feel as if the words are constantly about to spill out in person, on the phone and over email. She is with me every minute. It is as if I have a miniature version of her on my shoulder, and I want to tell her everything—not just the important things, but everything: some interesting new product I've spotted on the shelf at the drugstore, a funny moment in a TV show, some eccentric thing Zayde has said. I want to be able to turn to her—this mini, shoulder-dwelling Liz—and share every moment of my life. Either she has truly become my partner, or I am becoming delusional. I remember how Shakespeare compared the lover, the poet, and the lunatic in *A Midsummer Night's Dream*, saying that each was driven by the same wild imagination. I have never been a huge fan of the Bard, but I suddenly feel like he might be a man who really got it.

Zeke and Becca go back to Baltimore on Wednesday night. On Thursday, my mom takes me shopping at the mall; I hate the mall—all those teenagers in one place. The mall is like a time machine, transporting me back to anxious days of wanting to be thin enough and cool enough. As my mother and I walk in and out of stores, I feel myself regressing to a time of adolescent insecurity that I'd thought I'd outgrown. This state of mind does not serve me well in the conversation I have with my mother over lunch in the food court.

"Are you okay still living with Zayde, Rachel?" asks my mom, her head cocked to one side, her salad waiting.

"Yeah. Sure. Why? Has he said that it isn't good?"

"No, he hasn't said anything of the sort. I think he loves you being there. I'm just wondering if you are feeling too pressured. I know that you do quite a lot for him, and, Rachel, it's not your job. You are busy with school and no one expects you to be a caretaker to your grandfather—"

"He needs someone, Mom!" I am surprised by my sudden anger and raised voice. "He needs help with shopping and cooking. And he shouldn't be driving!" I am overcome with feelings—fierce protectiveness of Zayde, resentment over feeling obligated to continue to care for him, anger that I have to keep Liz a secret, guilt over my growing disagreements with Zayde over things at Beth El, exhaustion over trying to keep everything in balance. As is so easy to do in the presence of my mother, I start to cry.

"Rachel, why are you crying?" Her eyes are wild with something like worry. "It's clearly too much for you."

I wipe my eyes. "No, mom, really it isn't at all. I'm fine, I promise. I'm just PMSing today, that's all."

"Rachel, I understand that your grandfather needs more these days, and I'm prepared to get him help in the house. You don't have to be the person to do all that."

"But mom, I want to be that person. It's important to me."

She sighs, returning her attention to her salad. "Okay, but I hope you're taking care of yourself, too."

After packing on Friday morning, I check my email. I burst into a smile when I see Liz's name in my inbox and glance behind me to assure my privacy before clicking on it.

From: eabraham@alumni.yale.edu
To: rlevine@bscp.edu
Sent: Friday 4/25/97 9:12 AM
Subject: re:re:Miss you

My parents talked with us last night. My dad is sick. I'll
call you tonight.

L

I stare at the screen, both stunned by the content of the email
and by Liz herself. She has gone out to the library (at the minute it
opened) to write me this brief email that says almost nothing. It is as
if she needs to tell me this thing before the day goes on (a fact that
makes me feel close to her) but can't say more—nothing about how
she is feeling or what this means. It strikes me that this is quintessen-
tially Liz, connected in the most guarded of ways.

Back in Somerville that night, I kiss Zayde goodnight and wait
with my car phone under the covers. It is 11:15 before Liz calls.

"After the kids were all in bed, my parents sat down at the dining
room table with Alana, David, and me. I think my mom did all the
talking, at least at first. She said that my dad has been suffering from
kidney disease for the past eight years. His doctors had been treating
him with blood pressure medication and diet restrictions to keep his
blood sugar in check. Apparently, he had a test and it came back that
he is now in something called End Stage Renal Disease and that he'll
need dialysis several times a week."

"Wow," I say. "I don't know anything about kidney disease. Liz,
that sounds so scary. I'm sorry." I want to put my arms around her.

"Yeah, but that's not the bad part. Then she tells us that he is refus-
ing dialysis and that he is choosing to die rather than get treatment!
He just sat there, looking at us with this resigned expression, like
that was the end of the discussion. Rachel, I don't know how I didn't
see this coming. He was looking so swollen the whole time we were
there, and I just thought he'd gained some weight. It's like I couldn't
see what was right in front of me."

"Sweetie, you couldn't have known. How old is your dad?"

"He's seventy-nine. He says he's seen too many friends go through dialysis and it's no way to live. But, Rachel, eighty is the new sixty, especially down where they live. My parents have a very active life. He's not ready to die."

I realize that only her father himself can decide if he is ready to die but don't want to push her, especially not on the phone. "I'm coming over."

"Now?"

"Is that okay? I just want to hold you."

I think I hear her crying. "Yes. Please."

I can hear Zayde snoring loudly from the hallway so I don't bother peeking into his room. I leave a note on the kitchen table saying that my friend, Liz, is having a problem and that I am going to sleep at her house. I rationalize that I would do this even if Liz and I were just friends and leave her phone number if he needs me.

When I get to Liz's, it is after midnight. She's unlocked the door for me to come in and is in her bed facing the far wall. I slide in and curl myself around her warm body, kissing the top of her head. We don't speak. I just wait for her breathing to slow into the deep cadence of sleep before I let my eyes close.

Chapter 12

The next morning, Liz and I go out to breakfast and talk for a long time. I am conscious of trying not to play therapist with her but, the truth is, she is a master at avoiding her feelings. This stark difference between us has never been so clear to me. If my dad were dying (partially by choice), I would be a wreck. I would want, would need, to talk about my feelings with her. For Liz, it is like she doesn't know how to name what she is feeling—like I have to help her find the words.

"The doctor apparently told them that, if my dad didn't start dialysis next week, he might only live a few weeks, maybe six at the most. I have to book a ticket to go down there next weekend."

"Liz," I hold her hands across the table, "why don't you tell me how you are feeling about all of this?"

She sits and stares at our hands for what feels like minutes. She is so quiet when she finally speaks.

"I essentially disowned my parents, Rachel. I did that. I guess there has always been a part of me that believed a day would come when we would work it out. I always thought I had time to do that. And now there is no time. And the thing is . . . my dad doesn't care. He doesn't want to create the time, by getting treatment, for things to change."

I squeeze her hands tighter. "Tell me about what you want to say to him."

"I don't even know." She pulls her hands away, falling back against her chair. Then, leaning forward again, "Fuck, I want him to say it to me! To Michael and me! I want him to make things right with us before he just decides he's done."

"Can you tell him that?"

"I don't know. I'm just so angry. I don't know where to put all this anger."

Finally, a feeling word. The waiter places our check on the edge of the table.

"Rachel, I need to go for a run. That's all I can think of to do."

"I think that's a great idea," I say, knowing she is right, but slightly hurt that talking with me doesn't provide her with the release she craves. "I'll go home and change and get some stuff and come back over later?" I am anxious at the thought that maybe she doesn't want me there at all.

"Yeah, okay," she says, and I exhale.

"What are you cooking now?" Zayde peers over his *Wall Street Journal* at me clanking around in the kitchen.

"I'm just roasting a chicken to make a few dinners for the week. I'm going to be out a lot this week, and I just want to put a few meals in the fridge for you."

"You've been out a lot these days."

I stop what I'm doing and sit across the table from him. "Zayde, you know Arnie Abraham? Liz's father?"

"Sure, he used to be an ophthalmologist—"

"Right. It turns out he's very sick. It looks like he's dying. Liz is going to go down to Florida to see him on Friday and, well, she's just having a hard week, and you know that Liz and I have become friends, and she's just really struggling right now, and I think that maybe she shouldn't be alone this week—you know, just until she leaves for Florida. Anyway, she has this really great pull-out sofa in her apartment that I can stay on, and I think I may just spend this week at her place so that she doesn't need to be all alone." I realize that I haven't stopped to breathe since I started speaking. And also, that I used the phrase "really great pull-out sofa."

"That's a *shanda*." Zayde shakes his head using the Yiddish word for shame. "I'm really sorry to hear it. You're a good girl, Rachel. Elizabeth is lucky to have such a good friend."

"Thank you, Zayde. You won't miss me too much? I'll come by and fix you dinner each day, and anyway it's only for this week."

"You go. And if there's anything I can do for the Abrahams, you let me know."

I get up from my chair and walk over to Zayde, planting a long kiss on his bald, speckled forehead. I am relieved and guilt-ridden both.

Liz is unpredictable that week. One night she wants to make love, no, fuck—this is definitely fucking—up against the wall of her bathroom. The next night she wants to talk on the phone with her brother privately and goes into her bedroom and closes the door, leaving me reading journal articles for school at her kitchen table. One morning she gets up at five and runs in the rain for an hour and a half.

I suggest that she schedule a time to talk with Rabbi Stein. I am pleased that she takes me up on the idea and makes a time to meet with her on Thursday for lunch. Liz has never been to a therapist, and this is as close as she has been to being counseled in any kind of session. When I ask about the meeting later that night, Liz says that the rabbi was very helpful, and again I am full of conflict, both happy that she found the rabbi helpful and a little bruised that she seemed to find her more helpful than she finds me.

"I told the rabbi that I was just so angry at my father for choosing death over life, and she said that it was okay to be angry with him. She also said that I could still respect his decision even if it made me angry, that I could both have my own feelings and allow him to have his. I really wanted her take on it from a Jewish perspective, though. I said, 'Doesn't it say in the Torah to choose life?' She said that it does say that in the Torah, but that it might also be possible to define 'life' more broadly, that maybe for my father, he defines life by the quality of his living and not by the number of his days."

This is what I love most about Judaism. We can take a phrase from the Torah written some 3,000 years ago, "I have put before you life and death, blessing and curse. Choose life," and revisit it, reinterpret it, for our time and situation.

"We also talked about time," she went on, "and the fact that, when it comes to our relationships with the most important people in our lives, time can sometimes be, I don't know, an illusion. Like, it's possible to pick up conversations we may have never finished. Basically, she was encouraging me to talk with him."

I drop Liz off at Logan Airport the next morning. The wind is especially bitter, and she wears her hat with the braided ties. I tug them as I say goodbye. "Hey, I'm here if you need me, but I understand if you can't call."

"Thanks," she says, and I'm embarrassed for wanting more from her.

❧

That Saturday night, Zayde and I pick up Bess and go to the Union Diner for pot roast. I like Bess. I wonder if Zayde might, too—if he might be interested in her romantically. I even ask him on the car ride over to her house.

"Bess is so great. Do you ever think of her, I don't know, romantically?"

"Rachel!" he barks, scolding.

"What, Zayde? You are both widowed and have known each other for years."

"Bess is a friend, an old friend. She was close to your bubbe. I was close to her husband. There will never be anything beyond friendship between us."

I quickly understand that what I thought was a question about love and companionship, he heard as a question about betrayal. He grips the steering wheel and scowls at the road ahead.

Fortunately, he perks up during the meal with Bess. That is, until we start talking about Rabbi Stein.

Bess brings it up. "So, it looks like the board is going ahead with contract negotiations," she says matter-of-factly.

"Is that true?" I have the presence of mind to speak slowly, trying to hide my excitement.

"I spoke to Leonard Markley after minyan one day last week—he's one of the vice presidents, dear," she says, looking at me. I love that Bess always makes sure I am up to speed on these things. "Len said that between the town hall meeting and all of the conversations they've been having with members over the past months, it seems clear that the majority support the rabbi. So they are going to go ahead and start working on her contract."

"Asinine!" Zayde slams his hand down on the table and spits through clenched teeth. That is the word he uses when he's really reached his limit.

"Lew, listen, I've been giving this a lot of thought. We all have. I've changed my position on the rabbi. I think she is attracting a lot of new, young families."

I sit up straighter and smile at Bess. Might Zayde be able to hear this from her?

"Bess!" he snaps. "Those new, young families are hardly Jewish! What, do they think they can go to church on Christmas and synagogue on Chanukah? She thinks she can change the way things have always been done to make those families happy? What about those of us who built this shul? Those of us who are there every Shabbat? What about making *us* happy?"

His voice is getting louder, and I find myself slouching into the booth again.

"Lew, we're not going to be around much longer! The future of the synagogue doesn't depend on us—it depends on *Rachel's* generation!"

Shit, shit, shit . . .

They both look at me.

"Okay, Miss Future Generation," says Zayde, as if suddenly noticing I am there. "Do you agree with what your friend, Miss Abraham, had to say at the meeting last month?" This is the first time he's asked me how I feel about the issue and certainly the first time he's made reference to Liz's speech at the meeting.

"I think the rabbi is right," I say as simply and honestly as I can. "I don't think that making non-Jews more a part of our community dilutes it. I think it strengthens it." I pause, gauging my grandfather's face. "I'm sorry, Zayde."

We eat our pie in silence.

❧

I pick Liz up at the airport on Monday morning. She's taken the day off of work, and I decide to skip classes and spend it with her. It is a bright, spring day, and we walk along the Charles as she tells me the story of her weekend.

"When we all got to the house Friday night, it was weird, stilted like we were all being too careful. We ate a late dinner, and all I could notice the whole time was how tired and swollen my dad looked. He didn't say much, and when he did it was kind of wheezy. Then after dinner, Alana and my dad went into the family room while Michael and I helped my mom clean up. Michael told my mom that he and I wanted to talk with my dad after shul the next morning.

"She said, 'Oh. That'll be nice,' but not to us —she just kept loading the dishwasher.

"But Michael didn't stop. He said, 'I don't know if it will be nice. Lizzie and I have some things we need to say that might be kind of hard actually.' But she just kept loading that dishwasher and then before I knew it, I blurted out, 'Mom! We don't want to wait until you are dying to have the same conversation with you! You and Dad pushed Michael away when you found out he was gay. I pushed you away when I realized I was, because I didn't want to go through what he'd gone through.'

"Then she stopped and the three of us just sort of starred at each other. I don't know who started crying first, probably me. I said, 'We may be grownups, Mom, but that doesn't mean we don't need you to love us.' And then she just put a hand on each of our cheeks and said, 'I've loved you both every minute of your lives. I haven't always been a good mother to you. I'm so sorry.'"

"Liz," I say, stopping to look at her. "She apologized. What was that like?"

Liz huffs a little laugh. "You know, we hugged it out for a second, wiped our eyes and then basically went back to cleaning up the kitchen. I'm not even sure we spoke after that." She shrugged. "But I think enough had been said." With that we start walking again.

"So did you talk with your dad?"

"Yeah. I was bawling before I even started, but I had rehearsed what I was going to say." She puts her hand on my arm and we stand facing each other on the path. She takes a breath and delivers her monologue.

"'Daddy, I want you to know that I respect your decision not to do treatment. I know I was very unsupportive last week in Baltimore. I just didn't understand how you could not choose to live. I still wish you would change your mind, but I also know that this is your decision alone, and I do support whatever it is you want. I just don't want you to go. I want things between us to be different, to be better.'"

"That's amazing, sweetie. You said it just like that?"

"I think so—it took longer because I had to pause a lot not to cry. But then my dad just sort of stared at his lap. Maybe he was crying, I'm not sure."

She turned to keep walking. "But then Michael said, 'Dad, things haven't been good between us for thirty years. I thought I was okay with that. But the truth is, I have some things I need to say to you before you go.' I feel like I'd be scared if my kid said that to me. He might have been, I don't know. But Michael said all this really great stuff."

"Like what?"

"Like he said, 'Dad, I am really proud of the man I am. I have a successful career; I am a good partner to Barry and a good friend to my friends; I am a community organizer; I am a good Jew—I am an environmentalist, and I work to repair the world.' Then he said, 'And, I am Arnold Abraham's son. I have always wanted our relationship to be different. I know we don't have much time left, but I'm asking you if it can be.' He was fucking awesome."

"I think you were both fucking awesome." I take her hand.

"My dad told Michael, 'I haven't always understood you, but I've always been proud of you.' I thought Michael might explode, he was practically shaking. And then they were saying 'I love you' to each other and hugging, and I was like, 'Hello?' But then my dad looked at me and said, 'I didn't understand you either, Lizzy. You were always so angry.' And then he stopped to cough and spit into a napkin. I could tell it was hard for him to talk. Finally, he said, 'You are my baby, and I love you.' And I said it back."

For a minute, we just walk in silence.

"Rachel, it feels so surreal to me. The conversations were so brief.

In some ways they hardly touched the years of damage. But in other ways, they were exactly enough. Isn't it strange that it can be both at the same time?"

I don't answer her question, because I'm not sure I do understand. Instead I say, "I think you were so courageous to put it out there for them—to tell them what you needed to hear and to ask them if they could give it to you. I am so proud of you."

She kisses my shoulder while we continue to walk. I stop and turn to her, completely unprepared for what's about to come. "Liz, I always thought I'd wait for a romantic moment to say this to you, but you know what? The only difference between us and your dad is that your dad knows his death is imminent. For all any of us know, ours could be, too. So I want to tell you that I love you—that I'm in love with you." My face burns. It's almost scary to look at her face, but I can't turn away.

She's quiet a moment, then puts her hands on my face and kisses me, not unlike that first kiss in the snowy parking lot. "I don't know that I'm ready to take that risk—" she starts, pressing her forehead into mine.

"Don't," I interrupt, all the while thinking, *do, do.*

"But," she says sternly pulling back to look into my eyes, "I'm feeling very aware right now that love isn't about readiness. And I definitely love you, Rachel Levine."

Chapter 13

I don't know if Liz will want me to go to Florida with her when her father is close to the end, but it is so much what I want. I want to be a part of her family and to support Liz during this life moment. I don't mention it to her. But I do meet with Rabbi Stein.

The rabbi's office is small and cozy, the walls lined floor to ceiling with books. She gestures for me to sit across a low coffee table from her.

"Rachel, it's so nice to get some time with you. It sounded on the phone like you had some big things you wanted to talk about."

"Yeah, I suppose they are some big things. Specifically, I want to ask you some questions about shmira, but before I even get there"—I just jump—"I need to tell you, um, that Liz Abraham and I are girlfriends, uh, I mean not just friends—we're in a romantic relationship."

"Rachel, I had no idea! That's wonderful. Thank you for telling me."

I hate how visibly shaken I am. "Oh, um—you're welcome. But my zayde doesn't know. He can't know."

"I see." She nods and listens like a master therapist and, though I know she isn't one, it feels very much like a therapy session.

"It's just, I made a promise to my mother that I wouldn't tell him, I mean, not about Liz—my mother doesn't even know about Liz. I just don't think my grandfather would be open to the idea of his grand-daughter dating anyone other than a man."

"He's from a different generation, it's true. And Rachel, I will absolutely keep this information between us. But you should also know, that if you ever do decide to come out to him, I will support you in any way I can. I would try to help him understand that, while the Conservative movement has yet to change its prohibitions on same-sex unions, the issue is being discussed widely in Conservative rabbinic circles. Many of my colleagues and I are advocating strongly for changes in these rulings." Then, perhaps noticing the look of fear on my face, "But I also understand that your grandfather might not ever agree to talk with me about it, let alone find comfort in my perspective."

I smile apologetically, embarrassed that my grandfather's feelings about her are so evident.

"I appreciate your support. It really does mean a lot to me." I don't know what else to say, my head swimming with the image of rabbis sitting around a conference table debating about same-sex marriage. "Um, is it okay if I shift gears for a second?"

"Of course."

"So, about watching over a body after someone dies? My zayde has taught me a lot about it, and I went with him to sit with Ivan Resnik's body when he died last year."

She seems surprised. "Rachel, that's very special. The Chevra Kadisha does really holy work, and it can be overwhelming for someone your age. What was that like for you?"

"That's the thing," I say. "I found the whole concept of this non-re-payable mitzvah really moving. But I just don't think I can do it again if it means I have to read Psalms out loud for hours and hours. I really struggle with many things about our traditional writings—the gender stuff, the image of God as an angry dictator—I just have a very different approach to Judaism. And, I'm wondering if it is possible to do shmira in a different way. Maybe to talk to the person's soul or to be silent? Would it be somehow sacrilegious to do something other than the prescribed readings?"

"Different rabbis might tell you different things, but I think it's entirely appropriate to do something other than read Psalms when sitting with the dead. I think as long as you are both guarding the body and comforting the soul, you are doing a very big mitzvah. It isn't about what you say, but about the *kavanah*, the intention, behind the act."

I am relieved to hear this. I don't know if I'll be going to Florida with Liz or even if the timing will be such that I might sit with her father's body, but the idea of being able to do this for the father of the woman I love feels like a gift. And I need to know, before going, if I can do it in a way that feels both true to tradition and true to myself.

Liz's father's decline from one weekend to the next is staggering. There are hospice nurses coming to the house daily, and they are giving him medicine to control the pain. Her mother's reports are disheartening. I try to be as tuned in to what Liz needs from me as I possibly can, asking her often what I can do while trying not to be too overbearing. The best part is that, because we already said "I love you" to each other, we use these words freely and often. It feels like a small but powerful piece of verbal holding I can offer.

Three weeks after her trip to see her father, Liz calls me.

"The hospice nurse thinks he's close to death. I'm going to fly down in the morning."

I almost say, "Do you want me to come?" but then realize this sounds completely detached, like it doesn't matter to me one way or another. Instead, I say, "I want to come with you."

"Yes," is all she says.

Rain pelts against the windows that overlook the tarmac. It feels appropriate. "Liz, um, it would help me to know—what does your mother know about me?"

"Nothing at all until last night," she says. "I told her that I would be there as quickly as I could and that I was bringing my girlfriend, Rachel, with me. There was no room for discussion."

"Okay," I say, moved by her strength and resolve. "And Liz, the last thing I want to do is complicate things with my own needs right now, but," I hesitate, "they can't know that I'm Lew Kessler's granddaughter. Not yet. It's just too small a community and I'm too afraid that it will get back to him."

"Understood," she says, and then we sit quietly, listening for the announcement to board.

I see it as soon as we turn the corner in our rental car onto the Abrahams' street—a black hearse in the driveway of the house on the cul-de-sac. Liz must see it at the same moment because she stops the car in the middle of the street and just freezes, her hand over her mouth. I put my hand on her shoulder.

"Oh sweetie, I'm so sorry," I say.

"We didn't make it," she says. "We're too late," and she inches the car forward and parks in front of the house.

The front door opens before we are out of the car. A small woman, I'm assuming Liz's mom, in a navy velour sweat suit, comes down the walk toward us, her eyes stinging red as if she's been crying for many hours.

"Lizzy," she gasps and pulls her daughter to her, breaking into audible sobs. "I told them to wait until you'd come, but then the hearse just pulled up . . ."

"It's okay, Mom. I'm here now," says Liz. They hold each other for a few long moments before Liz pulls away and gestures to me. "Mom, this is Rachel."

I hug Mrs. Abraham. "I am so so sorry," I say, unsure of everything.

Arnold Abraham died only two hours earlier. The funeral home said they would hold off as long as they could, but they had to prepare the body if the funeral were to be held the next day. The hearse had arrived just ten minutes before Liz and I.

We go inside. Liz asks two solemn-looking men in dark suits if she can have just a minute with her father before they leave. She goes into the bedroom where his body is on a gurney. I sit with her mom in the living room while she wipes her eyes, her hands shaking violently. To my surprise, she takes my hands or, rather, she puts her hands into mine as if to ask that I help her still the shaking.

"Mrs. Abraham," I start.

"Please, call me Fran," she says, sniffing.

"Fran." I'm not sure what I will say until I hear my own voice. "Have you eaten at all today?"

"No. It was a long night. I can't remember when I last ate."

"Okay," I say. I want to find a way to be helpful but also in the background. "After they leave, why don't you and Liz spend some time together. I'll take the rental car and go get some sandwiches. I saw a deli when we were driving in."

She exhales slowly. "That would be great. Thank you, dear."

The next several hours are a flurry of planning. Liz helps her mother write an obituary for the morning's paper; the rabbi comes; a platter of food arrives from one of the neighbors; the time of the service is set for three o'clock the next day; I reserve hotel rooms for Michael and Barry, and Alana, David and the kids, all of whom will be arriving sometime after dinner. Liz says that she and I will stay in the spare bedroom. I don't know how her mother will feel about this, but I take my cues from Liz and don't question her.

When Liz's siblings arrive, they treat me with warmth and make me feel welcome—something for which I am immeasurably grateful. Despite everyone's immediate acceptance of my presence in the midst of this family scene, I am aware at every moment that I am very much a stranger to them. I want Liz to have time with her siblings and mother. They need to discuss who will speak at the service, and they need to be together without the distraction of a newcomer. This is when I pull Liz aside, into the quiet, carpeted hallway off the living room.

"Sweetie," I say, tucking a piece of Liz's hair behind her ear, "I'm wondering how you would feel if I ducked out for a bit. I'd actually like to spend some time sitting with your dad at the funeral home if that's okay with you."

Liz looks into my eyes, "You mean shmira?"

"Yeah. I mean, I know he's at a Jewish funeral home and that they have staff there that does that overnight. It's just, it would be an honor for me to sit with him."

"Rachel, you don't have to do this. You've been a tremendous help to us today. Don't feel that you have to do more."

"Actually," I say, "it would mean a lot to me. I want to do something to honor your father. Even though I never knew him, he is a part of you. I called the funeral home earlier and asked if someone could let me in if I came by late and they said it would be fine. It's really something I want to do."

Liz hugs me and whispers into my ear, "Where did you come from, Levine?"

I slip out the back door.

I am nothing if not a planner. I scouted out the funeral home earlier in the day when I went for sandwiches and have a map in my purse just in case I get lost. When I arrive, an overnight staff member, an older man with bad posture and a shuffle, lets me in and takes me into the room where the bodies are held. He checks a tag tied to the toe of one of the bodies and then says, "This one's him," motioning to the gurney. There are two other bodies in the room, each wrapped in a white linen shroud. I'd expected the bodies to be covered in a loose sheet, like Ivan Resnick's had been, but then realize that these bodies must have already been washed and prepared for burial. The shrouds are wrapped tightly around the bodies and the sight makes me think of King Tut. The old funeral man grabs a metal folding chair from against the wall and sets it up for me next to Liz's dad's body. He mumbles, "I'll be in the next room."

For several minutes, I just sit. The fluorescent lights are hard to adjust to and I notice that I am trembling slightly. The room is cold, and I wish I'd thought to bring a sweater. And then it hits me with a wave of nausea—I don't think I'm doing this for Liz or for her dad. I am doing this for me.

I think of how much I planned in order to make this moment happen—meeting with Rabbi Stein, telling Liz I wanted to be with her in Florida; I've even prepared what I want to say in the presence of the body. The word *manipulative* flashes in my brain and just as quickly, I wipe it away. No, I am not manipulative, not in the sinister way the word implies. And yet. I think of the Harvard trainee at the counseling center and the look of disgust on his face when he accused me of taking Charlie's moment and making it about me. I am so afraid of not knowing what my future with Liz holds. I want so badly to solidify my place in this family. *Is this what I'm doing here?*

I am suddenly flooded with shame. I pull my chair in closer to Liz's dad's head. I know he can't hear me (at least not through his ears), but I still want to be close so that I might speak my confession in privacy.

"I'm going to call you Arnie," I say in a half-whisper, not sure where to put my eyes and finally settling on speaking to the space just in front of me, Arnie's body to my left. "Fran said to call her Fran and, from what Liz has told me, you were the more laid-back one. My name is Rachel Levine. You know my zayde, Lew Kessler from Beth El? He's the one who taught me about shmira."

I am silent for a minute, rocking back and forth in my chair like I might be davening.

"Um, I had this poem I was going to read to you, but . . . it's . . . never mind. It's not right. It's just that . . . well, I'm actually here because I love your daughter and . . . I'm not sure how you feel about that, but you told Liz, Lizzy, a few weeks ago that you loved her and, if you love her, then you must want her to be happy. I want you to know that, for as long as she'll have me, I will do everything in my power to make her happy. I know that, to most fathers, that might mean providing for their daughter, you know, making sure she'll never have to worry about money or anything. The thing is, Liz is brilliant and hard-working and I don't think she'll ever need anyone to make sure she's financially cared for. What I mean is that I'll do everything in my power to make sure she laughs every day and is challenged . . . shit, sorry, I mean . . . Arnie? That's not the truth about why I'm here."

I am rocking hard now, and so queasy, and there is something like throbbing behind my eyes.

"Everything I just said is true. I want to make Liz happy, I do. It just isn't the whole truth. The whole truth is that I so badly want Liz to love me forever. And maybe I'm afraid of losing her. Maybe I just want to be here with you so that she'll see I'm the one for her. I don't know. I'm sorry, Arnie. I hope you can forgive me for being so confused. I'm supposed to be comforting you. I hope you can take comfort in knowing that someone loves your Lizzy this much and just wants it to last."

I close my eyes, tight, my arms folded and legs crossed and take deep breaths. Dr. Vargas says that when people sit with their arms and legs like this it may mean they are closed off, putting a barrier between themselves and something or someone in front of them. I think I am sitting like this because I am cold.

After a few minutes, I quietly fold my chair and return it to the spot against the wall from where the man had retrieved it. I stick my head in the little office where he's watching what appears to be a Nick at Nite rerun of *Sanford and Son* on a small TV. Is this what constitutes shmira behind the closed doors of a funeral home?

"I'm going to go now," I say.

When I get back to the Abrahams', Liz, her siblings and mother are still talking in the living room. I quickly say goodnight and slip into the guest room down the hall. When I get into bed, I am a little surprised to realize just how exhausted I am. As I drift off to sleep, I repeat over and over in my head, *I am a good person, I am a good person.*

The funeral is held in a small chapel in the Abrahams' large synagogue and is lovely. Is that a strange thing to say about a funeral? It is, though; friends and family gathered to pay tribute to a life of a loved one is a beautiful thing.

Liz agreed to speak and stayed up half the night writing her eulogy. Now, she approaches the podium next to her father's closed, simple pine coffin with the same dignity she had that first time I saw her approach the bimah to read the blessing before the Torah so many months before. And, like that day, she speaks in a clear, assertive voice and seems to look into the eyes of each person in attendance.

"Arnie Abraham was my father, my abba," she begins. "I use the Hebrew word for father, abba, with intention. It is not what I called him, but it is relevant, because what I want to share with you today is how my father raised me to be the Jewish woman I am.

"When I was a young child, growing up in Cambridge, Massachusetts, in a Conservative Jewish community, things were different for girls and women than they are today. Girls were allowed but not encouraged to learn Torah for their Bat Mitzvahs; women didn't count in the minyan; rabbis were always men. I went with my parents to Shabbat services every week, and I would ask them questions about where the women were in the leadership roles. My father often read Torah, and I was so proud of his participation in our congregation. I wanted to follow in his footsteps.

"When the time came to prepare for my Bat Mitzvah, my father became my official Hebrew tutor. He worked with me for months on end, teaching me trope so I could chant the tune for my Torah portion. I have a crystal-clear memory of the look of pride on his face during my Torah reading. I chanted a longer portion than any of my classmates that year, and that was because of him. My father instilled in me a love of Judaism as fierce as his own, and he made sure I knew that my voice mattered."

As she continues her eulogy, I listen on the edge of my seat. I hadn't known that Liz's dad had taught her as a child what I had only learned in college—that girls and women could play as vital a part in Jewish practice as our male counterparts. I envy her this.

The burial is difficult. I stand behind the immediate family (next to Barry, my new best friend). We say Kaddish together and take turns shoveling dirt into the grave. As always, I hate that sound—the thunk of a shovel-full of earth landing hard on the top of a wooden coffin. Still, I feel a reverent, humble respect over having the opportunity to participate in this tradition. It makes me feel connected to every Jew who has ever had to say goodbye.

Knowing I really can't take more time off from classes, the counseling center, and Zayde, and also worried that I might overstay my welcome, I fly home the day after the funeral.

Liz drives me to the little airport in West Palm in the rental car she's decided to keep for the rest of the week.

"I know it's a waste of money to keep paying for this car when we're just sitting at the house," she says on the drive. "I just need to know that I have my own wheels, you know? That I can get out of there if I need to."

When we pull up to curb-side check in, Liz comes around to help me get my bag out of the back seat. She takes my face in her hands, right there on the sidewalk in front of so many travelers. I think she is just going to kiss me goodbye, but instead she looks into my eyes and says, "Rachel Levine, you have been amazing through all of this. You have been my family. I love you so much." Then she kisses me, a quiet, dreamy cloud of a kiss that I am sure says, "*I want to be with you forever.*"

Chapter 14

I'm walking into Liz's apartment one evening a few weeks later and overhear the end of a phone conversation she is having with her mother.

"Okay, Mom! I'll definitely check my work calendar. Yes, it would be great to see you then."

I'm standing by the door, and suddenly a rush of tears overtakes me. I am so happy for Liz—for this new chapter she is beginning with her mother. But as I think about my relationship with mine, I find myself grieving. I haven't really done it—what we therapists call grief work—and it creeps up and grabs me from behind just as Liz is turning toward her mother for the first time in almost twenty years. At first I can't name it, the sudden catching of my breath in my throat, the rush of tears for no reason. I just know that I am experiencing a level of anxiety that feels primal in its intensity.

I am reminded of a day when I was about six years old and shopping for back-to-school clothes with my mother in Sears. We had lost each other for what might have been only less than a minute. I remember feeling swallowed by the tall, round racks of clothing as I called for her, a feeling of terror washing over me. I have no memory of the moment I found her, only of being lost in that sea of clothes. This feels kind of like that. Out of the blue, a wave of dread, weak knees, pounding heart. I want my mother and feel as if she is nowhere to be found.

I ask Dr. Vargas for the name of a good therapist. I have come to trust her and know that she will not think less of me for seeking my own therapy. She has also offered me, and I have accepted, a position as a second-year trainee at the college counseling center, which means I will be staying on for an additional year of training, working under Dr. Vargas again, during my third and final year of classes. As the counseling center is closed during the summer, all I have in the months ahead are a few intensive courses and time to work on my own issues.

Dr. Vargas refers me to a colleague of hers in Cambridge, a Dr. Kevin Miller, who practices out of his home office in a picturesque neighborhood near the Harvard campus. Though I have my car, I often choose to walk the half hour from Zayde's, relishing the private outdoor time before and after sessions. I smile when I think about Dr. Vargas talking about the frame of a session, thinking that my walks are how I frame the frame.

I spend the first walk to Kevin's (he goes by his first name) wondering how I feel about working with a male therapist. I have never pictured myself working with a man, perhaps because my two prior therapists were women. But Dr. Vargas assured me that he is "very smart and compassionate" and said she thought we'd be a good match.

I picture Kevin Miller as white-haired and bearded, though his voice during our phone conversation to schedule the appointment did not indicate age one way or another. I am surprised to find that he is youngish, maybe in his late forties, and strikingly handsome. From the kids' bikes on the porch, I deduce that he has a family.

I like Kevin right away. When he opens his office door to find me sitting in his small waiting area—not so much a room as a foyer—he stands tall and confident and says, "Rachel Levine, I presume?"

"You presume correctly," I say, standing to shake his hand. His quirky greeting reminds me of something Zayde might say and makes me feel at home. As I peer into the office behind him, I see a little, brown, fluffy lap dog standing exactly in the middle of the room. He cocks his head at me, his tail wagging frantically.

"Who's this?" I ask.

"This is Lucky," says Kevin, "my assistant." I laugh and give Lucky a scratch on his head. When I sit on the sofa across from Kevin's armchair, Lucky immediately jumps up and sits next to me. I've never had an affinity for licky, yappy dogs, but so far Lucky hasn't licked or yapped so I am open to getting to know him.

Kevin sits across from me holding a notebook in his lap. He takes a slow breath, and grins at me. "So who are you, Rachel Levine?"

I laugh out loud. "Sorry, it's just that that is the same question my girlfriend asked me on our first date."

"And what did you tell her?"

I smile, remembering our shivery walk to lunch. "I think what I said to her might be different from what I'd say to you."

"And why's that?"

"For one she already knew a little about me—I mean the basics. And secondly, I was flirting."

We both laugh a little. "Fair enough," says Kevin with a nod. "So how might you answer the question for me?"

I wait a moment before answering. "I miss my mom," I say.

❧

"My mom was asking about you today," says Liz one night. "She said you'd be proud of her for going to that book club! Turns out she really likes it."

I smile. I had been suggesting ideas of things for her mom to get involved in. Apparently I'd mentioned joining a book club.

"She's signing up for some lecture series too. She's really getting out."

"That's great, Liz." All I can think is, *My mother doesn't even know about you.*

I am constantly comparing my connection with my mother to hers. Where I had been so close to my mother growing up, the six years since coming out to her have been so distant. Where Liz has been so cut off from her mother for the past fifteen years, she is rebuilding a connection with her. And then I feel guilty for comparing. What Liz has endured, both through her brother's history and her own, is terrible, and I do not want to begrudge her the reunion she and her mother are having. And yet, I am filled with an envy I can only bring to Kevin each Friday morning at ten.

As I become clearer about what I am feeling, the anxiety attacks dissipate, and I am able to feel the sadness that has been fueling them. Kevin is instrumental at helping me stay with the grief, and I am beginning to think that his maleness—the fact that he is neither a mother nor a daughter—enables him to support me in a uniquely disentangled way. He is empathic without being sentimental, something that I struggle with in my own work with daughters who want to talk about their relationships with their mothers. In those moments in my work at the counseling center, I have to work hard to keep my own feelings about my mother out of the room, which I suppose is one reason why I need to be doing this therapy with Kevin.

That summer, I take an elective course in geropsychology where we get to do things like spend time at an assisted living community interviewing octogenarians about their perspectives on living and dying. While this population is so different from the late adolescents

I work with, it is a cohort with whom I also feel at home. Living with Zayde and being around his friends has me brimming with questions about the elderly. How do they make sense of the speed at which technology is changing? How do they make peace with their regrets? Are they more or less afraid than the rest of us?

The class only meets on Tuesdays and Thursdays and, with the summer off from clinical work, I have long, free days of biking, reading, and visiting Liz on her lunch breaks. I stay at her place about twice a week, making up different stories about my whereabouts, and we spend most Sunday afternoons in her bed. We have long talks, usually after sex and naked without covers as she has no air conditioning and her Cambridge apartment is stiflingly hot. With her bedroom window wide open to catch any breeze there might be, we are safely unseen by anyone outside as long as we are lying down; if we need to get up, say, to use the bathroom or get a snack, we have to use the skills of a contortionist, moving through the space of the room below windowsill height lest we put on a show for the people of Central Square.

As we lay on our backs one Sunday afternoon, flushed and praying for a breeze, Liz asks, "So what's your number?"

"You mean how many people I've had sex with?" I figure all couples have the What's-Your-Number conversation sooner or later.

"No. I mean how many people have you been in love with?"

"Of course that's what you mean!" I laugh. "Unrequited *and* mutual?"

She laughs out loud. "Um . . . both. I want both."

"Okay, my first love was my English teacher in eighth grade, Ms. Crowley. I think she was like twenty-six or something. I thought about her every day for about three years! When I graduated that year, she said I could call her Debbie, and when I was in high school, I used to go back to the middle school and visit her a lot and one time we went to lunch at the mall together!" Suddenly feeling as giddy as a school girl, I have flipped over onto my stomach and am propped up on my elbows.

"Oh my God, take a breath!" says Liz, laughing at my excitement.

"Wait, there's more. Remember that REO Speedwagon song, 'I Can't Fight This Feeling'? That was our song!" We are rolling around on the bed, laughing.

"Please tell me you didn't tell her that!" gasps Liz.

"No, I definitely didn't. She didn't know anything. But Liz, it was serious. I wanted to run off with this woman!"

"I believe you! Okay, who's next?"

"Next was Eric Posner. He was a counselor at this sleep-away camp I went to for a month when I was sixteen. He was like thirty and had this long, hippy hair and beautiful eyelashes. I wrote him a letter on the last day of camp, telling him that he had changed my life forever."

"Did you have a song?" asks Liz, smirking.

"Of course. It was 'The Boxer' by Simon and Garfunkel. Eric used to lead these sing-a-longs with his guitar, they were actually called 'mellow-a-longs,' and he used to play that song—"

"Mellow-a-longs?!?" She is pealing with laughter now.

"Listen!" I implore, feigning defense, "I loved him!"

"I'm sure you did, you silly, heartsick teenager! When did someone finally love you back?"

"Ah, that's Jason," I say with a sigh. "Jason and I were friends in high school and then became a couple senior year. We were together from about December until we left for college. And before you can ask—yes, we lost our virginity to each other and yes, we had a song." I wait a beat. "'Open Arms' by Journey."

"No!" Liz howls, rolling around again.

I pin her down. We are like bear cubs wrestling.

"But wait," I say, "there's more. Let me tell you how that became our song. A couple of weeks before we had sex for the first time, we were hanging out with a group of friends playing Truth or Dare, and he chose truth and someone asked him, "If you could have sex to any song, what would it be?"

"And let me guess, he said 'Open Arms.'"

"Right! So I bought one of those loop tapes where you can play it over and over without rewinding? And I recorded 'Open Arms' onto it so that it would play continuously? Anyway, I was house sitting a few weekends later for the family I usually babysat for—"

"They let you house sit at seventeen?"

"I know, wild, right? The mom, she even said I should sleep in their bed and that I could have a friend stay over with me. She knew I had a boyfriend—she was kind of cool that way. So, I set up a tape player with fresh batteries under their bed and, of course Jason stayed over with me, and then just as he was putting the condom on, I flung myself over the side of the bed, groping around in the dark for the tape player—he was like, 'What are you doing?'—and then I pressed play. And that's how that became our song!"

Liz cannot stop laughing.

"Okay, okay," I say. "What's *our* song?"

She thinks, then says, "I think it's the blessing before the Torah reading!"

I think all of Central Square can hear us crying with laughter.

We lay in a heap, catching our breath. Liz toys with my hair and says, "Tell me more about Jason."

"You know, we were seventeen and in love. We had a lot of clumsy sex and went to the prom." I became more serious. "Actually, I lost myself a lot in that relationship."

"What do you mean?"

"I just don't think I understood how powerful it all was—sex and being that vulnerable with someone. When he said he wanted to break up when we went to college, I sort of fell apart for a while. It's still really hard when I see him."

"When do you see him?" she asks.

I pretend not to notice the edge in her voice. "The last time was our five-year high school reunion. Here's the thing—I definitely don't want to be in a relationship with him anymore and, looking back, I know that we were supposed to end it after high school. But I just don't believe in falling out of love with people, you know? I mean, I think that once I love someone like that, I always will on some level. Even if I don't want to be with them, I feel all of those feelings when I see them again, both the rush of it all and then the hurt, too."

"Huh. So you'll always love all the people you've ever loved?"

"I think I will." This feels scary, like I am telling Liz I've cheated or something. I try to change the pace of the moment. "So if you ever break up with me, we can't be friends because I'll always love you."

"Okay, move on."

"Next? Nora in college, and I've told you about her already. And then you! Now you tell me your list." I suddenly feel desperate for the focus to shift.

"I loved one woman in college—Gabby Schulman. We were together for most of my junior year. She was a senior, and, when she graduated, she moved back home to Seattle and ended it. I don't actually know what she's up to now. Then Helen in Paris."

She stops. I want to know so much more.

"It's funny for me to think of you having a whole relationship in French," I say. "How did you and she break up?" That's what I really want to know.

"I found out that she was having an affair—with a man." That is all she says. Then, "What should we eat? I'm starving!"

Chapter 15

"**Y**ou're not going to believe this, but my zayde said to invite you to Shabbat dinner this Friday."

Liz's eyebrows seem to pull her eyes wide like little marionettes. "To what do I owe this honor?"

"You've got me, but he's been in a pretty good mood for the past few weeks. Must have something to do with the rabbi being away in Israel for the summer."

That Friday, I cook chicken in a crockpot and make roasted potatoes. Liz brings the challah and the wine. After dinner, we stay at the kitchen table and play two rounds of Rummikub, Zayde on one side of the table, bent over his tiles with his knit yarmulke that he only wears at home, and Liz and I across from him, stealing secret moments of pressing our legs together under the table.

"Elizabeth, you are quite good at this game. I didn't think many young people knew how to play it."

"Ah, Rummikub was always my parents' Christmas Eve tradition. They taught me very young, and I don't think a December 24th went by during my childhood when the three of us didn't play for several hours."

Liz keeps winning, but having them both at the table with me makes me feel like *I've* won.

A few days later, Zayde looks up from reading his paper in his recliner and asks, "Shayna meydeleh, have you met any nice boychiks in your classes?"

"Oh Zayde, I've met so many, I don't know how to fend them off!"

He shakes his head with a chuckle and goes back to his paper. I don't feel guilty about the lie. I am everything Zayde needs me to be—his aide, his cook, his companion. I am caring and patient and, in return, I receive my zayde's love and respect.

One Friday morning in July, Kevin wants to know more about my relationship with Zayde.

"I've always been close to my grandfather. I guess I put him on a pedestal when I was a kid. Maybe I still do."

"How so?"

"I don't know—it's like I feel protective of him. Like, I look up to him but also think of him as sort of fragile. I mean, he's old. He doesn't deserve pain at his age. That's why I can't come out to him—I don't want to cause him any pain."

"And what does that have to do with your mother?"

I look at the floor. "You therapists—you're always bringing it back to the mother!"

"You're good at that, aren't you?" he asks.

"Good at what?"

"At using humor when you are uncomfortable."

"I guess not," I say. "If I was good at it, I might have successfully thrown you off my trail."

He thinks about this. "No," he says. "That would have just made me a bad therapist."

We smile, then I start to cry.

"What was your question again?" I say between sniffles.

"What does all of this loyalty, this protection of your grandfather have to do with your mother?"

I sit thinking for what feels like a long time. "I want to say nothing.

I want to say that my relationship with Zayde is about him and me only—that I take care of him simply out of love and because it is the right thing to do. That I spend every Saturday morning with him at shul instead of sleeping in because that is where I want to be each week."

"I appreciate you telling me what you want to say," says Kevin. "I would think there is a lot of truth in all of that as well. I'm just wondering if it's the whole story."

More tears, more silence. Then, "Are you suggesting that I'm trying to win back my mother or something by taking care of her father?"

"Are you suggesting that?" he asks in his gentle voice.

"I don't know," I say. "I just know that I have to do the right thing."

⁓

"Can you spend all of next weekend with me?" asks Liz on one of our late-night phone calls. I smile under the dark covers.

"I sure can!" I whisper, not hiding my excitement.

"Great. Two of my friends from Yale are living in P-town this summer and they invited us down for the weekend."

I have always heard that Provincetown, at the very tip of Cape Cod, is a haven for gay people, but have never been there myself. Liz suggests we take the harbor ferry from Boston, a three-hour boat ride that, she adds, often includes whale sightings.

"Liz, I get very seasick. Really, even in the mildest of waves." I worry. When Zeke and I were young, my dad went through a "let's all take up fishing as a family" phase one summer at the Jersey shore. I still get queasy when I think about that boat ride off the coast of Ocean City.

"No worries," says Liz. "I've taken this ferry several times, and it is a big boat. I don't even remember there being any waves at all."

I agree to go, I pack Dramamine and some clothes, and we climb aboard on a humid July Friday morning.

We are about forty-five minutes out from shore before the waves start in earnest, and then it takes another twenty minutes for me to start vomiting. I take the Dramamine but am sick before it can even kick in. Liz feels terrible. She swears, over and over, that it has never been choppy on this ride, and I believe her because other sick passengers are saying the same thing. One woman is crying, telling her husband that she can't believe, after taking this boat so many times before, that it could be this bad. I'm sure Liz is relieved by this woman's testimony, lest I think she is a big liar.

When the boat docks in Provincetown, I shuffle slowly down the metal ramp with all of the other sick passengers. Each of us is careful not to make eye contact with one another out of the lingering embarrassment of having so loudly retched among strangers. My parents actually used to tell a funny story about one of their early dates when my mom drank too much at a party and vomited in my father's car. The lesson, besides the obvious dangers of intoxication, seemed to be that, if someone stays with you after seeing you barf, that person is probably there to stay.

I slump onto a bench near the ticket office for returning passengers and put my head in my hands. Liz sits next to me and rubs my back. "I'm so sorry, sweetie. Are you feeling any better?"

"Will you still stay with me after seeing me barf?" I ask, pouting out my lower lip.

"Which time?" asks Liz.

I groan and put my head on her shoulder, and we laugh for the first time that morning.

❧

Liz's friends, Jamie and Jenna, have been in P-town for a month, where they are subletting an apartment above a café on Commercial Street. Jamie, a freelance journalist, is working on a series of articles about the history of the Cape while Jenna, a graduate student in anthropology, has the summer off and is working at the café beneath them. Liz filled me in on their history before the trip, explaining that they have been together since their undergraduate days. They are coming up on their ten-year anniversary. I don't know any couple among my peers that has been together that long. I'm eager to meet Jamie and Jenna, to see what that kind of long-term relationship looks and feels like. Maybe I think of them as a sort of template upon which I can project my future with Liz.

Commercial Street is like gay heaven to me—same-sex couples walking hand-in-hand everywhere, stores with pink triangle stickers in their windows. Jamie takes us into one store that sells all women-themed things like goddess jewelry, Rosie the Riveter posters, and feminist books. As I flip through a stack of postcards, Jamie leans over to me. "They have a 10% lesbian discount." Liz leans in and whispers back, "She's bi—only 5% for her," and winks at me.

It is one of those moments when you don't know what's funny and what's not. On the surface at least, Liz is trying to make a joke. But her humor masks more, and I know that. I know she has a problem with my being bisexual; I know that Helen left her for a man.

I feel hurt by her making me feel "other," especially in front of Jamie. I feel confused by the "lesbian discount"; how do they know who to give the discount to? How does one claim said discount at the register? Is there a secret ID card I haven't been issued? I smile and act as if I find the whole thing funny, while inside I feel everything sinking.

That night we cook dinner together in Jamie and Jenna's apartment, which is cozy like a beach house. It reminds me of that first dinner at Liz's place when I felt so young and nervous. As we get into the cooking, though—each of us with a job, chopping vegetables or stirring the homemade pasta sauce, each drinking wine and nibbling on cheese while we do—I begin to feel more at ease. They try not to exclude me by talking about people only the three of them know, but in some ways that is inevitable. They have a long history together, and any attempt to make me feel like less of a newcomer is polite but doomed. I don't mind this—it gives me a chance to observe Jamie and Jenna's relationship as I had hoped to.

What strikes me most during our cooking together is their sameness. Unlike Liz and me, they seem similar in so many ways. Even their names suggest a set of twins from the kind of family where the parents dress their kids in matching outfits. They look a little like each other, too, with their cropped brown hair and similar heights.

I had a social psychology class as an undergraduate where we debated whether "opposites attract" or "birds of a feather flock together." I had been strongly in favor of the idea that opposites attract, believing that those characteristics in others that remind us too much of ourselves ultimately turn us off. Ironically, I'd never thought about this applying to gender. Sure, by definition two women would have more similarities to each other than a woman and a man, but only across certain domains. I think of Liz and myself not as opposites exactly but as having enough differences (both physical and in personality) so as not to mirror each other. Jamie and Jenna seem more alike, and they seem to gravitate toward sameness. I think about phrases my mother might use like "two peas in a pod" or "regular Bobbsey Twins."

What strikes me then is that perhaps I am attracted to people different from me not because I am avoiding characteristics that remind me of myself, but because I want to preserve my sense of self. When I picture myself in a relationship with someone very much like me—an extrovert, a psychologist maybe—I immediately feel a rising anxiety that I will somehow lose my individuality, will be seen as only part of a couple and not as my own person. Liz and I are both women and both Jewish and both feminists but would never be confused for each other. We come at the world from vastly different angles and have to work to find our common space. I suddenly realize that this is what allows me to love her and feel whole at the same time.

When dinner is ready, we make heaping plates of pasta and take them into the living room, gathering around the coffee table. Liz and I take either end of the sofa and balance our plates on our laps, while Jenna and Jamie each sit cross-legged on the floor. I look at the coffee table, which holds a spread of wine, cheese (what is left of it), and garlic bread, and feel a surge of warmth. I raise my glass in a toast. "I just want to share my gratitude for being among such cool women and such delicious food."

"Hear, hear!" says Jamie, and we clink over our feast.

"Sooo," says Jenna with wide eyes, "we have something to tell you." She looks at Jamie and smiles broadly. "We are having a baby!"

Liz, in her typically understated manner, makes a sound like "ohh" and rises from the sofa to hug her friends. "Is this fetus in the room with us?" Liz asks.

"Yes," laughs Jenna and says, "I'm pregnant!"

"But you've been drinking wine with us all night," says Liz, flashing Jenna a worried look.

"No," says Jenna. "You poured me wine, and I've been carrying it around with me so that you wouldn't guess before we told you!"

Jenna and Jamie tell us the story of searching for a donor, how they looked through binders and binders of handwritten applications from the sperm bank, and had finally decided on a man.

"He's from an Irish family like both of ours," says Jamie. "The form included all sorts of details—family medical history, athleticism, hair color, eye color, GPA. He's a smart guy!"

"How did you decide who would carry the baby?" I ask.

"That wasn't exactly easy," says Jamie. "We both want to have the experience. It's likely that we'll have a second child, and that I would carry that baby. We reserved a ton of this guy's sperm so that we could use it a second time."

I am riveted, also stuck on the image of a ton of sperm.

"Hey—you ever think about it?" asks Jenna with a nudge of her chin toward Liz.

Liz sits up straight as if she's just been unexpectedly called on in class and hasn't quite finished the reading. "Me? About having kids?"

Liz looks pensive, and I have stopped breathing altogether. Is Jenna asking about *us*, about whether Liz and I have thought about kids? Is she just asking Liz? Is Liz thinking about me right now? Is she going to say anything?

"Yeah," she says. "Yeah, I mean, I've always envisioned having kids someday. I don't know that I care though if I'm the one to carry a child. I don't think that's so important to me."

I smile unwittingly, picturing myself nine months pregnant with our future child.

The next day is sunny and beautiful. Jenna has the day off from the café, and the four of us load up beach bags with blankets, towels, an umbrella, sunscreen, and snacks and walk down to the beach talking about morning sickness and prenatal vitamins. Jamie and Jenna are the first of either of our friends to be having a baby, and both Liz and I are full of questions.

We stake out a spot on the warm sand for the day. I immediately take up my beach position—under the umbrella with my book. As I do, I realize that Liz and I have never been to the beach together, and that there are some beach-related things she might not know about me. The first is that I'm not a lay-in-the-sun kind of girl; I burn. I like relaxing near the ocean, especially if I am reading something good, but I love shade. The second thing, the thing I've maybe been keeping a secret as I don't think an athlete like Liz would find it so attractive, is that I can barely swim. I never go into the ocean beyond my calves and, even then, I tend to stare at my feet the whole time to make sure a jelly fish or other stingy creature isn't coming near. I am an oceanaphobe.

Liz, as I might have predicted, loves the water. She spends most of that day swimming, dipping under and through waves like a sexy dolphin. Though I feel a little bit Victorian with my pale skin and umbrella, I love watching her from my spot in the shade. I also feel a little bit victor*ious*. As I watch Liz shining in the ocean, her beauty more radiant than ever, I feel a sense of pride in having her. Having her. I wonder if this thought is inappropriate, or too possessive, or sexist. I think of boys who walk with their arms slung around their girlfriends' necks as if holding them on a leash. Does feeling proud of being with Liz make me like those boys? I don't think so, but I decide to keep these thoughts in my head just in case.

Just then, Liz comes out of the water and collapses on the blanket next to me, letting the sun dry her wet skin. I take the opportunity of being in safe Provincetown to roll on top of her. "You are a fish!"

"And *you* are too dry!" she says rolling me over, pinning me on the sand.

"Not even *remotely*," I say in my most suggestive tone. We lie there kissing until both Jamie and Jenna come out of the water and shake their short, wet hair at us.

"Get a room, you two!" says Jamie, plopping down next to Jenna.

We sit up, and I pull a bag of chips toward me.

"Do you not swim?" Jamie asks.

I guess I couldn't hide it. "I admit, I'm a little afraid of the water." Thankfully, Liz is smiling at me—it feels safe to go on. "Even when I'm washing my face in the shower, I hold my breath by puffing out my cheeks and scrunching my eyes closed like a toddler learning to swim." I have them laughing hard as I demonstrate. Maybe Kevin is right about my using humor to cover my discomfort.

But then things get more uncomfortable, and I manage to put the humor away and stay with the conversation in as honest a way as I can.

Jamie says, "Rachel, can I ask you a question? What's it like to be bi? I just have a hard time imagining what it's like to be attracted to men—and maybe a harder time imagining what it would be like to be attracted to *both* men and women."

She isn't being derisive; her question is honest and her tone respectful enough. I look quickly at Liz, wondering if she is going to rescue me, but then realize that Liz is probably eager to hear how I will answer. Jenna just looks at me and waits.

"I don't really know how to answer that," I say first. "I mean, I am attracted to some men, and I've had boyfriends. But I've also always been attracted to women and have had, and have, a girlfriend—"

Jenna cuts in, "I think maybe Jamie's question is more about lifestyle."

I wonder if Jenna's knowing Jamie's question means that they talked about me the night before in bed or something.

Jamie nods. "Right, I mean, how do you choose what kind of life you want? I would think that being in a long-term relationship with a woman and being in one with a man is more dissimilar than it seems. Your community, where you choose to raise your kids, your political involvement—they all change, right?"

I am suddenly reminded of the fact that Jamie is a journalist, accustomed to asking relative strangers probing questions, and I want to be as articulate as I can. I want all three of them to find my response thoughtful and wise, like I know myself perhaps better than I actually do.

"You're right, Jamie," I say, the use of her name giving me a little shot of power. "It probably is about more than just the gendered stuff inside of the relationship." And then I go blank. I realize that the truth is, I don't know what I think about choosing a life. I know I want to be with Liz, though, so I say, "I guess I don't think we have as much agency as you're suggesting. I think there is fate, and who you meet, and who you love—and then that becomes your life." I don't know if I believe what I'm saying, but I think it might at least get me off the hook. It doesn't.

"That's romantic," says Jamie. "I just don't really buy it. I think we have to own that we make choices all the time. I think you and Liz *chose* each other."

Jenna interrupts. "And let me say I'm glad that you did. We haven't seen our old college friend here this happy in a long time!" Thank God.

"Yes," says Jamie, softening, "I think you both made a wonderful choice in each other. I just don't believe that you were brought together by fate."

Liz knows I need rescuing then and gets up from the blanket. Shielding her eyes with her hand, she says to us, "I think it's time for more swimming." Then reaching out her hand to me, "Are you sure I can't pull you in?"

"I'm in," I answer, grabbing her hand and letting her pull me up. I am even willing to get in the ocean to end this conversation.

✺

The ferry ride back to Boston on Sunday is far calmer than Friday's trip had been. A heavy dose of Dramamine taken well before we departed has left me sedated to the point of dozing on Liz's shoulder for the first hour.

I blink awake, mortified by what can only be drool under my chin.

"Morning sleepyhead. You feeling okay?"

I wipe my mouth casually. "Yeah. Wow, I've been out!" Yawning, I look at Liz. "I really loved P-town, and your friends are great."

"I'm sorry about Jamie," she says. "I know she can be a little overbearing."

"No," I say. "She's just a journalist," and, still feeling the effects of the Dramamine, smile a little drunken half-smile at Liz. "I'm sorry I don't swim."

"Why are you sorry?" asks Liz, cocking her head at me.

"I don't know, I just felt totally uncool. Watching you—it was so clear how at home you feel in the water."

"Yeah, I do love swimming. I think I actually might feel most alive when I'm in the ocean."

I am surprised at her willingness to share this insight, though am not surprised when she turns to me and asks, "What makes you feel most alive?"

"Being on land," I joke. "No, actually, I feel most alive when I'm in love—when I'm limerent."

"Limer-what?" asks Liz

"Limerent. It's a psychology word. It means that state of being head over heels, you know, when you can't concentrate on anything else but that person?"

"Oh," says Liz, playing with my hair. "*That* state." And she winks at me.

Chapter 16

The week after our trip to the Cape, I am busy working on a final paper for my geropsychology class. The assignment is to choose a topic relevant to aging and do an in-depth interview with an older adult. The paper has to include a transcript of the interview along with an analysis of the data gathered. We have been discussing why some older adults seem to get more cognitively inflexible with age, while others seem to become more open to new learning and experience, contrasting the caricature of the crotchety old person who shakes their cane at the neighborhood kids with that of the wise, calm elder. I decide to make this question the focus of my paper and to ask Zayde's friend Bess if she will be my subject. She is happy to help—as I knew she would be.

I have never been inside Bess's home, an old Somerville house about the same age as Zayde's. Just inside the front door, I ask Bess if she minds if I take off my sandals—it is raining outside, and they are wet from the puddles and prematurely leafy sidewalk. I don't want to trail mud into what immediately strikes me as Bess's museum of a house—full of original furnishings like Zayde's, but with an even more preserved feel. I can see that the sofa in the living room to the left is covered in plastic. The house smells of dusting powder, the kind women of a certain age apply with a big soft puff in order to keep their makeup in place.

Bess leads me into her powdery living room with its floral wallpaper and plush mauve carpet that feels like moss under my bare feet. The room's shelves and end tables are covered in a mixture of Judaica (ceramic menorahs, Kiddush cups, decorative *tzedakah* boxes for collecting charity money) and photographs of her grandchildren. Bess takes me around the perimeter of the room, introducing me to each grandchild (of which there are nine) in each framed display, telling me each one's age and whereabouts.

I begin my interview with this. We sit in two formal armchairs at the end of the room that are not covered in plastic, and I put my little tape recorder on the small table between us. "Bess, you have such beautiful grandchildren. It seems like you love being a grandmother."

"Oh honey!" she exclaims, wrapping her arms around herself and giving a little squeeze as she might to a child. "My grandchildren are my precious angels! I tell you, they are what keep this old woman going."

"Bess, it's funny, I don't think of you as an old woman. Do you mind if I ask you how old you are?"

She chuckles and shakes her head. "I turn eighty-two next month, God willing. I think that does indeed make me an old woman, and a blessed old woman at that!"

I am so drawn to Bess. She is vibrant and kind. I think of the things she said at the diner that night when she told us she'd changed her mind about the rabbi. The contrast between Bess and Zayde is so palpable; while they are both elders, long-time congregants, and good friends, they have completely different ways of receiving the world. Where Zayde seems closed as if he is sitting behind a pair of locked shutters, Bess is like an open window. I want to know what makes her the wise elder—and maybe to better understand my zayde as well.

I have not prepared many specific questions. Rather, I want to have an authentic conversation with Bess that takes its own direction and has its own momentum. I look around the room at the mixture of Judaica and photographs.

"I can't help but notice that this room has two . . . I don't know . . . themes I guess. It is clear that you love being Jewish as well as being a grandmother. Maybe we can start by talking about those things— how they intersect?"

Bess sits back in her chair, looking up as if to find an answer. Then looking at me, nodding and smiling she says, "Rachel dear, they are one and the same to me!"

"What do you mean?"

"Well," she says, her eyebrows raised, "I raised a Jewish family. I made a Jewish home. This is really where Judaism thrives, isn't it? Don't get me wrong, honey, our synagogues and Jewish schools are very important places. But the home—that is where we live Jewish lives. Lighting the candles on Friday nights, saying blessings together with our children as they grow up—these are the things that I love the most."

I nod, more out of habit than agreement.

"So, when I think of my children and grandchildren, I think of those moments with them as the most special. I guess that is what I mean when I say they are one and the same."

I'm not sure what I am going to ask next, until I do. "Bess, when your children grew up and left home, did they continue to practice Judaism—both in their homes and in synagogues—as you had done with them?"

"All four of them certainly did." She straightens up and looks proud. "My Dottie was a religious school director for many years. Martin reads Torah regularly at his shul in New York." She pauses, and I wonder if she is feeling defensive. "They each married Jewish husbands and wives. They each made good, Jewish homes."

I uncross my legs, planting the soles of my feet into the pink of the carpet, and lean forward, my elbows on my knees. "And what about their children—your nine grandchildren? Do *they* practice Judaism in the way that you envisioned for them?" I notice my hands trembling. I am now talking about my own generation, and I fear Bess's possible disappointments.

She sighs a long slow sigh. Her cheeks seem to tighten at the sides of her mouth. "The way I envisioned? No." She shakes her head. "The two oldest, Nathan's girls, are both married to men who aren't Jewish. Neither wedding was in a synagogue. Oh, Naomi's wedding did have some Jewish parts—they broke a glass at the end and they had a *chuppah*, but then they did something with two candles coming together. It was—what did Nomi tell me? 'A combination of traditions.'"

I want to know more, and I want to stop at the same time. My mind jumps to Liz, who is Jewish, yes, but I know her being female would be taken far worse by Zayde than Bess was taking her granddaughters' interfaith marriages. And, in any case, I know that Zayde is the less open-minded of the two.

I am still leaning in. I take a deep breath. "I'm curious about how you have managed your discomfort with their choices." I stumble on *discomfort*, not knowing if it is the right word. "I hear you saying that the fact that they married non-Jewish men was upsetting to you, but I guess I'm wondering how it has affected your relationships with them. What I mean is, have you made peace with it?"

Bess doesn't speak right away and seems to consider my question carefully. The silence hangs in the room. When Bess finally does speak, she says, "You know Rachel, when you get to be my age, you realize that life is short. It's true, I may not understand or care for every choice my grandchildren make, but they are my loves." Her smile returns. "I guess what I am trying to say is, I don't always like what they do, but I love them anyways."

"I think they are lucky to have you," I say gingerly, suddenly knowing where I want to go with these questions. I cross my legs again, trying to relax. "A few minutes ago we were talking about family and Judaism. Is it fair to say, then, that when push comes to shove, you choose family? I mean, that you choose to stay connected to your grandchildren even if they ultimately don't lead the Jewish lives you would like?"

She looks surprised and sits up stiffly. "Yes, but it's not like they've rejected Judaism. Both of my granddaughters intend to raise Jewish children whether or not their husbands ever decide to convert."

I need to push harder, to see at what point Bess would draw the line, if she would ever draw a line. "Okay, but let's say—just hypothetically—that one of them decided to reject Judaism. What if they chose to raise their children with no religion or as Christians?"

Bess's eyes widen. She sits back again, letting out a slow exhalation. "That," she says more quietly, "would break my heart."

I lean forward again, closer to her. "I understand. I do. I'm just going to ask you one last hard question about this, Bess. If that happened, and if you felt brokenhearted about it, can you imagine that you could move past that pain and still be close to your granddaughter—still love her the same way?"

I hold my breath, my toes burying themselves into the thick fibers of carpet. Bess tilts her head to the side, just slightly, and looks at me as if she's seen something alarming.

"I want to tell you yes, that I could. But the truth is I just don't know."

∽

I have a hard time writing that paper. I end up making it more of a creative writing piece; I know that this particular professor is open to nontraditional styles of writing, and being creative seems to feel less scary. I call it "Space," because, as I listen to the recording of the interview, what strikes me most is Bess's silent pause—the space between my question about loving her granddaughter and her answer. I hypothesize about what was happening in that space and conclude that what she was doing was considering the possibilities—weighing the choices put before her—and that it was this consideration, this openness to possibility, that made her the flexible, wise kind of elderly person. Even if she couldn't say what she'd do, she was willing to take the time to imagine.

I further theorize that it is those people who are made too anxious by this openness who react harshly, with certainty, and who are not willing to learn or think about what other possibilities exist. I think again about that night at the diner, when Zayde slammed his hand down on the table and said, "Asinine!" For him, the idea of considering change or something new was too scary and there was no pause for thought. His reaction was immediate and fixed.

I sit at my computer and watch the screen go blurry through tears. Zayde will never accept Liz as my partner. There isn't enough space.

When I see Kevin that week, I talk about the paper and about what it is bringing up for me about Zayde.

"The thing is, I was never considering coming out to Zayde. I don't know why I'm suddenly so caught up in how he would react if I were to."

"For one thing," he replied, "your relationship with Liz is continuing to grow. I would imagine that, as you become more serious with her, you'll want to be able to share your happiness with the people you love."

"Yeah, what I need to do is start with my parents. It's funny, it's like coming out to them all over again."

"How so?"

"I think they think that bisexual just means 'confused' and that they are hoping, at least my mom is hoping, that I'm all straightened out now." I tell him about the conversation at the beach where Jamie asked me about choices. It isn't until telling Kevin that I realize there might be a connection between the questions she asked me and the pressure I feel to come out to Zayde.

Kevin listens carefully. "It sounds like Jamie really doesn't understand bisexuality."

"That was my first thought too, but honestly, I don't think anything she said was really off base. She is right that I have a choice about the kind of person I look for to make a life with. We all do that, right? Like how people decide whether they'll only date within their religion. There was this girl in my dorm one year who would only date men who were taller than her! So, I think what Jamie was pointing out was that—now that I'm in a stage of my life where people think about who they'll settle down with—I have the option of dating men or women, and that choosing men means that I get to live this accepted, conventional life where my family wants to dance at my wedding and I can have babies just by having sex. And if I choose a woman, I don't get those privileges, but I get this community and these progressive women to surround myself with."

"And there is no way to have both?" Kevin genuinely asks.

"I don't think so. I think if I'm with a man, our friends will be heterosexual couples. Every new person I meet will think I'm straight. I'll become a soccer mom."

"And your child if you have a woman partner won't play soccer?" He smiles.

"My child might play soccer, but no one would assume that I was straight."

"No," he says. "They would assume you were a lesbian. They still might only see half of you."

"Huh. I guess that's true. People always assume you're one or the other."

"And how would that feel, to know they only see half of you?"

"I would feel half-visible."

"That's not a feeling, that's a thought. What does being half-visible *feel* like?"

I sit for a minute, envisioning myself on the sidelines of some suburban soccer field. In one scene, I am cheering with a bunch of moms and dads, the women wearing barn coats and duck boots, the men sporting sweatshirts advertising our local NFL team. In another, I am on the sidelines with a group of short-haired, athletic looking moms.

"I think it feels half-lonely."

Chapter 17

As I'm driving to Bryn Mawr to spend a few days with my parents in early August, I remember a silly argument Liz and I had the previous week.

"I think I'm going to tell my parents about us when I'm home next week," I said.

"It's funny that you say that—home. You do know that Somerville is your home now, right?"

"Oh, I—" I'm embarrassed. I guess I am too old to call my parents' house "home" but it is still how I think of it. The only other places I've lived have been in a dorm or at Zayde's or at Liz's apartment. I've never picked out my own shower curtain, never chosen where to put the coffee maker. "I guess it's just an old habit," I say.

On my first night visiting, my parents and I sit around our kitchen table, and they fill me in on the local gossip I've missed. Mom ran into Shelby Seller's mom at the grocery store, and it was clear she'd had "work done." Dad saw our family dentist and found out that his son is getting married to a British woman and moving to London. I take this as a good opening and segue with seeming nonchalance.

"So, listen—speaking of relationships, I, uh, wanted to let you guys know that I've been seeing someone pretty seriously in Boston."

They both look up with what I can only call expectation. By this time my mouth is, conveniently, full of food.

"That's wonderful, Rach," my dad replies. "Tell us about . . . this person."

I swallow then don't let myself hesitate. "Her name is Liz Abraham she's twenty-nine she works for a Jewish non-profit . . ." It all comes out in a rush.

My mother is looking at her plate, pushing food around. Then she speaks. "And where did you meet this Liz?" Still no eye contact.

"We actually met at Beth El. She's a Saturday morning regular like Zayde and I are—"

"At Beth El?" she interrupts, clearly shaken.

"Mom, listen, Zayde doesn't know a thing. I mean, he knows her but he thinks we are just friends. I have been very discreet."

"And how long have the two of you been . . . seeing each other?"

I can hear the shaking in her voice now. I don't want to be in this place again. "For about seven months."

My dad smiles a too-big smile. "Goodness, seven months? Why are we just hearing about her now?"

I love my dad for trying to be normal, for pretending that my mother isn't on the verge of tears, for asking to hear more.

"I guess I didn't want to say anything at first because I didn't want Mom to worry about Zayde finding out." This is partially true. "I wanted to make sure we weren't just, like, a passing thing, you know?"

My mother looks up this time. "And what does that mean? That you're not a passing thing? You're a permanent thing?" Now she seems angry.

"I don't know, Mom," I say a little louder, wishing I had waited until dessert so that I could have a quicker exit. "We love each other. It *could* become a permanent thing, but obviously I can't know that yet." I hate that I am dignifying her homophobia with a response.

Again, my father takes the high road. "We would love to meet her sometime sweetie."

I thank him and continue eating, but nothing tastes right after that.

∾

The only other time my mother speaks about Liz is several days later. I have been throwing her name in regularly to ensure that I am not being silenced, things like, "Oh, I saw that movie with Liz," or "Do you like this shirt? I bought it when Liz and I went to the Cape one weekend." We are eating bagels for breakfast in the kitchen together when she turns to me and says, "Rachel, I'm very concerned about your grandfather finding out about your relationship with Liz." Her voice is low, like someone might overhear us.

"Mom, I understand your concern, I really do. All I can tell you is that I'm being extremely careful. I don't know what else I can do."

"Maybe it was a bad idea for you to live with him."

I don't know what to say, so I don't say anything at all.

∾

I wait until I am back in Boston to tell Liz about the experience with my parents. We are eating dinner at our favorite Indian place in Central Square. When I get to the part about permanence—when I told my parents that we didn't know yet but that it could be permanent—I act decidedly casual but look into Liz's eyes after I say it, looking for some clue as to what she is feeling. I have no doubt that Liz loves me, but we never talk about the future. Does she picture herself living with me? Raising kids with me? I try to remind myself that we haven't been together long enough to be talking this way but then remember the old joke about two women in a relationship:

What do lesbians bring on their second date? A U-Haul. Women are known to move fast into commitment. It isn't so unreasonable for me to want to talk with Liz about our future, right? To hear her say that she wants to grow old with me?

The other piece of the puzzle is that, in the coming months, I need to be applying to internship sites for my fourth year. I have to decide if I am willing to leave Boston for the year, which will begin the following summer. This is a conversation I need to have with Liz.

Her eyes reveal nothing, so I just ask. "Liz, do you *think* about it?"

"Think about what?" she asks, looking up from her saag paneer.

"About us. About what our future might be." I notice that I am shaking and think of that first day when I sat next to her at Shabbat services, the pages of the prayer book trembling in my hands.

Liz cocks her head and looks into my eyes. For a long time she doesn't speak. I can't stand the silence.

"Forget it—we don't need to talk about that—" I say, wishing I'd never brought it up.

"No," she interrupts, taking my hands across the table. "I do think about it, Rach. I just don't know if I'm ready to talk about it—not just yet."

I tell her I understand. I am lying. I don't really understand a thing.

I am feeling a lot of anxiety by the time I see Kevin. I don't even want to talk about the time at home with my parents; I just want to talk about the dinner conversation with Liz.

"I can't stop thinking about what she said: 'I just don't know if I'm ready to talk about it.' What does that mean? Does it mean that she wants to break up with me but just isn't ready to yet? Am I doing something wrong? Am I reading too much into it?" I sound like a runaway train and can see that Kevin is just waiting for me to stop, so I do.

"Are you done?" he says with some humor, his eyebrows high.

"Yes," I mumble. I've been spewing out what therapists call one cognitive distortion after another: mind-reading, personalization, catastrophizing.

Kevin takes a slow, deep breath as if to say, "Let's just take a minute to calm down."

Without even realizing it, I slow my breathing to match his. "I know, I'm jumping to all sorts of conclusions and you're probably going to want to *challenge* those thoughts with *evidence—*" I am showing off my newly acquired cognitive therapy jargon but stop when I notice that Kevin is shaking his head. "No?" I ask.

"No. Actually, I was going to suggest we do some exposure and response prevention around the uncertainty."

"Like what Zeke does to treat his OCD? But I don't have OCD."

"No, but we can still approach your anxiety about Liz in the same way. We can think of the intrusive worries about her wanting to end the relationship as an obsession, right?"

"Okay. I mean, the thoughts certainly make my anxiety rise in the same way that an OCD obsession would. But I'm not doing any rituals."

"Sure you are. You want to bring the anxiety down, so you do two compulsive things. First, you analyze the data over and over, looking for clues as to the 'right' answer, correct?"

I consider this. "Yes. I replay things she's said to try to convince myself one way or the other about what she's feeling. I even reread old emails looking for hints."

"And the second thing is that you check with her, right? You fish for ways to bring up the future so that she'll reveal more."

"Sometimes. I create little openings, like saying something about how great it is that Jenna and Jamie are having a baby or wondering out loud about whether Zeke will propose to Becca in the next year, as a way of seeing if she'll say something about us. I always sort of hold my breath in those moments."

"Do you ever really get the certainty you're looking for?"

"No," I admit. "Never certainty."

"So the treatment is not different than what Zeke does when he has to sit with not knowing something. You have to accept that you just can't know yet what the future will bring for you and Liz, and then you have to tolerate the anxiety that that uncertainty brings up."

"I think I really understand the appeal of marriage better than I ever have," I say.

"How so?"

"There's your certainty, right? I mean, there's a contract and jewelry exchanged. You can finally relax into knowing that you are both equally committed."

"You do know that something like 50 percent of marriages end in divorce, right?" He isn't trying to be rude; he's trying to push me.

"I know. Even marriage doesn't offer complete certainty."

"Rachel, the notion that we can have complete certainty about anything is a lie."

Kevin always cuts through my bullshit and makes me look at the truth. In that moment I both hate and love that man.

Chapter 18

I don't really believe in coincidences, and I especially don't that afternoon when I receive the following email from Becca:

From: bkramer@alumni.jhu.edu
To: rlevine@bscp.edu
Sent: Friday 8/15/97 3:22 PM
Subject: Help

Rachel,

Hi. I really wanted to call you but I don't have your number at your grandfather's house and I didn't want to worry your parents. Zeke is in a really bad place, and I don't know what to do.

It started just after his first few weeks of classes in July—at first, he seemed okay and excited about med school, then things seemed sort of off but I think he was in denial or something. He kept telling me he was fine but I could tell he wasn't. Now it's like he's just

crashing. He's told me about his OCD. I've just never
seen it and don't know how to help him. Will you call me
at my apartment when you get this email? (202-423-
8794) Thanks, Rachel.

Becca

I call Becca right away, worried and a little angry at Zeke for
not telling me he was having such a flare up. It is true that I haven't
spoken much to Zeke since he started classes; he seems so buried
under the work. As I dial Becca's number, I berate myself for not
having predicted that this transition could be triggering for Zeke. I
know that stress can often be a catalyst for an increase in symptoms.
I failed to think about how this could affect my baby brother. This is
how I think of him when he suffers—as my little guy, my responsibility. My parents never put this expectation on me; it was more of a
position of pride I'd taken on as the oldest and as Zeke's biggest fan.

"Rachel," Becca says after answering, "thank you for calling me. I
just don't exactly know what to do. He just gets really distant—like
he's in a trance or something."

"Becca, when does this happen? When he's studying?"

"Yeah, but not just then. At first, I thought he was ignoring me.
Like, I'd say something to him, and he just wouldn't respond or even
seem to hear me. I was getting really pissed. But then I realized he was
lost inside his head, that he wasn't really hearing anyone or anything."

"What happened when you pointed this out to him?"

"I tried for weeks to talk to him about it, and he was just so defensive. He kept saying he was fine. But then finally this week, he just
sort of broke down. He cried and said that he can't remember his
OCD being this bad. He said he's scared."

I fight my own tears. "Becca, listen, I have about another week
before my classes start. I'd like to come down for a few days. Would

that be okay with you?" I struggle with the fact that I am asking her permission; on one hand, I don't need it—he is my brother after all. On the other, I don't want to step on her toes and know that this is a test of sorts for her—if she is going to spend her life with my brother, she is going to have to learn about OCD and how to help him fight it. Though I sometimes begrudge Becca her seeming perfection, I have to admit I like her answer.

"Um . . . I, uh . . . yeah, I'd appreciate that. I want to understand this part of him Rachel, I really do—but I don't think I can understand it *from* him right now."

❧

I don't tell Zeke I am coming. I just show up, like a fairy godmother from the land of mental healing, armed with referrals for specialists in Washington and Zeke's favorite chocolate chip cookies. He is pissed.

"Rachel, why are you here?" he asks in a whine when he opens his apartment door to find me standing outside of it. Fighting with each other is a skill honed over years of siblinghood.

"It's good to see you, too," I shoot back, placing the cookies in his hands and pushing past him into his open studio room. I turn back to him and shrug. "Surprise!"

"Did Becca ask you to come? Because that was totally unnecessary." He shakes his head at me. "Couldn't you at least have *asked* me first?"

"No, Zeke, I couldn't ask you because I had no idea you were having a hard time. Why didn't you tell me?"

"Rachel, did it ever occur to you that this isn't about you? I can ask for help when I want it—*if* I want it."

I don't know how to respond to that. Of course, it isn't about me. Of course, I should have asked Zeke if he wanted me to come down. I sink into one of his kitchen chairs, deflated. "I'm sorry, I just thought

. . . when Becca contacted me, she sounded really worried about you. She said she didn't know how to help you."

Zeke flops angrily into the chair across from me. "Rach, if I'm going to fuck up, you have to let me! You're not my mother! But I'm on it—I have an appointment at an OCD treatment center later today, I've talked with my professors about the classes I've missed and have gotten a few extensions, and I've been communicating better with Becca. I'm figuring it out—without my family swooping in to help. Can't you understand that that's important to me?"

I sit there, taking in everything Zeke has said. I don't know how I've landed in this place again. I think I am giving, but really I'm taking. Or, I'm doing both at the same time but just can't be certain about which part is driving me.

"Give me those cookies," I say, reaching out for the Tupperware container that I'd just given to him. "I'm starving." We sit there and eat cookie after cookie, not speaking but clearly forgiving. Finally, I look at my baby brother—who suddenly doesn't look like a baby anymore—and say, "So you don't need to be rescued. Duh."

⟡

That night, Zeke, Becca, and I go out to dinner at one of their new favorite hangouts in Georgetown. Zeke is quieter than usual, but he does tell us about the appointment he had that afternoon.

"I explained to him that the feeling is similar to my old OCD but that now it's just all about med school. Like when I read something in a textbook, it just never feels like I've understood it correctly. I keep rereading the same paragraph over and over until it feels right."

"But babe," Becca says, covering his hand with hers, "the stuff you're reading is hard, not to mention totally new. Anyone would need to reread it more than once."

Zeke shakes his head. "That's not it, though. It's not that I *actually* don't understand. It's just this feeling like I haven't taken in all the words correctly—almost like an itch—but scratching it means reading it over and over until the feeling is gone. I do the same thing with my notes. I rewrite them over and over until it feels right."

I watch Becca taking this in. I can see she's trying to understand, trying to wrap her head around what she can't quite imagine in his. "I think I get how that works when you're studying, but what about when we're just hanging out at night, talking or whatever? You seem so far away sometimes. It's like you don't even know that I'm there." I see the muscles of her cheeks tense and wonder if she's afraid of crying.

"Becca, I'm so sorry. It's just that it's with me all the time. Like, when we're watching TV together or something, all I'm thinking about is an exam I took that day, going over the answers in my head trying to figure out if I'd actually written what I thought I did. Sometimes I'm just thinking about some reading I just did and going over the content in my mind to see if I remember it exactly right. I'm not trying to ignore you; it's just really really hard to be present right now."

Becca nods and brushes his cheek with her hand, while I, still stewing in the shame of having swooped, busy my eyes by looking around the restaurant. That's when I see them—Jared Coplon and Melissa Levitt. Melissa Coplon? I'd heard they'd gotten married. Jared lived in my dorm our first year at Wesleyan and started dating Melissa that spring. I stayed casual friends with both of them throughout our time at school, but haven't kept in touch since graduation. I excuse myself from Zeke and Becca and, somewhat shyly, approach Jared and Melissa's table.

"Hey strangers!" I say, feigning a confidence that I'm not really feeling.

"Oh my God, Rachel Levine!" shouts Jared, quickly followed by Melissa's similar words of surprise.

They ask me to sit, which I do, saying, "Only for a minute, I'm just in town for the night visiting my brother and his girlfriend, right over there, and I just noticed you two and thought I'd say a quick hello." *Why do I talk so fast when I'm nervous?* "So, what's going on with you guys?"

Melissa jumps right in. "We got married ten months ago!" She says this while extending her left hand to show off a sizeable engagement ring stacked on top of a circle of little diamonds.

"Wow," I take her hand, as this seems to be the expected next move. "That's beautiful." All I can think is, *This is what a sanctioned relationship looks like.*

Jared adds, "We bought a townhouse in Rockville because it's closer to work for both of us, but we try to get into the city as much as we can on weekends."

"We have the nicest neighbors—just a ton of young couples in the area."

"Yeah, we really lucked out. It's a great neighborhood."

"Rachel, can you believe our five-year reunion is in less than two years? It's going to be so great to see what everyone's up to! Oh my God, we haven't even asked you what *you're* up to! I'm so sorry!"

"Um, well I'm living in Boston and getting my doctorate in clinical psychology actually." I nod in that awkward way and don't say anything about Liz. "It's really great," I add, wanting to escape. "Listen, I'd better get back to my table, but it was really great running into you both," I say, standing up. Really great. Twice.

⌒∾

The best part of this unsolicited trip to Washington is my slumber party with Zeke. After dinner, Becca goes back to her place, and Zeke and I put on our pajamas, make microwave popcorn, and sit cross-legged on his bed for hours talking about our respective relationships.

"Is it hard for you," I ask, "telling Becca all about the obsessive thoughts? It seemed like you might be a little tense when you were answering her questions."

"Yeah, you know? I mean, on one hand, she and I are way past the 'impressing each other' stage. On the other, I'm worried that she's going to think I'm crazy. Who wants to marry a crazy person, right?"

"Zeke, you're not crazy! OCD is not—"

"I know, I know," he cuts me off. I am trying to fix it again. "But I really think she's the one. I mean, I'm not proposing now or any-thing—I don't even have the money for a ring—but I think about it a lot, and we talk about it, too. But will she still want to marry me after seeing what a total mess I can become?"

I stop myself before saying anything overly reassuring. Instead, I ask, "Wouldn't you rather know that now?"

"I guess so," he says, looking distant and tired. "Okay, enough about me and Becca—you've spent the whole night with us. Tell me more about Liz. When do I get to meet her?"

"I don't know. When are you coming to visit?"

"No time soon, if our mother has anything to say about it. The other day I said something to her on the phone about wanting to take a weekend in the fall to go up and see you, and she was like, 'You don't have enough time off to go all the way up there! Why don't you just come home and Rachel can come home too so that we can all see each other?' Not that it's up to her, but she seemed to want us all under her roof. Either that, or she doesn't want me to meet Liz."

"Did she say anything to you about Liz?"

"Oh yeah, I got an earful—about how she's so worried Zayde will find out. Sounds like it was an eventful trip home for you."

"It kind of sucked. It was a little like time travel—Dad saying all the right things, but more to placate Mom than anything else. Mom getting that tense look, you know, where her jaw gets all tight—"

"Oh, I know!" he says, clenching his teeth and flaring his nostrils in his best imitation of our mother.

I laugh, though nothing about it is funny to me. "She hasn't really changed at all, Zeke. I mean, she doesn't moan and groan and cry like she used to—at least not in front of me—but she's just as intolerant. Or maybe that's not true—maybe *all* she is is tolerant. She tolerates me but she doesn't embrace me anymore."

"I'll embrace you," jokes Zeke as he hugs me. "Now tell me about Liz—is she hot?"

"So hot!" I say, laughing and wiping tears from my eyes. "She's like fire, you know?"

"I don't know! Tell me already!"

"Well, she has this tiny, compact, like, boy body—"

"This is getting less hot for me."

"No, no, listen—like she's all muscle and strength but little, too. And she has this gorgeous jet-black hair that's all short and wispy and *always* looks good. She doesn't even get bed head! And then her eyes? They are this piercing green that practically glow they are so awesome."

"Okay, so now she is like an alien boy."

"Stop it!"

We are both laughing now.

"Wait, I'm not done." It feels so freeing to be able to talk about Liz in this way. "She's incredibly smart. She went to Yale and got a Fulbright to study in Paris, and can read Hebrew way better than anyone we know. And she has this amazing job where she can be an activist and an organizer and get paid to do what she's passionate about. Oh, and she's a runner and a swimmer and a photographer."

"So, she's pretty much perfect?"

"Can you tell I'm wild about her?"

"No, not at all," teases Zeke. "Is she wild about you?"

I pause. "I know that she loves me—I really do believe that she does. But she is holding back in some way, and I haven't quite figured out what that's about."

"How do you mean?"

"I don't know. I mean there is a part of herself that she's not giving to me, that she's protecting. I think I just need to be patient."

"You haven't even been together a year, Rach."

"I know, but with women every day is like a year!"

"U-Haul?"

I punch his arm. Brothers.

Chapter 19

September brings with it a rush of new things—new classes, a new training year with Dr. Vargas, the crowding of Boston's streets with the influx of so many students, the turning of leaves, the return of routine.

Dr. Vargas has me lead some of the orientation for new trainees this year, which makes me feel smart and experienced. On top of my caseload of ten, I will also be supervising one of the new trainees on a clinical case, while Dr. Vargas supervises me on my supervision. I love that she has become my mentor.

I find myself so excited to reconnect with my client Charlie. Rather than going home over the summer, Charlie sublet an apartment in Boston with some friends and worked at a restaurant in the South End—the hot neighborhood for gay men. When I see him for our first session of the semester, I hardly recognize him. He has a cool haircut and is dressed more stylishly than I've ever seen him. The real change though is that he seems more comfortable in his own skin. He walks in with a huge smile and hugs me.

"Rachel," he says, "I have soooo much to tell you!" He spends that hour telling me about his glorious summer—the gay bars, the friends he made, his first "real boyfriend" who he saw exclusively for six whole weeks. I think he might actually be glowing.

"Charlie, I'm curious. If you could send a message to your freshman-year self, when you were at school in Virginia, what would you say to him?"

He thinks, the smile never leaving his face. "I would say, 'Just hang in there, kid. Better days are on their way!'"

The irony of being a therapist is that you are always trying to put yourself out of a job. That is, you want your clients to become well enough, self-reliant enough, to leave treatment. I know Charlie won't need me much longer but am not sure if it is my job to bring this up with him. I take my question to Dr. Vargas.

"So, if a client is really doing well," I ask in our next supervision meeting, "do I suggest that he stop coming?"

"Are we talking about Charlie?" she asks with a knowing look. She knows that I've come to love him something like a little brother and knows that it will be hard for me to terminate with him. I hate that word, termination. It sounds like I am planning to kill him rather than say goodbye.

"I *am* talking about Charlie," I say returning her glance, grateful for the trust she and I have built. "I think he's just coming in now to hang out with me. It's like he uses the sessions as his journal, as his way of recounting and recording his story. I love being the recipient of that, but is it appropriate?"

"What do you think?" she asks, ever the clinician.

I hesitate. "I think that not wanting to lose him is *my* need. I think he enjoys coming but that he doesn't really need me anymore. I think I need to bring it up."

"Okay then," she says. "But I like what you said a moment ago—about how you've become a place to document his experience, like a journal. Perhaps you could explore that a bit with him in the termination process."

The termination process. I picture myself sharpening knives.

⁓

When the rabbi returns from Israel, Zayde stops going to Shabbat services. Just like that. He says that now that the board has officially decided to renew her contract, he just can't stomach her anymore. He will go to High Holiday services in October, but that the rest of his davening will have to be done at home.

"Zayde, really? Just come with me. I miss you sitting next to me."

But he won't budge.

The truth is, when Zayde doesn't come, I sit with Liz—and that is pretty great. Even though our relationship is a secret, when I sit next to her, I pretend that it is years into the future and that we are there with our kids (who won't stop squirming!). We are a well-known and respected family at Beth El.

Even though Liz and I don't live together, our menstrual cycles have synced up, just like mine did with my college roommate's, who was on the pill and made me like clockwork. I love this about women's bodies, how we can speak to one another in this secret pheromonal language, linking arms so that we all cycle together like a group of friends packed into the same car on a Ferris wheel. What this means is that Liz and I ovulate together, and we've noticed that, without fail, mid-cycle we become ravenous for sex. Okay, maybe not ravenous— but really really interested in sex.

One particular September Saturday happens to be a mid-cycle libidinal surge. As I sit next to Liz in services, every brush of our arms, every whisper, every glance seems drenched in desire. We are electric in our energy, and my body hums with the current of it. Just as the Torah service is concluding, which means there is still the better part of an hour left to the service as a whole, Liz leans toward me and whispers, "Meet me in two minutes in the classroom at the top of the stairs."

I look at her with a sharp inhalation. "No!" We can't possibly do this in shul! She just stares me down. A dare.

I sit there for two long minutes, thinking that I'll have to look as if I, too, have the sudden urge to use the restroom. *How does one look when one needs to pee during services?* I try knitting my brows together slightly. *No, that is a constipated look. Should I walk out with my hand lightly resting on my bladder?* Ugh! I give up and just leave.

The staircase to the upstairs classrooms is in the back of the building. I sneak past the bathroom and coat closet, past the social hall, and find myself tiptoeing like a thief up the steps. When I get to the first classroom, the door is open just slightly. I slip in and close it behind me. Liz is sitting in the teacher's chair, her feet up on the desk, smacking a ruler against her open palm.

"You are not serious!" I say. Maybe I really am vanilla when it comes to sex.

"About the ruler?" she asks with a sly look. "No." Then rising to meet me, she puts her hands on my waist and pulls me to her. "You know sex on Shabbat is a mitzvah, right? It is written."

I lean into her and, half kissing her, say, "Whoever wrote that definitely did not have this in mind." And then we are at it, like wild animals. Like two nice-Jewish-girls-in-their-Shabbat-clothes wild animals.

We are still at the desk when the classroom door opens five minutes later, except I am splayed across the top, my head hanging off the edge, my back arched toward the ceiling, and Liz is in the chair, her face buried deep inside me. I'll never forget the look on the old woman's face. I am surprised to see a huge smile spread across her face as she makes sense of what she is seeing. Then I remember that I am upside down.

"What on earth?!" is all she says through her grimace.

We scramble out of the room as fast as is humanly possible, Liz wiping her mouth and me pulling down and smoothing my skirt.

"Sorry," I say under my breath as we pass her. I never look her in the eye.

We just keep moving, right down the stairs, out the back door, past the playground, finally stopping at a bench around the block. Collapsing onto the bench, Liz is hysterical with laughter.

"It's not funny!" I whisper-yell at her, tears springing to my eyes.

"Of course, it is!" she gasps. "Did you see the look on her face? We will be telling this story for the rest of our lives!"

"Liz!" I sit next to her, grabbing her shoulders so that I can look at her squarely. "You don't understand! What if this gets back to my grandfather?" I am starting to hyperventilate.

Liz wipes my tears with her fingers. "Sweetie," she says in a soothing tone, "Pearl Zimmerman just had the most uncomfortable moment of her life. I seriously don't think she's going to prolong her discomfort by telling people about it."

"What do we know about her?" I ask, trying to wrap my head around what Liz is saying.

"We know that she's a long-time member who has taught in the religious school forever. We must have been in her classroom. She's very traditional, but she's an introvert. She's not gossipy."

"What makes you think introverts aren't gossipy?!"

"Fine, I'm not speaking for all introverts—I just don't think that Pearl Zimmerman is gossipy."

I slump against the back of the bench and close my eyes. "Okay," I say, blowing out a slow, controlled exhalation. "I'm counting on that."

When I get back to Zayde's that afternoon, I feel like the whole house is littered with eggshells. Every step I take feels like risk, like maybe the phone has already rung, and Zayde already knows. Of course, it hasn't. And, of course, I know this, but the real possibility of Zayde finding out about Liz and me suddenly seems to hang heavily in the air. I lie down on my mother's old bed, staring up at the water-stained ceiling, playing through scenarios in my head. Zayde crying. Zayde screaming that I am a disgrace to our family and our community. Zayde saying I am dead to him.

Would he? Would he go so far as to sit *shiva* for me?

And is there any possibility he might surprise me and be okay with it? I think about my mother's words from six years ago.

*

"I feel like an appendage has been cut off!" My mother, gripping the kitchen island counter as if to keep herself from collapsing.

"But Mom, I was never an appendage. I have always been a separate person." Me, sitting at the table, staring at salt and pepper shakers.

*

"I don't even know you anymore!" My mother, slamming a car door.

"I'm the same person I've always been." Me, calling after her through the open passenger-side window.

*

"I feel like I've been to your funeral." My mother, pale and thin.

"I am alive. I am here." Me, unconvinced.

*

I cry myself to sleep and stay asleep all afternoon.

Chapter 20

When I see Charlie the next week, I ask him if he's ever kept a journal.

"Like a dah-ree?" he asks in his Southern accent.

"Sure, yes. Journal and diary mean the same thing. I was just wondering if you'd ever had the experience of writing about your own life, about the things you go through."

"Nope," he says with a shrug. "I'd be willing to try it though if you think it's a good idea."

"Let's back up a second and talk about how you're feeling about coming here—to see me." I am very nervous. I don't want Charlie to feel that I am in any way rejecting him. "What I mean is, you're doing really great, Charlie. I enjoy meeting with you each week and hearing all your stories. I'm just wondering if you still *need* to be coming, though."

"Wow," he says. "I guess I am doing really well this year. I mean, coming out was the best thing I ever did."

"Yes, but remember, coming out is a process. Coming out to yourself and to your friends is one part of that process. Coming out to your family or to coworkers can be very different."

"Oh, believe me, Rachel, I have no intention of coming out to my family any time soon. Can you even imagine? No way!" He laughs too hard.

"What's funny?" I ask, tilting my head the way Lucky the therapy dog at Kevin's sometimes does.

"Huh? I mean, it isn't funny really. It's just the farthest thing from my mind. I'm perfectly happy being out at school and letting my family think I'm dating some girl from the Campus Crusade for Christ." Here he laughs again, but with a hint of sadness. "Coming out to more people isn't really on my college to-do list. I just really like coming to talk to you."

"I want to make it clear, Charlie, that I like it, too. It will be hard for me to say goodbye to you. But part of my job is to help you know when you no longer need me. And I'm just wondering if you still do." I say this with a wincing shrug, showing all of my insecurities. I feel like I am the client and he is the therapist. Is it okay that I said it would be hard for me to say goodbye to him? What will Dr. Vargas think when she hears the tape? "I brought up the journaling because it occurs to me that, in some ways, I've become like a journal—a place to put your story. I'm wondering if you might benefit from actually keeping a journal."

"I get what you're saying—"

"Here's the thing," I interrupt. "We wouldn't have to just stop therapy cold turkey. In fact, it might make sense to meet once a month for a while to sort of taper off, you know." I have no idea if this suggestion is more in Charlie's best interest or in mine. I find myself wishing I'd rehearsed this.

But then Charlie seems to take the reins. "I like that idea," he says. "What if we met once in October, and once in November, then once before break in December? Then we could see if we wanted to stop or what for the second semester?"

"Sounds like a plan," I say, relieved.

When I bring my tape of that session to Dr. Vargas, I simply say, "Don't even bother listening to it."

"Uh oh," she says, somewhat mocking my hyperbole. "Didn't go so well with Charlie?"

"I mean, it went okay. I was just a mess—when I listened to the part of the session where we talked about termination, I was really nervous." I am surprised that my eyes are welling up. "I'm sorry," I say. "I'm just having a tough week and I don't want to say goodbye to Charlie, and I'm afraid it's all about what I need."

"I see," she says with her calm, centered demeanor. "I'm sorry you are having a hard week. Why don't we listen together and see if it's really as bad as you think."

As I listen to myself on the tape, the tears that had been welling start streaming. I hear myself being so tentative, so worried that I will hurt Charlie by making him feel abandoned. And maybe I am feeling abandoned at the idea of Charlie not needing me anymore. And maybe it is about Charlie, and me, and Zayde, and my mother all at once.

Dr. Vargas doesn't push or even ask. She just lets me sit and cry. Finally, I say, "This termination thing is really harder than I'd expected. Specifically with Charlie, I mean."

"Do you want to talk about it?" she asks with what feels like the utmost respect for my privacy.

"Not really. Thanks," I say, blowing my nose. "I see Kevin on Friday. But is it okay that Charlie and I meet monthly for the remainder of the semester?" I know that, by November, there will be students on the wait list for the counseling center. "I would still take on a new client, it's not like he would fill a whole slot—"

"It's fine," she reassures me. Then she coaches me on how we might use these monthly sessions to look at his progress over time and move away from his weekly anecdotes, so that we might both have some closure.

I stay anxious around Zayde through the High Holidays. My parents come up for Rosh Hashanah, and we all go to Beth El together as we always have. Zeke can't get away from med school. I have horrible dreams on the nights leading up to the holidays, things like Pearl Zimmerman shrieking and pointing at me as I sit with my family during the silent meditation. In one, the rabbi (who, in the dream, is male) gives a sermon about the evils of homosexuality and asks Liz and me to come up to the bimah as Exhibit A. Liz is spending Rosh Hashanah with her mother in Florida, and I have to wonder if she's planned it this way—if she just understands that I'm not ready to have her, my parents, and Zayde all in one room. I say "I wonder" because this is not a conversation we've had; in fact, I have consciously avoided it. I believe that if I pretend I am more comfortable being out than I am, she might love me more. She might see that I am marriage material.

When the holidays are through and nothing terrible has happened, I start to calm down and am able to enjoy my favorite season in New England again. I especially love my walks to Kevin's on Fridays, shuffling my sneakers through the dry fallen leaves on the sidewalks of Somerville and Cambridge.

Kevin's office has become my weekly refuge. When he opens his office door to find me in the waiting area, Lucky, who has become a part of what feels so right about this space, runs out first to greet me. Lucky lies on the floor through most sessions, but when I am really upset—like if I am crying—he will jump up on the soft, brown sofa and curl up next to me or in my lap; he knows I need a little extra love right then. Kevin's office envelopes me in safety, and in that room, I can name the fears and feel the sadness that I have worked so hard to conceal.

Liz doesn't really get it. Dar Williams just released a song about therapy where she says, "When I talk about therapy, I know what people think—that it only makes you selfish and in love with your shrink." Liz loves to quote this to me, though I point out to her that the song is actually very pro-therapy.

"Are you suggesting I'm in love with Kevin?!" I ask.

"Are you suggesting that?" she replies, eyebrows up.

"That is the most ridiculous question you've ever asked me! Of course, I'm not in love with him." I won't even entertain the conversation with her and abruptly change the subject. "Is your mother still coming up next week?"

"Yes, she just bought her tickets. And she wants to take you out to dinner."

"Just me?" I ask in a sudden panic.

"No silly, both of us. She likes you. She wants to know you better."

I am cognizant of how afraid I feel to let a parent—anyone's parent—know me better. Like if they really knew me, they'd be sure to disapprove.

The following Thursday night, Liz, Fran, and I go to dinner at the Border Café in Harvard Square, which feels, to me, like too loud and collegiate a place to bring one's mother. But Fran, sipping her second margarita, goes on and on about how being with us makes her feel young again. She even calls our waiter "yummy" behind his back. Fran keeps referring to Liz and me as "you girls," as in "You girls are living in such a different time, what with the electronic mail and this whole World Wide Web I keep reading about. I can't even wrap my head around it! So Rachel," says Fran, turning to look at me. "How many more years of graduate school before we get to call you doctor?"

I smile at the idea of Fran looking into my future and seeing herself there to call me doctor. "I'm in my final year of classes now. Next year, I'll do a full-time clinical internship. Then, of course, I'll have to finish my dissertation before I can graduate. I don't even know what my topic will be yet."

"So you'll work full-time next year at your counseling center? Lizzy tells me that you are very good with the college students."

I smile at Liz. "Actually, no," I say, aware of the fact that Liz and I haven't been discussing my plans for the following year. "In the fourth year of my program, you do a full-time internship at a site approved by the American Psychological Association. There are only so many in each state, and it's pretty competitive."

"So you won't necessarily be in Boston?" asks Fran.

"No. I do want to continue to work with college students, but there are only two training sites like that in Boston. I'm sending applications all over the country. Then I have to go interview at the ones that are interested in me. Then I find out what my options are."

Liz, seeming to consider this for the first time, asks, "So is it a match system like med students use?"

Zeke was just explaining that whole process to me—where you rank your choices and the programs rank theirs and then through some algorithm, the computer spits out your match.

"No," I say, looking at her. "I'm guessing that the APA is moving in that direction, too, but for now, I have a little more choice in the matter. I think I find out where I've been accepted in March and then have, like, twenty-four hours to choose or something."

"No pressure," says Liz with a roll of her eyes.

"No. No pressure at all," I answer, concentrating on my plate.

Chapter 21

Charlie practically bursts into my office when the time comes for his October appointment.

"Rachel!" he shouts, not even yet seated. "I am a journalist! No—not a journalist, but a lover of my journal. I am 'one who journals,'" he says with air quotes. In his hands, he clutches a black, hardcover book with "Journal" inscribed in gold lettering.

"I'm so glad to hear that, Charlie!" I'm relieved that I'm not leaving him with nowhere to put his stories. "Tell me."

"So I found this *fat* journal in Harvard Square—"

I look at its thickness, which isn't considerable.

"—and I've been writing in it every day since."

"That's awesome. What kinds of things are you writing about?"

"Just stuff—like about guys I like or a club I went to or whatever. Then I get to go back and relive it, you know, by re-reading what I wrote? It's like, there is so much happening for me right now, you know? I love getting it down on paper. You are a genius for suggesting it!"

I laugh. "I don't know if I'm a genius, but I think what it shows us is that you don't need therapy the way you once did. Now, you get to process stuff in your journal, and the best thing is, you get to keep it forever. It's all yours, Charlie."

"Rad," he says gesturing in what I think is a hip hop move. He is a boy who's found his stride and I beam at him, as if he were my own.

∞

I dream that I have sex with Kevin. Actually, it is worse than that—and isn't the first time. In this rendition of the "sex with Kevin" dream, we are in his office and Charlie is hiding behind his couch. That's right, me, my therapist, my client, and sex. I feel like Freud would put me to the top of his waiting list.

So, in the dream, Kevin and I don't know that Charlie is there until he pops up from behind the couch and goes off on me. "You are such a *liar*, Rachel Levine! *This* is what you call being queer?"

Apparently, Charlie doesn't know that I am Kevin's client or I'm sure he would have had some words about that, too. I am devastated but also defensive. "Charlie, you just can't understand this," I say. "I love this man." And then the alarm clock begins to buzz like a slap across the face.

I see Kevin that Friday.

"I'm dreaming about sex with men," I say with obvious worry knitted between my brows.

"Okay," answers Kevin.

"No, it's not okay. It's not. Because I'm *not* a fence-sitter, and I'm *not* confused, and I definitely do *not* want to have my cake and eat it, too!" I say, invoking every bad bisexual stereotype I can think of.

"*I'm* confused," says Kevin. "I thought that if you're bi, you're attracted to men and women. So, why can't you have sexual dreams about either one?"

He is right, of course. And, really, what I am upset about is that I am dreaming about *him* and that this makes Liz possibly right about my ability to fall for him. But I don't want to tell him that so I say, "I know. I've just been arguing lately with Liz about bisexuality, and I think the dreams just make me feel vulnerable to losing the debate with her."

"What would losing that debate look like?"

"I don't know. Maybe proving that she is right in thinking that bisexuals can't be trusted or that we're attracted to too many people to make committed partners."

"We've talked about this before," Kevin reminds me. "You told me that that was Liz's baggage, not yours."

"I know, but I want to be with Liz long-term, and if she is going to want to be with me, I can't be her baggage."

"Unfortunately, we have no jurisdiction over what Liz thinks or feels. This is the uncertainty of being in a relationship, remember?"

I look over at Lucky who, sensing this, lifts his head to me. I address those little round dog eyes directly. "Damn uncertainty."

I desperately want to avoid Beth El after the spread-eagle-on-the-desk incident, but, not wanting Rabbi Stein to think that I have changed my mind about supporting her, I force myself to go to Saturday services. I sit with Liz but avoid eye contact with Pearl Zimmerman or anyone who looks like they might know her—which, in our small community, is just about everyone. I stay only a short time for lunch, just long enough to chat with the rabbi for a few minutes and grab my bagel.

On one early November Saturday, Bess comes up to me at the luncheon. "What's your Zayde up to this afternoon? I'd like to talk with him."

"I don't think he has any plans. I'm sure he'd love to visit with you."

"I may just stop by," she says. "I don't think he's going to like what I have to say though."

I have the sudden thought that she's found out about Liz and me and is going to tell Zayde. My heart pounds.

But she says, "I'm tired of his tantrum-throwing about the rabbi. He's been coming here all his adult life and he needs to get his *tuchas* back into shul!"

I exhale but it is too late to stop the shaking in my hands; I hope she doesn't notice. "Bess, I think that's a great idea. He certainly won't listen to me about it."

"Will you be home later, dear?" she asks.

I have plans to see a matinee with Liz at the Somerville Theater. "No, I, um, have plans to meet up with a study group from school."

"Maybe that's better. Maybe he'll listen to me if I corner him alone."

I am a little surprised by Bess's aggressiveness and find myself wanting to say, "You go girl!" Instead I just smile at her and say, "Good luck."

I begin to turn away, when she says, "Oh and Rachel?"

I turn back.

"I've been thinking a lot about that question you asked me a few months back . . . about what I would do if one of my grandchildren converted."

I wait, still shaking.

"I think it would be very hard for me, it's true. But just because I don't understand, doesn't mean I would love them any less."

Tears spring to my eyes. "Thanks, Bess," I say and leave to get my jacket and my girl.

∽

I see Charlie for a session just before he leaves to go home to Virginia for Thanksgiving break.

"So, how are you feeling about therapy these days?"

"I really do like talking to you," he says. "But I've also done some thinking—and some writing—about what you said . . . about how I don't need therapy the way I did a year ago. I guess I am feeling ready to stop coming. I mean, you can't say I'm not happy these days!" His smile is infectious.

"We have today's session and then one more scheduled in mid-December. Should we make that one our final session?" I ask, still anxious about not wanting him to feel that I am kicking him out.

"Yeah, okay," he shrugs, nodding his head.

"Okay then. I'm going to give you some homework between now and that last session. I want you to think about the ways in which you've changed since first coming in here last fall. How have you grown? I think it will be nice to sort of review your journey in here."

He takes this in and seems to agree that it makes sense.

"Also," I say, "I want to get feedback from you about my role as your therapist. It will help me to grow as a clinician to hear what worked as well as what didn't."

"Okay," he laughs, "but I don't think I'll have anything bad to say!"

"Oh, I'm sure we can come up with some things I could have done better. Really, it will help me in my training to hear what your experience of me was in here." These are all of the things Dr. Vargas has taught us about how to do a termination session. I surprise myself when I suddenly add, "And let's plan a sort of goodbye party while we're at it!"

Charlie's eyebrows rise in curiosity.

"I mean, let's mark the occasion with something special. I think I'll bring brownies." Brownies have never been a part of termination protocol or part of what happens inside of the frame of therapy. I don't know what Dr. Vargas will think, but I am clear that I want to celebrate this moment with Charlie and don't particularly care about the frame.

"Awesome," he says. "I have to think about what I want to bring. I'll surprise you."

Every year we have Thanksgiving dinner at my parents' house. Just as I have the previous two years, I drive down to Bryn Mawr with Zayde. As we near the New Jersey border, Zayde says suddenly, "So Bess paid me a visit a few weeks ago."

"She did?" I ask, my hands suddenly gripping the wheel just a little tighter.

Zayde is looking out the windshield off to the right. "Yes she did. She wanted to talk to me about coming back to shul."

"And?" I ask, holding my breath.

"I told her how I felt about the rabbi. And she said 'I know *exactly* how you feel about the rabbi—you haven't shut your mouth about it for *months!*'" He says this in a high-pitched, imitation Bess voice. "But then she said some other things. About your bubbe. She said, 'Lew, you have to look beyond yourself. What would Esther want?' May her memory be a blessing." This last part is in his own voice. "She said that your bubbe would want me to continue going, especially since I get to go with you." He never looks at me.

I feel my eyes sting to hear Zayde talk about getting to go with me like it is a privilege. And I miss my bubbe. "Zayde, I love sitting next to you at shul. I miss you. I wish you would come back."

"I will," he says, very seriously. "But I'm not doing it because I've changed my mind about that woman rabbi. I'm doing it for you and for your bubbe."

◠◡

Thanksgiving dinner is never a simple affair. My mother cooks for days in advance, outdoing herself year after year. By the time we all arrive for the four o'clock meal, she is exhausted, tense, and in no mood for visiting. She just wants everyone to eat—a lot—and to shower her meal with lavish compliments.

My father sits at the head of the table, though I've never really understood why. Besides the carving of the gigantic kosher bird, he's done nothing to help. This was one of those things I'd started noticing during college Thanksgiving breaks. I would come home and demand to know why we all just bow to the patriarchy. For several Thanksgivings after that first angry one, Zeke would whisper to me at some point during the meal, "Are you going to use the word patriarchy again?" I would just stamp on his foot under the table.

This year, everyone wants to hear about my applications for internship, which I've just finished mailing off.

"What kinds of sites are you looking at?"

"How many did you apply to?"

"Did you apply to any here in Philadelphia?"

I explain that I've decided to apply to only college counseling centers, that I ultimately want to practice with adolescents and maybe direct a counseling center someday. I've sent out ten applications, all over the country at both big universities and small colleges. I say that I'll be hearing back in February about interviews and then will travel to any of the sites that offer me one.

"Are there any in Boston?" asks Zeke, perhaps wondering about Liz—who they all seem careful not to mention.

"There are two in the Boston area," I say. "The farthest one is the University of California at Santa Cruz."

"California?!" gasps my mother, just coming into the dining room with a pot of coffee. "That's too far, Rachel."

"Mom, it would only be for a year. Besides, these internships are very competitive. I'll be lucky to get an offer anywhere."

It is true that I'd be lucky. It is also true that I don't want to leave Boston and Liz, even for a year.

"You keep us posted, sweetheart," says my dad. "That coffee smells delicious."

Chapter 22

A few weeks after Thanksgiving, Zayde comes downstairs just before bed to find me baking brownies.

"That smells delicious, shayna meydeleh!" he exclaims with surprise—I'm not exactly a baker.

"Thanks, Zayde. They're for share—half for us and half for me to bring in to work tomorrow."

"If that doesn't make those students feel better, I don't know what will," he says, skimming off a finger-full of batter from the rim of my mixing bowl and licking it clean. I know that Zayde doesn't really get what I do. His generation doesn't know from psychotherapy, and he isn't about to understand it now. That's okay. I don't need for him to understand what I do as long as he is proud of me for doing it.

My session with Charlie is scheduled for ten. I check the small desk clock in my office against my watch, thinking that perhaps the batteries are dead. The clock says 10:05, and Charlie is never late. By 10:15, I'm a little worried. Did he forget? That would be so unlike him. I check my email and there is nothing waiting from him in my inbox. At 10:30, I go and knock on Dr. Vargas's partially open door.

"Come in, Rachel," she says, turning from her desk in her swivel chair and peering over her reading glasses.

"Um, quick question," I say sitting. "I know that when clients don't show we generally don't contact them and we wait for them to contact us. But Charlie didn't come to his final session today, and I'm a little worried about him."

"Hmm," she says. "We do know that not showing for a final session is not uncommon. What do you think it could mean, clinically?"

"I know that it's often a form of avoidance—you know, the whole 'I'll leave you before you can leave me' thing, but that just doesn't feel like Charlie to me. I don't think he'd do that."

"Why don't you give it the day?" she says. "If you haven't heard from him by tomorrow morning, give him a call in his dorm room."

I don't wait until the next morning. Something just doesn't feel right about not hearing from Charlie. I take his phone number home with me and tell myself I'll wait until after dinner to call.

I get the answering machine. "Yo, it's Pete and Charlie's room. You know what to do." It is Charlie's roommate's voice. At the beep I say, "Hi, Charlie, this is Rachel calling." I don't leave my last name or indicate anything more about who I am, being sure to protect Charlie's privacy. "Please give me a call or drop me an email. Thanks."

We have team supervision the next morning. Because I am in my second year of training and am focusing on supervision, I tend not to present cases to the group. Rather, my role has been to offer support to the first-year trainees. But I am so worried by the time I get to team that I bring it up.

"It hasn't been that long," says one of the women in the group, a trainee from Harvard that I generally like. "I mean, he probably forgot, right? I know that it's not so unusual for my clients to miss sessions now and then."

I can tell she is concerned that perhaps she's been too cavalier about her clients' no-shows and that maybe I am exhibiting a more appropriate response. I am quick to explain, "No, I think it is common for college students to miss sessions—perhaps especially because they don't pay for them—but this is different. This client never missed sessions, and he was looking forward to our final meeting. I made brownies." I hadn't planned on sharing this but it slips out before I can help it. "I mean, we had set the session up as a kind of celebration/goodbye meeting. I just have a bad feeling about it."

Dr. Vargas speaks next. "Rachel, what are you afraid of?"

"I'm not sure," I say. "If he, or any client for that matter, were hurt or in a car accident or something, how would we know? Because of the confidential nature of our relationship, no one would know to call us."

Just the tenor of Dr. Vargas's voice feels grounding to me. "So," she says, "that is another tricky part of the therapeutic relationship, isn't it? We develop this intimate connection to another person and, not only is there no mutuality in the relationship, but we aren't even linked to this person once they leave the office. People in our clients' lives may not even know we exist. How are we to know if they are safe when they leave us?"

"We have emergency contact information on their intake forms," suggests one of the other trainees tentatively.

"Yeah," says another. "When is it appropriate to use that?" They all look at me.

"I . . . I don't know." I have Charlie's file with me and flip to the intake form, the one on which he'd left his reason for seeking treatment blank. "He has his mother listed as the emergency contact, with their home number. I don't think she knows he comes to the counseling center. He's not out to his family."

Dr. Vargas jumps in. "Rachel, why don't you wait another day and then try his dorm room again. You can also send an email to his school address and see if he responds that way. I don't think we have reason to break the client's confidentiality at this point. How does that feel to you?"

I nod and shrug a bit, enough to show that I understand. I have to sit with my own anxiety about Charlie's wellbeing without doing anything impulsive.

Liz turns thirty on Saturday. While she is pretty indifferent about the whole "big 3-0," I think this is the most exciting thing that could possibly be happening.

I left Charlie an email and two more messages on his dorm machine and still haven't heard a thing. I am worried and confused but decide that I can set it aside for the weekend in order to focus all of my energy on making Liz's birthday special.

I suppose it feels like a bit of a test I have to pass—if I am the one she chooses to spend her life with, I should know how to make big life-moments special. I have a vision of us in our fifties and Liz saying, "I'll never forget that weekend in New York you planned for my thirtieth, remember? Oh and then the fortieth surprise party, and our trip to Greece on my fiftieth . . ." It is a lengthy vision.

I told her a few weeks ago to clear her calendar for Friday afternoon through Sunday. I told her to pack a bag that was to include comfortable walking shoes and a hot outfit for a night on the town. I didn't tell her anything else.

I have been planning for weeks. Actually, Zeke helped me plan when we were home for Thanksgiving. His old college roommate, Sam, is living in the West Village in New York with another friend of theirs. Since the two guys had been planning to find a weekend to visit Zeke in D.C. anyway, they arranged to go the weekend of Liz's birthday, and Sam agreed to let me use their apartment.

We prearranged every last detail—that Sam would leave his key with a friend who worked late on Fridays at the video store on the corner, that I'd leave it under the mat of the old woman who lived one floor below him (she'd never know) when we left. I'd been a sleuth of celebration, making dinner reservations at the most hip bistro I could find, researching the hottest lesbian dance clubs in the Village, studying and committing to memory a street map of lower Manhattan—the numbered streets go up as you go uptown, SoHo is South of Houston Street, which is pronounced like "House-ton," not like the city in Texas. I told Zayde that we'd be driving down to New York City for the weekend with a bunch of friends, making me sound like one of a large group. It wasn't a total lie—there are many people in New York.

When I pick Liz up at her apartment Friday after work, I stand awkwardly in her living room waiting for her to pack a few last-minute things. When she comes out of her room pulling a little wheeled bag behind her, I hand her a rose and a card. Inside the card, I've written this itinerary in the fancy calligraphy I'd learned at camp when I was twelve:

Liz's 30th Birthday Weekend
Wild Women Take the West Village

Friday night
Drive to "our place"
(Stop at Rein's Deli in Vernon, Connecticut,
for dinner en route)

Saturday
Sleep in
Explore
Dinner at 8:00 at Art Bar
Dancing at Henrietta Hudson's Bar and Girl

Sunday
Sleep in

Brunch
Drive home

I bounce a nervous bounce on my heels while watching her read through my plan. She smiles a soft, surprised kind of smile and looks up at me over the top of the card.

"You know how to plan a weekend, Levine!" and she kisses me slowly.

"Let's go!" I shout, too loudly for my proximity to her face. I want her weekend to be perfect, and for that we need to hit the road.

It is after eleven by the time we walk into Corner Video to get Sam's key. I imagined that I would be very mysterious, not telling Liz why we were starting our adventure in—what turned out to be—a kind of a seedy video store, but I impulsively spilled everything before we'd even gone a few miles on the Mass Pike.

Sam lives in a shoebox. I'd heard that New York apartments were tiny and very expensive, but I hadn't quite pictured anything this small. There is a little main room with a futon, where I think the roommate sleeps, and bookshelves made out of plastic milk crates like we used in college. Off the room is a little galley kitchen, a bathroom with a shower stall, and a bedroom just big enough for a twin bed, a small chest of drawers, and a bike hanging from the ceiling.

"Oh," I say when we open the double locks and switch on the lights, immediately worrying that Liz will forget for a minute that I am a poor grad student and instead think I've been cheap in picking our lodging.

She must sense my concern because she walks right into the shoebox and says, "This is perfect!"

"Really?" I ask, so grateful. "There's hardly room to walk around."

"Rach, this is New York! You don't pay rent to have a spacious apartment, you pay rent for the experience of calling this city your home!"

"You do?" I say, a little surprised to hear her speak with such fervor about a city she hadn't chosen to live in.

"Yes! You pay to live among these wild throngs of people. To be a part of the energy."

"'. . . the New York city rhythm,'" I add, quoting the Barry Manilow CD we'd listened to on the drive down.

"Right!"

We both laugh.

"I've never heard you love up New York so much," I say. "How come you've never talked about wanting to live here?"

"Because I don't," she says matter-of-factly. "I love to visit New York. I appreciate it. But I'd be constantly agitated living here—too much stimulation."

I take my winter scarf from around my neck and lasso her with it, pulling her to me. "I'll show you too much stimulation," I say in what Liz always teases is my "bedroom voice." ("Like the Bangles sing about in 'Manic Monday'?" I asked the first time she accused me.) I kiss her hard as we hurriedly strip each other of our winter clothes, letting them drop around our ankles. We melt down on top of them and, as midnight strikes on the dawn of Liz's special day, we are all fingers and tongues and limbs, on a nest of wool layers, in a little nook of a home, amid the throngs and the rhythm of the city.

∽

We sleep curled up in Sam's twin bed (on which he's assured me he's left clean sheets) until 10:30 the next morning. When I see how late it is, I pounce on Liz and implore, "Get up old lady," straddling her on my hands and knees, my nose and forehead pressed to hers.

She opens her eyes to my bulging eyeballs against hers and makes a sound that I translate as a cross between "Good morning my love," and "Why? Why are you waking me like a cat?"

I jump up. "Time to explore! We have an agenda to stick to!"

Stretching out her tiny Liz body to wake her muscles, she says in a yawn, "The agenda didn't say *where* we're exploring."

"That's because you get to choose," I say jumping into my jeans and nearly hitting my head on the bike hanging from the ceiling. "We can stay in the Village, go to SoHo, head up to Midtown—"

"Wow, someone's been learning about New York, huh?"

"Okay, so I've been doing a *little* researching," I say climbing back onto the bed. "My parents didn't exactly expose us to New York much as kids. To them, 'the city' meant Center City Philadelphia."

"Ouch," says Liz in that tone that New Yorkers or those who love New York use when talking about Philadelphia.

"At some point, I think in eighth grade, I realized I was practically the only kid at Bryn Mawr Middle School who hadn't seen the Statue of Liberty, and I begged them to go. I remember when we got off the Amtrak in Penn Station, my mother clasped her hands in mine and Zeke's, as if we might be snatched from underneath her nose as soon as we hit the platform. My dad was two steps ahead of us with his map already held taut at eye level as he looked up at the signs for an exit to Seventh Avenue."

I imitate him holding up the map, which makes Liz laugh out loud.

"Then Zeke's like, 'Ow! You're hurting me!' and he's all wrestling his arm back from my mother, who's then not just holding our hands but pinning our arms against the sides of her body with her elbows. She's yelling, 'We need to stick together! We discussed this!'"

"You'd discussed it?"

"Oh indeed! My mother sat Zeke and me down the afternoon before the trip and told us about the 'dangers of New York'—the violent muggers, the kidnappings. She said that we would not be taking the subway under *any* conditions. She said we needed to stick together no matter what. Which we did—until we found the exit to Seventh Avenue and saw that it was a revolving door."

"Please tell me she unhooked you and allowed you to go through it."

"Sure, but as soon as we got outside, she snatched us up again. This was us headed toward the taxi line—" and I jump up and pantomime a tipsy three-legged race, this time actually bumping my head on the bike tire.

"Ooh, you okay?" laughs Liz.

I fall back onto the bed laughing and holding my head.

❧

I am a little surprised (and secretly totally psyched) that Liz picks Midtown Manhattan as our destination for the day. I have never seen the tree at Rockefeller Center or the ice skaters, or the windows and lights on Fifth Avenue. I just hadn't expected Liz to pick Midtown—it seemed so mainstream of her, so touristy. But she says she hasn't seen the traditional New York Christmas sights in years and she wants me to experience them with her.

We dress in all our winter layers, grab coffee to go from a little place down the block, and take the subway (the subway!) from Washington Square up to Rockefeller Center. It is dirtier and smellier than the T in Boston, and I feel both a little scared (my mother shaking a finger at me in my head) and triumphantly cool.

Liz sits watching my face as we chug through the dark tunnels. "You've never been on the New York subway, have you?" she says with a teasing smirk.

"What makes you think that?" I say, disappointed that my coolness is not as evident to her as it is to me.

"The look on your face," she says with a hint of "duh" behind it.

"You look like you just boarded Space Mountain for the first time at Disney World."

"That's enough out of you," I say and focus on reading a poster for ESL classes that is mounted above the window across from me.

I can't imagine, if I look like a kid at Disney World on the subway, what I must look like when we get to the ice rink. As I stare up at that tall Christmas tree, Liz gently puts her mittened hand under my chin and pushes my jaw closed. I just keep staring.

We spend hours doing all the things I've ever wanted to do in New York—watching the skaters, walking through St. Patrick's Cathedral, looking at the blown glass creations in the windows of Steuben's. The crowds are so thick, we have to hold on to each other tightly so as not to lose sight of each other. My mother might even approve.

What happens next is not on my agenda. As we head back toward Rockefeller Center on the opposite side of Fifth Avenue, I see him. Underneath the enormous statue of Atlas holding up the heavens, I see him with his arm around a girl. My pulse quickens before I am even sure it's him.

I grab onto Liz's arm as we approach. "That's Jason, in the red hat," I yell-whisper into her ear.

"Jason who?"

"Jason, my high school boyfriend."

"Oh! Your first requited love? Introduce me!" and she pulls me right up to them.

"Hey!" I say, all smiles and calm.

"Rachel?!" And he hugs me, tightly. "What are you doing here? This is too funny!" Liz and the girl next to Jason just smile and stare.

"Hey," I say. Again. "Um, we were just, you know, visiting New York. What are you doing here?"

"Same, uh hey—this is my girlfriend, Sheri," and he puts his arm back around her the way guys do when they are showing off pretty girlfriends. "Sheri, this is Rachel, my ex!" *Wow, he doesn't miss a beat.*

Sheri puts out her hand for me to shake. "Oh, so nice to meet you!" she says with white, straight teeth and the word "unthreatened" flashing across her forehead in neon lights.

"Hi," I say. "This is Liz."

Liz sticks out her hand to Sheri first. "Her girlfriend," she adds for me.

It's not that I didn't mean to say it. I am just so confused—seeing Jason, and with this girl, still feeling the heat of his hug pressed into me, smelling him.

"Hey, that's great," says Jason, all sincerity. "Do you guys live around here?"

"No," answers Liz before I can. "We're just down from Boston for the weekend. You?"

"We're actually living in Hoboken and just decided to come into the city for the day," says Sheri. So they live together. There is silence, and a lot of nodding.

"Listen, Rach, it was great to run into you. And Liz, so nice to meet you," says Jason.

"You, too," I say, feeling that old feeling of saying goodbye to him flood over me. Even all these years later. Even in this skin.

❦

On the subway back to the Village, Liz watches my face again.

"What's going on with you, Levine? Did seeing Jason freak you out?"

"No, it didn't freak me out exactly. It's just amazing to me that, after all this time, after having moved on, he still elicits so much old stuff in me."

"Like what?"

I want to be honest with Liz. She is my best friend. I want to say that it makes me want him, and that I want him to miss me, and that seeing him makes my heart feel broken all over again. I want to tell her that I am clasping my mittened hands between my knees not because I am cold but because I don't want her to know that I am still shaking. But it is her birthday, and this is her trip. So instead I say, "It just makes me feel young and catty and like I want to be better than his new girlfriend. Stupid stuff."

She kisses me on the cheek and says, "Sheri seemed nice. But I pick you."

I want to be present. I want this weekend to be all about Liz. But as we sit across from each other at this trendy Art Bar, eating small plates of calamari and spring rolls, I am somewhere else—one of memories and longing and fear. I had loved Jason, deeply. And, as I told Liz, I don't really understand the concept of falling out of love. I still love Jason. It doesn't make me love Liz any less or question my connection to her. It just makes me marvel at the reality of it all—the fact that there are people out there in the world to whom I have given my whole self, to whom I still feel I belong—that they will always be out there and that we will run into each other in big cities and cross paths at unknown moments. And that I can live my singular life with all that love walking around in the world.

It is easier to conceal my distraction at the dance club. I read about Henrietta Hudson's in a lesbian magazine and, true to the description, it is packed with dykes of all kinds. I am able to lose myself in the music but find myself wishing I was more of a drinker. I want to be drunk, to get out of my head, but my body reacts to alcohol the way it does to sun. I don't tan; I go straight from pale to vomiting. So I just keep dancing and let the bass be my drug.

Chapter 23

On Monday night, I try Charlie's dorm room again.

"Yeah," answers a brusque-sounding boy. Pete.

"Um, hi. I'm wondering if Charlie is there," I ask, tentative hope in my voice.

"Uh, no he's not. Hey, can I ask who this is?"

"My name is Rachel. I'm a friend of Charlie's, and I have been having a hard time getting a hold of him. Is he around?"

"Uh, Rachel, right? Listen, he never came back after Thanksgiving break. I totally don't know what's going on. I've left two messages on his home phone but no one's called me back. I'm kind of freakin' out."

My heart is thrumming against my rib cage, images of gurneys and Charlie with tubes in his mouth and nose flash before my eyes. "Listen, it's Pete?"

"Yeah. Hey, do we know each other?"

"No, we've never met. I'm going to make some calls and see if I can find out what's going on. When I get some information, I will let you know, okay?"

"Yeah, okay. Thanks."

I hang up and look for the piece of paper on which I'd written Charlie's mother's name and their home number. I don't call Dr.

Vargas; I don't deliberate about what is the professionally responsible thing to do. I just dial.

The answering machine picks up. It is Charlie's father's voice in a mellow Southern drawl asking me to leave a message at the sound of the tone.

"Hi, my name is Rachel Levine and I am calling from Student Affairs at Concord College." This isn't really a lie—the counseling center is under the auspices of the Dean of Student Affairs and it is the only way I can protect Charlie's confidentiality. "I understand that Charlie has not been back to campus since Thanksgiving break, and I am calling to—" I am interrupted by the clatter of someone picking up an extension mid-message.

"This is Charlie's father," says a voice matching the one from the outgoing message on the machine.

"Oh, Mr. Lindon?"

"That's right. What office did you say you were calling from?" He sounds inconvenienced. Not angry exactly, more tired and distracted. I think I hear a game on the TV in the background.

"I'm um, I'm calling from the office of Student Affairs about Charlie's absence."

"Charlie's not coming back to your college, ma'am. You can go on and notify his professors that he's withdrawn. His mother and I will come up and get his things before the semester's out."

"Sir?" I ask, my voice shaking. "Can I ask you why?"

"We've just decided that your *college* is not the right kind of learning environment for our son. We understand that we'll have to pay for the semester. Thank you for your call, ma'am." And he hangs up. He said "college" like it was a lie—like it was a front for something else, something sinister. I sit on my bed and let the tears wash over me. They know that Charlie is gay.

The next morning, I sink into Dr. Vargas's beige sofa with the weight of a much heavier person. My worry, my guilt, the previous night's sleeplessness all feel like bulk, like my body is swollen with all of what I am feeling. Dr. Vargas leans forward in her chair, her elbows on her knees, looking deeply into my eyes in that holding way, and I cry and cry.

"How could I have just sent him back there without warning? How is it that we weren't talking about the possibility that they would pull him from school, reject him? I don't even know what kind of hell he is going through beyond not being able to return to school . . ."

"Take a deep breath," soothes Dr. Vargas. We sit for a moment, just breathing. My temples pound and I grab for a tissue to catch the drips from my nose. "Rachel, did Charlie ever talk about plans to come out to his parents?"

"No! In fact, he had clear plans *not* to. He said that it was just not a bridge he wanted to cross any time soon. I guess that made me feel relieved. I was afraid for him to come out at home and I certainly didn't push it. He was just in such a phase of loving his own self-discovery, it seemed like the last thing he needed to be taking on right now."

"Rachel, if that was something you'd discussed in treatment—that he was not planning on coming out to his family right now, then it makes sense that you wouldn't have been warning him or talking through how they might react. This is not something you missed."

"But if he didn't tell them, how would they have found out?" And then I see it, as clear as if it were actually sitting on Dr. Vargas's low coffee table. That shiny, black book with "Journal" in gold lettering.

∽

For weeks I live in my head. I mean that everywhere I go—class, out with Liz, watching *Wheel of Fortune* with Zayde—I am present in body only. In my head I am turning Charlie's story over and over, looking for possibilities, the worst-case scenario, the best. Would his parents eventually come around? Would he go to community college and find a small gay community there to support him? Would he go back into the closet? Would he hurt himself?

In Kevin's office, I sit with my feet tucked under me, hugging a throw-pillow to my chest, which feels tight all the time. Lucky lies curled against my thigh.

"How are you sleeping?" asks Kevin, with a slight tilt to his head.

"I'm falling asleep okay, but I wake up around five with panic. Actually, I don't know that I wake up with it—when I first open my eyes, I'm fine, but within just a second it hits me like a wave."

"Where do you feel it in your body?"

"My heart starts pounding. There is this weird, tingly sensation in my arms. But mostly I just feel really sick to my stomach."

"Are you eating?"

"I can't."

It's not that I don't want to eat. It's that there's a constant nausea in the pit of my stomach that seems to swell when I sit in front of food. Liz is worried. She says she doesn't like making love to my ribs and shoulder blades and hip bones. I smile at this. Then cry.

What Liz doesn't know, what I can't explain to her now, but what is slowly coming into focus for me is that this isn't just about a client. Yes, Charlie is my most present worry, but what I am feeling is a lack of control over everything. I don't know where I'll be for my fourth-year internship, I don't know what Liz thinks about our future, I don't know how to feel about my shifting connection with Zayde, and then on top of it all, I don't know where or how Charlie is. I feel a disconnection with the world that I later learn is called "derealization" in clinical terms and is a symptom of extreme anxiety. It hits me while driving Essie through Harvard Square, veering left around the T stop as crowds form at the crosswalks waiting for the light to change. It is as if I am enclosed in a glass bubble and the world outside isn't quite real. Everything is muffled—sounds, sights, feelings. It's like, even if I could reach through the glass and touch the arms of those pedestrians, they would feel like vapor.

On a freezing cold morning during the second week of January, I get a phone call at Zayde's from Dr. Vargas. The counseling center is closed for winter break, but she'd stopped into the office to get a few things done and found a letter addressed to me in her mailbox. Actually, she says, it is simply addressed to "Rachel—Psychology Intern, Counseling Center, Concord College, Concord, MA 01742." The envelope bears no return address but is postmarked from Chicago. She says that she'll be in for a few hours if I want to come and get it.

I haven't showered. I am reading in my flannel pajamas and drinking chamomile tea in the kitchen while Zayde reads the *Wall Street Journal* across from me. I jump up and throw on yoga pants and a sweatshirt, put my hair in a ponytail and grab my keys.

As I speed west on Route 2, I think about what Dr. Vargas said about the way the envelope was addressed. No last name. Charlie knows my full name. And no street address for the college. Surely, Charlie knows that. I wonder with disappointment if it has nothing to do with Charlie at all.

The Center is dark when I get there, except for a rectangle of light shining into the hallway from Dr. Vargas's office. As I knock on her door jamb, I realize that she's never seen me without makeup or pro-fessional clothes. My yoga pants are tucked into my snow boots, and I can feel that half my hair has escaped its elastic. She, too, looks different. She has on jeans and a pullover sweater. I have that funny kind of shock, like when you are a kid and you run into your second grade teacher while shopping at the grocery store with your mom, and you realize for the first time that your teacher has a whole life outside of the time she spends in the classroom with you.

"Hi, Rachel," she says in her soothing supervisory voice. "The letter is there," and she gestures to an envelope on the coffee table. "You are certainly welcome to read it here if you'd like, but I also understand if you'd prefer privacy."

I pull my arms out of the sleeves of my puffy winter jacket and lay it down on the sofa before I slowly lower myself beside it. I take the envelope. Sure enough, just "Rachel" and of course my title isn't really "Psychology Intern"; I am still an extern or practicum student. The handwriting is neat and careful. The letter can't be from Charlie. "I'll read it here, thanks," I say, still examining the writing on the envelope.

I slide my finger under the fold and gently open it. Dr. Vargas has turned back to face her desk. The letter, in that same careful writing, fills one side of a lined piece of paper.

December 28, 1997

Dear Rachel,

I hope this letter finds you. We don't know each other and I only had a bit of information from which to write your address. My name is Adrianne, and I am a graduate student in psychology as I think you are. I am training this year on an inpatient psychiatric ward at a hospital in Chicago. I recently treated a client of yours named Charlie L. on our unit. Rachel, this story doesn't end well. I just felt that you deserved to know this information. I do not have a release to disclose it to you, so please be aware that I'm doing so off the record.

Charlie was admitted to our unit through the emergency room in mid-December. He had been brought to the ER when someone called 911 after finding him overdosed on pills. It is not clear who it was that called the ambulance.

Charlie was on our unit for five days. In that I time, he shared with me the following things:

~ that he came out as gay at college over the past year and that he worked with "Rachel, an awesome therapist even though she was just an intern" (his words).

~ that, while he was home with his family over Thanksgiving, his brother found his journal and read it. His brother then gave it to their parents.

~ that his parents were furious to find out that their son was "sinning against God" and was "practicing perversion" (again, his words).

~ that they refused to pay for school any longer. He says he had no money of his own and that they demanded he stay in the house and renounce his sins.

~ that he didn't know what to do and ran away. He hitch-hiked to Chicago and got mixed up with some older guys here. He said that they were taking care of him (giving him a place to stay, food, spending money, etc.) in return for sex. I think he was with them for a couple of weeks.

~ that he couldn't live this way, felt he had no choices, and took an overdose of some of their drugs while they were out.

Rachel, I feel like we failed him. We finally got him to agree to let us contact his parents and we discharged him to their care. When one of our social workers called a week later to follow up on his treatment plans, his mother informed her that he'd killed himself in their basement with his father's gun.

I am so sorry to be telling you this news. I wanted you to know what happened and to know that Charlie spoke so highly of you. I thought that, if I were you, I would want to know.

Best,

Adrianne

I sit frozen with the letter in my shaking hands, rereading it to make sure I've understood correctly. Dr. Vargas turns toward me as I let it fall back onto the coffee table. Her eyes look at me, searchingly.

"He's dead," I say with a slow, confirming nod. As if I've known it all along.

Chapter 24

"At least I have an answer," I say in Kevin's office, holding the pillow to my chest. "At least I don't have to *not* know."

"Is knowing this better than the uncertainty of not knowing at all?" His voice seems deeper than usual, as if he is matching pitch with my sorrow.

I sit, frozen in his question. If I say yes—if I feel that I would rather know that Charlie is dead than sit with not knowing, then what does that say about me? That I would choose to feel grief over anxiety? That seems okay, but am I also then saying that I would choose certain death for Charlie so that I could be spared the discomfort of my own fear? I look at Kevin and shake my head slowly.

"I don't know," I whisper.

The terrible truth is that, after I find out about Charlie's suicide, I can eat again. I am no longer plagued by that constant queasiness. Not only do I no longer have to wonder how the story ends, but there is a template for this ending. There are instructions about how to feel. When a beautiful young person kills himself because he feels hopeless in a cruel world, you feel sad and angry. You are so sad and so angry. But at least you know.

"Most people find that knowing allows them to grieve," Kevin says with kindness in his voice.

"Yes, but that's when someone is known to be missing, when finding a body means an end to the terror in their imaginations. For all I knew, Charlie might have been okay. I wasn't envisioning the worst."

"Maybe not consciously, Rachel, but perhaps some part of you was. Maybe you can let yourself off the hook for struggling with this particular uncertainty."

"Maybe."

I don't stay with the guilt. Yes, there are moments of self-blame, mostly of the why-didn't-we-prepare-for-this-possibility variety. Also something bigger. Something like, why wasn't Charlie more resilient in the face of crisis, and if he wasn't, then why didn't I see that lack of resiliency in him? Dr. Vargas is all over me about taking on any blame. She feels confident that not only could I not have seen this coming, but that the work I did with Charlie was competent and therapeutic.

"But if Charlie had really been in a good place, was really ready to discontinue treatment, then wouldn't he have had better inner resources? I know he didn't have money and was dependent upon his parents, but couldn't he have gone to a shelter, or contacted a gay organization, or called me?" This is what I really want to know. Why hadn't Charlie contacted me?

"Rachel, what would you have done if he'd called you?" Her voice is calm, inquisitive.

"I don't know . . . I would have tried to connect him with someone safe."

"We'll never know why Charlie didn't try to contact you or anyone at the college—his resident advisor, his roommate. We can only guess that something about how trapped he felt made that kind of outreach seem impossible. But that is not your fault."

I know it isn't. I tell Dr. Vargas and the team at the counseling center and my peers at school (all these people so worried about me) that I am not harboring blame or guilt. I am just sad and angry.

Liz is the one who helps me channel that anger.

"I have an idea," she says, leaning in across from me at Café Algiers in Harvard Square a couple of weeks later. She's just taken off her winter hat, and for the first time I realize that maybe she does have hat head. "There is a new queer youth center opening downtown called The Neighborhood. They need a ton of adult volunteers. Maybe you can do some stuff with them. You know, put your anger into action?"

"What kind of queer youth center? What will they do there?" I am staring into my coffee, picturing kids in an arcade like the kind on the Boardwalk at the Jersey Shore.

"They're going to have hangout hours, you know, where kids can come play board games or just read. They're planning social events. I'm sure they'll have support groups, that kind of thing."

"Wow," I say, looking up. *Could I lead a group?*

"I know. Can you imagine if we'd had something like that when we were in high school? I would have *lived* there."

"Yeah." Though I wouldn't have lived at such a center, had there been one in Bryn Mawr. I wouldn't have even noticed it. I was happy in high school. Maybe I'd been different from other kids in that I'd had crushes on boys *and* girls, but I just dated the boys and the rest was a secret I didn't give much thought to. My adolescence was so different from Liz's.

"Why is it called The Neighborhood?" I ask. "What does that mean?"

"It means that kids can go there without saying anything that will out them. 'I'll see you later at The Neighborhood' is a whole lot less risky than, 'I'll see you later at the gay youth center.'"

"Oh right." I hadn't gotten it. I call them right away and set up an interview for the following week.

∽

The Neighborhood is on the third floor of an old building on Mass Ave near Tower Records. I wear a crisscrossed white ballet sweater with a long, peasant skirt that I think might say both "mature, adult interviewee" and "crunchy lesbian." When I walk in, I quickly realize that my outfit really says, "country girl out of place in cool urban scene." There is a butchy white woman in her forties working on a computer at a desk. Her hair is buzzed with a little cowlick sticking up above her forehead. A very hip-looking, attractive Black woman is on the top of a ladder hanging some sort of light fixture. She has on jeans and an ACT UP T-shirt. At the base of the ladder, a young, flamboyant string bean of a white, gay adolescent boy is telling a dramatic story with his hands. I wonder if he is supposed to be holding the ladder. Across the room, four kids who look to be in high school are going through a pile of donated books and pealing with laughter. I glance quickly at them and can't decipher their genders but see that they all have short hair and T-shirts. The heat seems to be blasting and the room is too hot. A boom-box on the floor plays something techno that I don't know.

"Um, hi," I say to the woman at the desk. "I'm Rachel Levine. I'm here to meet with Brenda about volunteering." Just at this moment, the song that was playing ends and everyone in the room seems to turn and stare at me. I want to melt through the floor or hide my shoulder-length hair or change my clothes.

"Hey there." She shakes my hand. "I'm Brenda. Listen, make yourself at home. I'm just finishing up something here and then we can talk."

Make myself at home? I can feel beads of sweat pushing through my pores. *Why is it so hot in here?*

I walk over to where the teenagers are sorting and laughing. "Hey," I say. "I'm Rachel. Can I help you guys out with anything over here?"

"Nah, we're good," says a smiling androgynous teen. "I'm Stevie." I am so grateful for Stevie.

Just then, I hear Brenda right behind me. "You know I'm kidding myself if I think I'm ever going to get that computer figured out any time soon. Why don't we go chat over here."

I follow her to a separate room that contains only a small sofa and coffee table, both a little battered but functional.

"Have a seat," she says. "As you can see, we're just starting to pull together some furniture to get this place decorated." She sits on one end of the sofa, placing a bulky three-ring binder on the coffee table.

I sit, turning toward her, and cross my legs under that godforsaken skirt.

"So, tell me why you're interested in helping out at The Neighborhood," she asks, right to the point.

I already like Brenda. I decide to just be honest. "I actually went through a pretty bad experience about a month ago. I'm a graduate student in psychology, and I work with students in a college counseling center. A student I'd been working with—a young gay man, about twenty—he, uh, committed suicide after being outed to his parents."

She nods the kind of resigned nod that says she knows this story— not of Charlie in particular but of so many others.

"Anyway, I've been feeling very sad and angry, and my girlfriend actually suggested that I do something positive with that energy and volunteer some time here. You might know her? Liz Abraham? She works at Makom?"

"Oh, I know Liz!" she says brightening. "I was just at a training she was running over at their place a few weeks ago. She's a spitfire!"

I am so relieved. Everyone who knows my spitfire loves her, and if they love her, they might love me, too. I also know that I am using Liz as a bit of a ticket in. By making it known that she is my girlfriend,

I don't have to prove my status; I don't have to be "just bi" or have people look at my clothes and wonder if I'm straight. Liz makes me legitimate.

I take in a deep breath. "I'd be very interested in facilitating a support group for teens."

"Isn't that serendipitous?" says Brenda, and a rolodex of SAT word scrolls through my brain: *serendipitous, serendipity* . . . all I can come up with is a restaurant by that name where I drank an enormous frozen hot chocolate. "I was just saying to the staff that we need to find someone with a counseling background to run a support group, and here you are!"

Ah right, serendipitous—found by accident, fortuitous. "I envision the group being a place where kids could talk about coming out, and being out—you know, the challenges and anxieties around family dynamics and school, that kind of thing. I think between my personal experiences and my clinical work, I could create a space for them to really explore their feelings and support one another."

I notice Brenda's smile and realize that I can stop selling myself; she is happy to have me volunteer in this way. I feel my limbs soften and my breathing slow down.

"Is there a particular day that works best for you?" asks Brenda, flipping open the binder and pulling out a master calendar and pages of handwritten lists.

"Um, my best evening is probably Wednesdays." Now I am racing through my schedule in my head—could I get back from the college on time to get to the T to get to the Neighborhood at a reasonable hour? "Would seven o'clock be too late?"

Brenda scans the calendar in front of her. "I think that could work." Then, looking up at me, she says, "Let's plan to start in three weeks. I just need a little time to get everything up and running. We'll handle all the publicity from our end. All you have to do is show up."

I feel a shocking relief at the simplicity of this instruction. All I have to do is show up.

I find myself thriving on routine the rest of the winter. It feels important to know exactly where I am supposed to be when. Classes on Tuesdays and Thursdays. The counseling center on Mondays and Wednesdays. Wednesday nights at The Neighborhood. Therapy with Kevin on Friday afternoons. Saturday mornings at shul. Saturday nights and Sundays with Liz. I like getting up and knowing exactly what my day will hold. I depend on it.

Kevin wants to talk about this. He wonders out loud about what I am getting from being so reliant upon each week's looking like the next; he wonders how it "serves" me.

"I just feel better when I know exactly what the script is, you know?" I say, still holding the pillow but perhaps a little less tightly.

"I do know," he says. In therapy this means he hears me, but that he wants me to push harder, to understand why.

"It's not like I don't know what it's about for me," I say, straightening up, my voice perhaps a little louder. "I just need to simplify right now. Last semester was so intense—applying to all those internships, getting caught in that classroom with Liz, not knowing where Charlie was, Zayde pulling away from the synagogue, him being so angry with the rabbi all the time. It felt like there was nothing solid underneath me."

"And what did that feel like?"

Lucky lifts his head, cocks it to one side.

"It felt like anxiety all the time, like there was an engine in my chest constantly revving. Like my stomach was always churning. Like no matter how deeply I tried to breathe, I couldn't get quite enough air." My eyes are brimming.

"And now?"

"Now, there is something solid. I know what's happened to Charlie. Zayde has come back to shul, and I'm feeling confident that if word hasn't gotten back to him by now about Liz and me, it isn't going to. My schedule is full and I'm busy and I know what each day looks like."

"But how does it *feel*?"

"Better. Quieter inside." Nothing for several seconds.

"Okay."

"Okay?"

He shrugs. "It sounds like that's what you need right now—stability, structure."

"But that's not a long-term solution?"

"What do you think?"

I think.

"I think I'd probably get bored if I lived my whole life with such predictability."

He chuckles lightly. "I don't know if you'd be bored or not. But since when is living a life of predictability something we get to choose?"

Chapter 25

This is how the mail-dance goes each day at Zayde's: Philip, Zayde's mailman of nearly thirty years, drops the mail through the slot in the front door sometime between two and three each afternoon. The little flap of the mail slot creaks its familiar creak as it's opened, alerting Zayde (who is listening for it). Zayde quickly shuffles over to the door and opens it so as to catch Philip and wish him a good day; Philip (who by now is at the sidewalk) turns back to wave and say, "And you have a good day, too, Mr. Kessler!" When Zayde closes the door again, the mail is splayed across the floor of the little entrance, having been pushed by the bottom of the door. Zayde bends over, picking up one envelope at a time. He carries the little pile into the kitchen, goes through it item by item, and puts anything for me in a neat pile on the Formica countertop just in front of the toaster. I know this dance from having witnessed it since I was young, and as I come home to Zayde's each evening in late February, I approach that little pile in front of the toaster picturing all the steps that have preceded it.

Internship sites will be sending written responses to all applicants. The first three letters I receive are rejections, and I begin to panic. Then I get an invitation to interview from the University of Vermont in Burlington, then one from Emerson College in Boston, and one from Santa Cruz. Then three more rejections and finally a last interview invitation from American University in D.C. Four interviews. I tell myself that is not so bad. And when I compare notes with my classmates who are also receiving letters that week, I realize it really isn't so bad. Four is good. The competition for internship sites is fierce, and I feel lucky and relieved. I contact the schools and set up interviews for the second and third weeks in March.

The first thing I do is go to Filene's and try on a new pants suit. It is a very dark navy, but under the florescent lights of the dressing room it almost looks black. I wear it with a crisp white-collared dress shirt and navy heels and leave the privacy of the dressing room to look at myself in a three-way mirror and better light. A saleswoman about my mother's age stops and says, "Don't you look smart." Sold.

The Emerson interview is first and the one I'm most nervous about. Landing the internship at Emerson is my only chance at staying in Boston, at being with Liz next year. I practice with Dr. Vargas.

"Ms. Levine," she says, sitting across from me in her office, pretending to be an interviewer among a panel of interviewers. "Tell us why you want to specialize in working with the college population?"

I take a deep breath. "Developmentally, I've always thought of the college years as a time of great possibility, a watershed moment—"

"Rachel," Dr. Vargas interrupts. "I'm sorry to cut you off. Try to stay away from clichés. Just be yourself. Be real."

"Okay," I say, and take a breath. "Let me try again." I think for a minute before beginning. "It's no secret that I am not very many years out of college myself. When I think of what those years meant for me, psychologically, they were really about getting to know myself for the first time outside of the context of my family. This is how I think about the college students I work with—they are experiencing themselves in a completely new way. For some, this can bring up a myriad of challenges. I think having the opportunity to work with adolescents in this phase is really a gift. They are at the height of discovery and change is all around them. To be able to partner with them at this moment in their development is, professionally, a gift. Wait, did I already say it was a gift?"

"Rachel, you are so on the right track. That was great! Yes, you said 'gift' twice."

We laugh.

"Let's try another question. We are also curious about your theoretical orientation. As what kind of therapist do you identify?"

This is an inevitable question at any clinical site. Interviewers want to know what type of therapy you practice. Psychodynamic, cognitive/behavioral, gestalt, relational, solution-focused—there are so many therapeutic approaches. In my graduate program, we've studied them all and are expected to have chosen a theoretical orientation by this point in our training.

"I really identify as eclectic, meaning that I have a strong foundation in several theoretical approaches and that I pick and choose among them depending on the needs of my client . . ." I can tell by the wince on Dr. Vargas's face that I should stop. "No?" I ask.

"You know, Rachel," she says almost apologetically, "this is such a toughie. I know what you are going to say—that you blend the best of what each modality has to offer in order to tailor your treatment to the individual."

I nod; we've discussed this in the past.

"But there's a way in which, in interviews at least, that answer can be interpreted as not knowing who you are as a clinician. They want to hear that you have a clearly developed sense of yourself as a certain type of therapist. That you've chosen an orientation by which to practice."

I sit for what feels like a long time, looking down at the coffee table between us, where my tape recorder so often is, and where once laid that terrible letter. I shake my head and look at Dr. Vargas. "It would be a lie though. I could pick a label—could call myself 'psychodynamic' or something, but I don't think I could pull it off with any sincerity. The truth is that I integrate those approaches. What if I developed an answer that was honest but also addressed their fears? Like, what if I could explain that, when I say eclectic—it doesn't mean undecided, it means a carefully thought out melding of techniques?"

"If anyone can do that, I believe you can."

I let myself take in her pride in me, let it feel maternal.

"Why don't you think about it," she says, "and we'll tackle that one again next time we meet. Let's try one more question: Now, I'm wondering if you can tell us about a particularly difficult case you've treated—both what made the case difficult, and how you approached it."

I sigh and look at Dr. Vargas. We both know my most difficult case. "What do I do?" I ask.

Her answer surprises me. "I think you don't talk about Charlie."

"Why not?" *Does she think I am at fault?*

"I want to be clear, Rachel, that it isn't because the fact of Charlie's suicide means anything about you as a therapist. It is just that the interview panel is going to have such a short time to get to know you—they'll get just a snippet of who you really are, and frankly I don't trust them to understand what good work you did with him. I don't know that they will have enough context. And I would hate for them to become focused on the suicide and not really hear about *you* as a skilled clinician. Do you understand what I mean?"

"Yes, I think I do," I say. "Also, I don't know that I'm ready to talk about Charlie anyway."

Dr. Vargas sits quietly with me, holding me in a way that only her silence can.

I do talk about Charlie with my kids at the Neighborhood during our first meeting that very same week, only I call him a friend instead of a client. Actually, playing the Liz card again, I say he'd been a friend of mine and my partner's. I tell them that I loved Charlie and that his death was a waste of a beautiful future. I make them promise that, no matter how badly they might feel, they will contact an adult at The Neighborhood if they ever think they might hurt themselves. We circulate copies of a contact list for this very purpose.

I can't believe how many kids show up to the first meeting—eleven, counting the quiet girl who sneaks in for the last fifteen minutes and stands against the wall in the back. They sprawl on the old sofas and on the floor. The other three girls and two of the seven boys drape themselves over one another in the manner of teenagers who want you to know how irrevocably connected they are. Two of the other boys seem to know each other too but in an awkward, self-conscious way, sitting together and chatting but avoiding eye contact. One boy, maybe fourteen years old, sits alone with enormous eyes and never says a word after sharing his name during our initial introductions. The energy in the room vacillates between electric, with all of us laughing at funny stories, feeling safe and understood, and solemn, like when one of the girls, Mona, tells us about her father.

"I remember the first time I heard him use the term 'stupid dykes.' He was watching some sports show on TV and the sportscaster was saying there would be a professional women's basketball league starting. So of course, after that I started sneaking to the upstairs TV to watch WNBA games!"

Her friend, over whom Mona's legs are draped, slaps her a high-five with a smile. "He would fucking kill you if he found out about you," says the high-fiving friend.

Mona shrugs. "I don't think he'd actually kill me, but he'd definitely hit me."

The room is quiet then.

"Mona," I ask, "has your dad hit you before?"

"Nah, I mean he's definitely hit my mom. Not me, though. I know to stay away from him."

❧

Jenna and Jamie's baby is born on the first day of March. Jamie calls Liz from the hospital in Brooklyn where Jenna has given birth to baby girl Taylor Grace. I am excited for them—and relieved they didn't choose a J name.

"What do you think of this?" Liz asks that Saturday, holding up a onesie that says "Nobody Puts Baby in a Corner." We are spending the afternoon in Harvard Square, mostly to distract me from my fast-approaching Emerson interview on Monday.

"I can hear Patrick Swayze's voice just looking at it. Why don't we get a book to go with it—like *Goodnight Moon* or something?"

"Oh, yeah, okay," says Liz with an almost imperceptible flash of confusion, which she quickly replaces with a smile.

"What?"

"No, nothing—I just hadn't been thinking that we were sending it from both of us. But no, of course, we can send a gift from both of us. Let's go look at the books." She is acting caught. Like I caught her not thinking like a part of a couple.

That night, in her bed, I don't come. Not as an act of dissent exactly, but perhaps one of self-preservation. I just can't let myself go, let myself be that vulnerable. I feel guarded.

"Where are you, sweetie?" Liz asks, stroking my hair long after she is done and it is clear I'm not that into it.

"I'm here," I say. "Just kind of tired tonight." The truth, if I were to let myself speak it, is that I am feeling terrified again. I can't let myself get in touch with the fear of losing Liz, not right now. I have four interviews in the coming two weeks and I have to be focused. I tell myself that we can talk about us after they are over.

"Will you spoon me?" I ask.

As I let myself fold into Liz, her arm tucking around me, I repeat these words to myself: *She is right here. She loves you. It's all going to be okay.*

Chapter 26

I arrive at the building housing the Emerson College counseling center twenty minutes early that Monday morning. It's too early to show up for the interview, so I stroll up and down a few blocks of Tremont Street reviewing some of the topics Dr. Vargas and I had discussed. I check myself out in the reflection of the dry cleaners on the corner and tell myself I look sharp in my new suit.

When I go up to the counseling center, I am welcomed by the receptionist and asked to wait in the waiting room. I want to pick up a magazine—to look casual. *People*? No, that makes me look shallow. *Glamour*? Too vain. *Good Housekeeping*? Barf. Finally, I decide on a pamphlet called *Depression: When it's More Than Just the Blues*. I have only just opened it when a tall, lanky man with neatly trimmed facial hair comes into the room.

"Rachel Levine?" he asks, looking at me—the only one there. I rise, shake his hand. "I'm Dr. Ketchel. We'll be meeting in the conference room."

"Thank you," I say, not quite sure what I am thanking him for. *Should I have said, "Pleased to meet you"? Did I make eye contact?* I follow him down the hall. We enter a long, narrow conference room where three women, who had been sitting at the table, stand to shake my hand. One is a current intern, the other two, Drs. Eagan and McDade, are staff psychologists. They welcome me and motion to a chair for me to sit in, between Dr. Ketchel and the intern. The group banters with me a bit about Somerville (Dr. Eagan lived there) and about BSCP where Dr. Ketchel says he'd taught a course several years ago. I can tell that they are eager to dissipate my interview anxiety, and I am appreciative. When the questions start in earnest, I feel ready.

They ask about the kinds of diagnoses I've treated and about my growth over my first three years as a practicum-level trainee. They wonder why I'd decided to stay at the Concord College counseling center for two years of training rather than try another site. I talk about how much I value quality supervision, and about my rapport with Dr. Vargas. I notice a look of recognition on Dr. McDade's face when I describe Dr. Vargas and realize that they very well might know each other. I know Dr. Vargas attends conferences with supervisors from other college counseling centers. The thought of this gives me a boost of confidence, as if Dr. Vargas herself has just come up behind me and given my shoulders a squeeze.

And then they ask about my "theoretical orientation."

Now, I had practiced my answer with Dr. Vargas several times, talking about how I believe in integrating different approaches to fit the specific needs of the client. I learned how not to use the word "eclectic" in describing my approach, how to express my thoughts about interweaving theoretical models without sounding ignorant or, worse, ambivalent.

What comes out of my mouth, though, is nothing I've ever heard before. Without hesitation, really without thought, I say, "In my heart, I'm a behaviorist."

I have never said such a thing. I'm not sure I have even thought it. But what comes out next is as succinct a description of my clinical perspective as I think I've ever prepared.

"I say, 'in my heart,' because I want to be clear that I believe in—and often practice—an array of theoretical approaches in my work. I believe that understanding one's childhood experience is essential and that psychodynamic inquiry provides clients with a road map for understanding their young adult selves. I believe in challenging core beliefs and that cognitive approaches help clients to question their most basic convictions about themselves. But, in the end, I think that all suffering is best treated by behavior change. I explain it to my clients this way . . ."

And here I begin to lie a little. I haven't done much of this work with my clients, yet. What I find myself explaining is actually the work Kevin has been doing with me—it is relatively new, called Acceptance and Commitment Therapy, and I wish Kevin could be a fly on the wall of this conference room, because as I am answering the interview committee's question, it is as if I'm finally getting it, as if I'm suddenly making sense of months and months of our work together.

"I explain to my clients that thoughts, feelings, and behaviors are separate things and that each affects the other. While we can *challenge* our thoughts and feelings, really they are beyond our control. Feelings and thoughts just come unbidden. But our behaviors are always within our control, and by changing our behaviors, we are able to create change in our thoughts and feelings as well."

Dr. Ketchel interjects, nodding, "I find that behavioral interventions are most successful when a client is being avoidant of something—perhaps avoiding social situations if they are socially anxious or avoiding going out in the case of agoraphobia. Is this the kind of behavioral change you're talking about?"

"Yes, but not exclusively. There is a new behavioral approach called Acceptance and Commitment Therapy, or ACT." (Thank God for Kevin being so cutting edge.) "ACT essentially says that we all avoid, and that what we avoid is our inner experience. For example, we avoid discomfort; we avoid sadness; we avoid anxiety and pain; we even avoid the physiological sensations we don't like, like our stomach churning or our heart rate escalating. The formal name for this is experiential avoidance, but I often describe it more simply— that we do anything we can to avoid feeling bad."

Here I pause, to gauge if they are with me, to gauge if *I* am with me. Dr. Eagan looks fascinated. She asks, "So what does that look like, say for a college student who comes in with depression or anxiety?"

"Well," I say, biding my time to formulate an answer. "An anxious student might be avoiding something in the physical world that elevates her anxiety—like avoiding talking in class or being around large groups of people. But she might also be avoiding the *feeling* of anxiety simply by worrying about its existence. For example, imagine a client who is experiencing a lot of anxiety. Not only does this particular client *not* avoid places or situations, she makes sure she is busy and distracted all the time. She runs from one activity to another in order not to be alone with her anxious thoughts. She doesn't look at first glance like a typically avoidant person, but really she is avoiding the experience of her anxiety. She is exhausted and exhausting to be around. The behavioral work for her would be learning to sit with the experience of feeling anxious, rather than running from it all the time. If she could stop fearing her anxious thoughts and feelings, she could slow down, be present, and let her body heal. For her, the constant running is like throwing lighter fluid on the fire, and only by discontinuing this behavior can the fire have the opportunity to die out on its own."

Still, I am in disbelief. I have never talked with my clients quite this way. This was what Kevin has been teaching *me* all along.

"I like that example, Rachel," says Dr. McDade, "but I'm wondering about the depressed client. How do you think someone in the throes of depression is avoiding their inner experience?"

I feel stuck and unprepared to answer this question, because of course my own experience is as more of an anxious person than a depressed one.

"To be honest," I say, "I've had less experience treating depression using ACT. I suppose though, I would want to try to understand what the client was *doing*. Were they stuck in bed? Were they withdrawn from friends? Were they over-eating or self-medicating in some way? By starting with their behaviors, I would try to discover what they were avoiding. I might ask something like, if you weren't in bed or eating all the time, whatever the case may be, what might you be feeling?"

"Thank you," replies Dr. McDade, as if satisfied with my conjecture.

"I'm going to play devil's advocate for a moment," says Dr. Ketchel, leaning back in his chair and stretching his arms behind his head. "I'm not very familiar with ACT, though it does sound like a very promising new approach. My question is, how is it not just Buddhism? Said another way, what makes it different from what the practice of Buddhist meditation aspires to? That is, trying to be present with one's experience and the transience of that experience?"

My armpits are dripping. I suddenly wonder if I'd forgotten to use deodorant. I do know some about Buddhist philosophy and about meditation from the class I'd taken as an undergraduate. I do see the similarities, though I haven't thought about them before. But then, I haven't really thought before about much of what I've said so far.

"My guess is that there are more similarities than differences. I would also not be surprised if the researchers who developed ACT have not given enough recognition to the Buddhist roots of their theory." I wonder if I am sounding too apologetic or not apologetic enough. "I think maybe the difference is in the presentation. ACT uses Western, psychological language in order to deliver its approach to a Western, psychological audience. I think it would be really interesting to look further into the intersection between the two." (A professor once told me, if you don't know how to answer an interview question, flatter the interviewer by saying that you'd like to research his question further.)

Drs. Ketchel, McDade, Eagan, and the intern all seem pleased with my answers and, as the interview winds down, there is lots of hand shaking and smiling. I leave feeling buoyant and like I have no idea what I've just said. I spend the following hours recreating the conversation and taking copious notes; I have three more interviews to go and a new script to study.

I take the train to DC two days later for a Thursday interview at American. My brother Zeke meets me at the train station, and we grab a quick dinner before heading back to his place. It isn't until we're blowing up an inflatable air mattress that he addresses the elephant in the room I've been so careful to avoid.

"I notice you haven't asked about my OCD," he says with teasing edge to his voice.

"Oh that!" I say jokingly. "I'd forgotten all about it! How's that going anyway?"

"Really well, thank goodness," he says, more seriously. "This guy I'm working with is really good. Kind of a drill sergeant, actually."

"Like how?" I wonder if any of my clients would say that about me.

"Like, he has me working with a lot of scripts. I write them with him during the session and then I have to read them over and over for homework during the week. Sometimes we record a script onto a loop tape, and I listen to it on repeat for days on end."

I try not to think about "Open Arms" by Journey. "Hey, would you play one for me?" I ask.

"Really? It's kind of weird . . ."

"No, seriously. Think of it as a training tool for the next time I need to do imaginal exposure work with a client." Imaginal is what exposure therapy is called when it involves writing up a pretend scenario rather than confronting something in the real world, or "in vivo."

"Okay," he says shrugging. He rifles through a shoe box near his bed, takes out a two-minute loop tape marked "Script #3," puts the tape into his stereo, and presses play. I realize that I've been expecting to hear the therapist's voice and am surprised when it is Zeke's.

> Hey man—it's me. So this is what could happen. I could do the reading for class and think I'm understanding it but not really understand it at all. I could understand it imperfectly and then when I get to the test, I could bomb it. I could think I know the answers but really, I could get them all wrong. And then I could fail the class. And then I could study really hard, and the same thing could happen with all my other classes. And then they'd kick me out of med school. And I'd feel so dejected that I'd just become totally depressed. I'd spend days on end in bed and wouldn't be able to hold down a job because I'd always oversleep, and I wouldn't even care anyway. Then Becca would see that I'm really a mess, and she'd leave and then I'd be all alone, jobless, no relationship. I'd end up living in Mom and Dad's basement forever. And everyone would say, "It's such a shame. That boy had such a promising future."

Zeke stops the tape. "Wow!" I say, genuinely amazed at the things Zeke has put into this script.

"I know, pretty gruesome, huh?" he says with a smirk. This is how I know he is really better. He can listen to his own voice telling him that his worst fears could come true and then smile about it.

"Is it hard to listen to?"

"You know, it's like all exposure—it's hard the first few times then it just gets easier. I'm habituating to my fears." He says it with an air of pride in his progress.

I hug him. "Hey, let's make one where I tell myself that I could go into this interview tomorrow and suddenly forget how to speak English!"

"Excellent. What do you speak instead?"

"Um, Klingon! I can only speak Klingon." Our dad was quite the Trekkie when we were growing up.

"Oh, you'll definitely *not* get an offer at that site."

"I'll be lucky if they don't kick me out of the interview."

∾

The interview at American actually doesn't go so smoothly. I do remember how to speak English, but my responses feel stilted and over-rehearsed. I leave feeling disconnected from the interview committee members and fairly confident that I will *not* get an offer.

The University of Vermont interview is the following Monday. I drive up to Burlington with a BSCP classmate who also got an interview there. I am grateful to have the company for the trip but am anxious about competing against her. The interview format is very different; we meet throughout the day but in groups only. I can't even pretend that we aren't competing since we are literally interviewing side by side.

Santa Cruz is at the end of the second week and is my last interview. It is also, by far, my strongest. One of the staff psychologists on the interview panel is a huge proponent of ACT (which I have thoroughly researched in the time since my Emerson interview), and I know he will pull for me even if the others on the panel don't. But, really, I feel good with all of them—they are kind and funny and warm. I wonder if what they say about West Coast people being so much nicer than those of us back East is true.

The American Psychological Association adheres to a uniform response date, requiring all training sites to call those applicants they've accepted by noon on Monday, March 30, just a week after the last of my interviews. If you haven't received a call from a specific site by noon, it means that they haven't chosen you. Once you know which sites, if any, have accepted you, you have until that Wednesday at noon to accept a placement.

I hardly sleep the night before that ominous Monday morning. I am sitting at the kitchen table nibbling nervously on a bagel when I hear, "Good morning, Esther" coming from the staircase and suddenly realize how long it's been since Zayde and I have had breakfast together. He is up early to keep me company, and I jump up and hug him.

As Zayde finishes his Cream of Wheat (which he calls Farina), he suggests that we watch *The Today Show* together to keep my mind off waiting for the phone to ring. We move into the living room and sit next to each other under the afghan that has been draped over the back of my zayde's couch for as long as I can remember and watch as Katie Couric and Matt Lauer banter about their weekends.

At 9:30, the phone rings. Zayde's eyebrows shoot up. I answer the heavy black rotary phone that is sitting next to me on the couch, the extra-long wire snaked over from its usual spot next to Zayde's armchair.

"Is this Rachel Levine?" asks the woman on the line.

I take Zayde's hand and squeeze. "It is," I say, trying to place the voice.

"Rachel, this is Dr. McDade from the counseling center at Emerson College. I'm calling to invite you to join us as an intern next year."

My voice cracks as I say, "Thank you so much!"

"We'll expect you to let us know of your decision by noon on Wednesday," she adds.

"Yes, I will let you know. Thank you again. I feel very honored to have been chosen."

Zayde beams at me and squeezes my hand tightly. I hang up and throw my arms around his neck.

"That was Emerson, Zayde! The one in Boston!"

"You mean you're staying here?" he asks, still a bit confused about how this process works.

"I think so!" I can't wait to tell Liz.

As the morning news shows turn into morning talk shows, Zayde and I stay parked under the afghan waiting for more calls. When hours pass and the phone doesn't ring, I tell myself that it doesn't matter if I don't get any other offers—as long as I have one and as long as it is here. But at 11:45, as I am dozing, my head on Zayde's shoulder, I am jarred by the phone once more. It is Santa Cruz. They apologize for calling late in the morning, noting the time difference, and say they would love for me to join their training program. I feel honored to have a choice to make, though I know where I want to be.

Back up in my bedroom, I call Liz at work and get her voicemail.

"Liz, it's me," I practically squeal. "I got two acceptances—Emerson and Santa Cruz! I'm so relieved! I can't wait to celebrate with you. I'll be over at seven with Indian food. I love you. Ahhh, see you later! Love you, bye."

Chapter 27

When I get to Liz's apartment, Indian takeout in hand, I am so tired from the emotional roller coaster of the past weeks, I just want to curl up with her on her cozy loveseat. I want to hear her say, "I am *so relieved* you are staying in Boston." I expect a toast over wine, maybe congratulatory sex, and all of the peace of having one more unknown known.

But Liz is wholly preoccupied with the business of setting the table. She ricochets between her overflowing drain-board and the little table like a silver ball stuck between two bumpers of a pinball machine: Get two forks; put down two forks. Get two glasses; put down two glasses. Get two plates; put down two plates. I sink into my usual seat, talking very fast about the whole morning, telling her about sitting between Zayde and the old phone, waiting for it to ring, trying to be distracted by Gene Shalit's review of the latest movies.

As soon as everything is on the table, Liz plunges a serving spoon into the container nearest her, starting to dole out the Chana Masala before she is even fully seated. "So, which internship will you choose?"

I realize she has not looked at me once.

I force a smile as if she might be joking and I find it funny. "Um, I was hoping we might make that decision together?" Silence. "I mean,

I think where I am for a year might matter to you. too." It becomes suddenly clear to me that this is not going to be a conversation about my internship choice.

I wait.

Nothing.

The ticking of the clock on her wall seems to get louder. "Liz," I start, my voice catching in my throat, "why do I feel like you're breaking up with me?"

She breathes, a full inhalation and exhalation without answering, then, looking into my eyes, she says, "I think I am."

"You *think* you *are*?!" Tears spring to my eyes. "What does that *mean*, you think you are? Why?"

"Rachel, I've been giving this a lot of thought." Now she is looking into my eyes without blinking, as if we're in a staring contest, as if I am suddenly a small child. "I love you, I do. I just don't see us staying together forever, and, if we're not going to stay together in the long run, then maybe this is the best time to end it. I don't want you to choose to stay in Boston because of me."

"I don't believe you," I say, feeling a surge of anger. I stand up, unable to contain the flood of adrenalin. "You clearly *don't* love me. If you love me, then why don't you want to love me *forever*? You don't break up with someone you love!"

"Rachel, you need more than love to build a lifetime together."

"Like what? It's not like were not compatible—we're even both Jewish!" I hate the tears streaming down my face, hate that they give her the upper hand.

"Like . . . like trust, Rach."

"Trust?!" I stop pacing to stare at her. "Have I ever given you a reason not to trust me?"

"No, not explicitly. It's just . . ." She stops, breathes again, her tear-less face collecting itself as she looks past me, then back. "It's just that I have a lot of issues about bisexuality—you know that. When Helen left me for that guy, I swore I'd never date another woman who liked men. But then I did, you know? I thought I could be okay with it." Silence. "I just don't think I can really ever be totally okay with it."

"You told me it was your baggage and that you were going to *leave it* at the door!" I shout, quoting that first email from over a year ago.

"I know, I know I said that. And I meant it—I thought I could be okay with it. But Rachel, I know you and—"

"You *know* me?!" I interrupt, my nose dripping. I drop back into my chair.

"Yes. I know you," she says, her voice all calm and reasonable. "I know that you love falling in love more than anything in the world. I know that once you've fallen in love with someone, you always love that person. I've seen it—when we ran into Jason in New York. And Rachel, these qualities are gifts!"

Here she reaches across the table and takes my hands. I hate that I let her but I don't want to pull away.

"These are the parts of you that shine! I do not begrudge you the fact that you love deeply. But you are also very entrenched in the straight world—it's what your family wants for you, it rewards you, it's the easier choice. Can you imagine how scary that is for me? I live 100 percent in the gay world, without a choice. Don't get me wrong, I love it and I wouldn't change who I am for anything, but for me to plan my life with someone who can move so freely between worlds, who can be so easily pulled into the sanctioned, glorified arms of a man . . . it's just too hard for me to live with that kind of threat."

"What does that even mean? The 'sanctioned, glorified arms of a man'?! What are you even talking about?" I feel dizzy, like she is moving too fast and I have motion-sickness.

"Think of this scenario, Rach. You and I have been together for years and the honeymoon period is over. And that period *would* end— it always does. Our lives are about paying a mortgage and taking kids to the pediatrician and farting in bed."

"Yeah, so what?"

"Rachel, listen to me. I am just saying that when the rush of falling for each other ends, relationships become more mundane—companionate. There's nothing wrong with that, it's just life. But that's when someone like you—someone who thrives on that kind of falling in love—gets restless. And, normally, I could take that risk—that you might get restless and be attracted to others. I think that happens in all long-term relationships. But for you and me, there will always be the weight of the culture pulling you to fall in love with a man. That's what I mean by sanctioned and glorified. That kind of union is celebrated in every facet of our culture! How could that not be enticing? To find yourself attracted to someone you can tell everyone about and have them respond by asking to see photos and giving you gifts?"

"So, let me get this straight. You are leaving *me* because you are afraid I am going to leave *you*?"

She lets my hands go, sitting back in her chair. "It's embarrassing when I hear you say it like that. But, in its simplest form, yeah—I guess that is what I'm saying."

"Don't call me simple!" I almost add, ". . . you ivy league bitch."

"Rachel, I'm not calling you simple, I'm just saying that, for me, it doesn't feel simple. This is about my deepest fears of abandonment. I've tried to learn to let it go, to believe that bisexual women can be just as capable of lifetime commitment as lesbian women. I just don't feel like I can be fully trusting. And, if I can't feel that trust, even though you've done everything to earn it, then it doesn't matter that I love you. I can't feel safe enough to make a lifetime commitment."

I suddenly have to get out of there. "You know, Liz," I say, standing and putting on my jacket that is hanging over the back of my chair as if waiting for me, "I used to think you weren't afraid of anything. I loved you for your *courage*. Now I think you might be one of the least courageous people I know." I feel powerful, if only for a brief moment.

"Rachel, wait," she says, following me to the door.

I don't. I fly down the stairs, my hand over my mouth, and just barely make it out the door before vomiting all over the sidewalk.

❧

I tell Zayde that I have a stomach bug. For the next thirty-six hours, I stay in my bed fitfully sleeping in between periods of crying and turning it all over and over in my head. Liz calls my mobile phone once, and I unplug it and let the battery run down. Zayde knocks on my door a few times, asking if I want soup but I tell him that I just need to sleep and will be fine.

But I'm not fine. I am stricken with a kind of grief that I'd forgotten I was capable of feeling. Everything inside me feels like it is falling, like there is no bottom to anything and the force of gravity has grown. I think about how ironic it is that we say "falling in love." Realizing you love someone doesn't feel like falling at all. It feels like flying. It's the end that feels like falling.

Liz never planned to spend forever with me. All those daydreams I had about babies and anniversary trips had been mine alone. I replay her reasons again and again trying to understand. It isn't that I don't intellectually understand her fear—shit, that is my job, helping people understand their fear. I get it. I just can't believe that, on a scale weighing her love for me against her fear, her love doesn't weigh more.

I have until Wednesday morning to make a decision about internships. A part of me wants to stay, just in case she changes her mind. But a smarter part of me knows that she never will—that when Liz makes a choice, she makes it for good.

With shaky fingers, I call U.C. Santa Cruz on Wednesday morning and accept their offer.

◠⃯

From: rlevine@bscp.edu
To: eabraham@alumni.yale.edu
Sent: Wednesday 4/1/98 11:27 AM
Subject: Things you should know

Dear Liz,

I want you to know the following:

I accepted the internship in California. I will be moving out of Somerville in early June.

Until that time, I would like to attend Shabbat services with my zayde. Please do not come to Beth El on Saturday mornings until I leave. It is only a few months and I don't think this is too much to ask.

I am furious with you. I trusted you with my heart and you were careless with it. If you felt so strongly about not being involved with a bisexual woman, then you should have bailed the minute you found out I was one—not over a year later.

I hope you find someone you can trust, but I think that is less about finding the right woman and more about you.

Rachel

I hit the send button hard, less like dispatching a letter than throwing a rock. For the first time since Monday night, I feel a surge of power, a reprieve from the pain in my chest and the knot in my stomach. For just a moment, I feel strong.

I take a long shower—letting the water burn as hot as I can take it. I don't care about Zayde and the water bill. When I get out, I put on my favorite work outfit. This is something I learned from my mother one day in sixth grade when Andy Hoffsteter told me that he was breaking up with me because he liked Kristen Moskowicz better. I cried a lot that afternoon, and that night, before bed, Mom said, "Let's pick out your favorite, prettiest outfit for tomorrow. You're going to walk into that homeroom with your head held high and feeling good about yourself!"

I need to go to work, to be in a familiar place, to see Dr. Vargas and to tell her I am going to Santa Cruz. When I go downstairs, Zayde is asleep in his easy chair. I kiss him gently on the cheek, feeling the bristles of his whiskers and he stirs, opening his eyes.

"Shayna meydeleh, I've been worried about you," he says in a sleepy voice.

"I'm fine now, Zayde. I have to go to work."

"At least let me fix you some lunch?" he asks.

I am so moved by his wanting to take care of me. I can feel the hot tears threatening to gather. Straightening up and turning toward the kitchen before he can notice my eyes, I say, "No, but thank you. I'll grab something on my way in. I'll see you for dinner."

"But it's Wednesday. Don't you have the group you lead at that clinic downtown?"

The Neighborhood. I have totally forgotten. I don't know how I can make it through that many hours. I will call in sick from the college, ask Brenda if she can cover the group for me.

"No, Zayde, I forgot to tell you—the clinic is closed today because they're um, remodeling the office. I'll be home by six." I'm not feeling strong anymore. I am shaking from having not eaten, but don't want to look at food either. All I want to do is get through four hours at the college and then get back into bed.

∽

I'm not sure how I see the two clients I do that afternoon. My mind keeps wandering to Liz, wondering if she will email me back and what it might say. I catch myself, bring myself back to the client in front of me, then a minute later, catch myself again. It's like trying to meditate when your mind is racing, coming back to the breath over and over.

I knock on Dr. Vargas's door at four-thirty and she greets me with a huge smile. "Rachel, I've been waiting all day to hear your news. Come in here already."

"Well," I say with a forced grin, "I was accepted at both Emerson and U.C. Santa Cruz, and I accepted the offer at Santa Cruz."

She opens her arms wide to hug me, making me think for a split second of my Goddess with the quilt wings.

"Oh, I am so proud of you," she says, wrapping me in those strong arms.

That's when I lose it. I just bury my face in her shoulder and cry. When she helps me down onto the sofa and sits next to me, holding my hands, the imploring look on her face asking what it is, I tell her that, while I am grateful for having been accepted, all I am feeling is rejected.

Dr. Vargas has known about Liz from my various stories over the year. I tell her everything, the story spilling out of me so fast. I can't not tell her. She waits until I am done and simply says, "Rachel, I'm so so sorry."

"Yeah," I sniff. "Me, too."

"What do you need right now, Rachel?" asks Dr. Vargas in the gentlest of voices.

I think, but my head feels filled with only empty space. "I don't know."

❦

From: eabraham@alumni.yale.edu
To: rlevine@bscp.edu
Sent: Wednesday 4/1/98 5:14 PM
Subject: Re: Things you should know

My dearest Rachel,

I was glad to receive your email. I tried calling once but thought you might need some space. It has been a terrible few days. I want you to know that. Yes, ending our relationship is my choice and maybe that gives me no right to say that I'm suffering. But I want you to know that I do love you, and that this is a huge loss for me, too. I am desperately sad. At the same time, I know that this is what I need to do. I am so sorry.

Of course I will respect your wishes about Saturday morning services.

I understand and am deserving of your anger. I just hope one day you will forgive me.

You will make a brilliant psychologist and, if you ever feel that you want to contact me, I'd love to hear about your West Coast adventures.

Love,
Liz

When I see Kevin on Friday, I am silent for much of the hour. I hold the pillow to my chest, my feet tucked up under me, and just let the tears stream, rocking. Lucky curls tight against me, and I feel grateful for his warmth. Like Dr. Vargas, Kevin says little. He just witnesses my grieving, which is, I suppose, what I need most from him. It isn't until the following Friday, following a sluggish week of reengagement, putting one foot in front of the other through classes, clients, Wednesday night at The Neighborhood, that he offers an interpretation of sorts.

"You know, Rachel, I've been thinking about uncertainty."

"That's shocking," I say, deadpan, a little surprised by my own sarcasm.

Kevin smiles. "I suppose it has been a theme for us, hasn't it? You've been working so hard on managing your response to the uncertainties in your life. When I think about how you've grown in this way—how you've learned to tolerate the uncertainties of living a Jewish life that doesn't play by all of the prescribed rules of your grandfather's generation, how you worked so hard to sit with the unknown in the time before you got that letter about Charlie. But maybe, most importantly, how you have tolerated the uncertainty around your future with Liz. That might have been the most uncomfortable thing of all, and yet you let yourself feel the anxiety of not knowing where she stood and were able to stay present, in the relationship, despite all of that anxiety. It's really quite remarkable."

"Thanks," I say, shyly, not sure how to take this compliment.

"And, you know, you've always described Liz as somehow wiser than you—older, worldlier."

I nod.

"But the thing is . . . Liz can't sit with uncertainty at all. She ended the relationship because she *couldn't* tolerate the anxiety of not knowing what the future might bring for the two of you."

I let this sink in. "I know what you mean," I say. "I even said as much in that email I sent her—that finding someone she could trust was really about her own growth. I guess I never thought about it, though, as a way in which I've grown *more* than her. It's a little empowering to think about that."

"Keep that in your back pocket, and take it out when you need to remember," he says.

I thank him. It is a lovely gift.

In Shabbat services that Saturday, I find myself thinking about shmira. I think about how, when a person is alive, their soul knows where it lives—in the body. And then, when the body dies, there is this time between living in the body and moving on to the World to Come, where the soul is a bit lost, hovering near the body and, as the sages suggest, confused. I feel like that. I feel like, when the relationship with Liz was alive, my soul—or at least my heart—lived in the relationship. And, intellectually, I know that there will be a next world, that I will move on, though at this moment I may not fully believe it. But in this time in between the relationship and moving on, this time of confused hovering, I need shomrim—people to guard and soothe my soul until it is ready to take flight again.

This is when I am able to answer Dr. Vargas's question about what I need. I need guardians—witnesses to my sadness—to simply be by my side. I think about the way Kevin and Dr. Vargas both sat with me quietly. I think about Zayde sitting next to me here in our usual seats and take his hand. It doesn't matter that he doesn't know I am grieving. He is by my side. When I go back to Zayde's after services, I call Kara and Doreen and cry to them over the phone. I ask for shomrim, and my guardians are there.

Chapter 28

As the first flowers push their heads up out of the earth, I hang back. I don't want to smell them. The arrival of spring feels like an affront to my preferred darkness of bed. I listen to WBOS on my clock radio, just an arm's length away from my pillow. The weather forecasters have been talking for days about the possibility of a spring snowfall, saying that it's been years since they've seen a snow storm as late as the third week of April. Between songs, they are interviewing shoppers exiting a local Star Market with milk, bread, nor'easter essentials. Then, as predicted, just as the last of the winter's slush is drying up, down comes over a foot of heavy flakes. I watch in disbelief out my mother's old, foggy bedroom window, my hair frizzy and too many days unwashed.

When the weather reports say it is really over, I get on my snow boots, waterproof gloves, puffy ski jacket, and hat and head out to Sandal Street with Zayde's snow shovel and ice scraper in hand. The big white Mercury and my little Escort Essie are buried; the street is hushed and still. I've dug out our cars many times over the three winters I've lived here and I know how to do it—clearing the wheels and being careful not to scratch up the paint with the shovel. So as I start the chore of tackling all that snow, it feels familiar. Until it becomes rage.

I attack each new mound of heavy, wet snow with all of my might, bending my knees so that I might heave each shovelful out of the way. I work fast, breathing hard, letting the icy air sting my lungs. I don't stop when our cars are clear. I shovel the sidewalk and the steps. I clear the sidewalk in front of Mrs. Frank's house next door. I shovel until my back is burning with ache and my arms are like lead. And all the while I sing those lines from that Dar William's song I'd heard her perform on that snowy night the previous winter. *"This is where I let my pain go. This is where I let my pain go."*

Of course, I don't really let it go that day. But I do turn a gentle curve of a corner and feel ready to live my last weeks in Boston fully. And just as quickly as that blizzard came, the snow begins to melt, and the sun appears, and it is spring again.

During the first week of May, Kara calls and answers my "Hello?" by jumping into monologue. "Clear your calendar for this Sunday. Doreen and I are coming up to Boston for the day and picking you up at ten! Oh, and bring some money. Or just a credit card."

"Who is this?" I tease. "Where are you taking me? And how much money are we talking about?"

"Never mind about that. See you Sunday." Click.

They arrive at exactly 10:02 on Sunday morning. It is sunny, and the forecast says that it is going to reach 67 degrees.

"Okay, where are we going?" I ask as I climb into the back seat of Kara's old Jeep Cherokee. I realize that they must have picked up the car at her parents' house in Connecticut after taking the train there from New York the night before. I notice how much they've planned for this.

"Rockport!" they scream in unison.

"Where's Rockport?" I scream back, mimicking their excitement. *Isn't Rockport in Maine?*

"We researched it—it's just up the coast," says Kara. "Word is, it's the cutest little beach town ever, up above Gloucester on Cape Ann."

"Seriously? Why have I not heard of this place?"

"Neither have we," says Doreen, turning from the front passenger seat, her red curls bouncing over her left shoulder. "But you haven't because you've been buried in graduate school and applications and your grandfather and Liz stuff. And now, you get to experience a day in one of Massachusetts's most quaint towns. Because we are wild like that."

I laugh. "Awesome. But what about the money?"

"Oh, that's to buy your ring," says Doreen, all business, carefully placing her steaming cup of Dunkin Donuts coffee back in the cup holder.

"You guys are buying me a ring?"

"No," says Kara, pulling onto the on-ramp for 93 North. "*You* are going to buy yourself a ring. There are apparently lots of cute little jewelry places in Rockport—funky stuff by local artists."

"Okay, but why exactly am I buying myself a ring today?"

"Oh, that comes from Shelley—this woman in my office?" says Doreen, now fully turning in her seat so that I can see her. "She has this ritual, that whenever she breaks up with a guy—"

"It doesn't have to be a guy," interrupts Kara, shooting Doreen a chastising glance.

"Right, well for her it's a guy, but whatever—whenever she goes through a break-up, she buys a 'commitment to herself' ring. Like, a ring to remind her that she is always her own best friend and that that counts more than anyone who may come or go in her romantic life."

"Huh." I sit with this. "You know, if you had told me this a month ago, I would have yelled at you to turn this car around. But actually, I'm kind of into it. I kind of love it."

"We thought you might," says Kara.

I can see her wry smile in the rearview mirror. She cranks up her tape player and the three of us belt out our favorite song from *Rent*.

> *In daylights, in sunsets*
> *In midnights, in cups of coffee*
> *In inches, in miles, in laughter, in strife*
> *In five hundred twenty-five thousand six hundred minutes*
> *How do you measure, a year in the life?*

❧

There is no finer present than this day in Rockport. We eat home-made ice cream, feel the sun on our faces, laugh with the squawk of seagulls. As the afternoon begins to stretch toward evening, I take in a long deep breath of salt air and say, "You guys, this day has been like balm to me."

"Rach, it's 'da bomb' not 'like bomb.'" This, Doreen.

"I think she said it's like 'balm,' weirdo." Kara.

I laugh. "Yeah, like salve you know? Like just the healing kind of day I've needed."

"But you still haven't found a ring," says Doreen, pouting out her lower lip.

"There's one store left that we haven't explored," I say, motioning toward a little boutique up ahead with a porch and a rustic, New England-style wooden sign with the words "The Treasure Chest" burned in. It is, indeed, full of treasures of all sorts—hammocks, wall art, shells, some clothes (loose, gauzy beach things), and jewelry. I know right away when I see it—in a little glass case that says, "Recycled Sea Glass Jewelry by Aviva Stackman, Cape Ann." There, among a beautiful collection of sea glass pieces, is my ring. It is a thick silver band, inlaid with chips of pale green sea glass, handcrafted by a local Jewish woman no less. I try it on. It fits my right index finger perfectly.

"Oh, it's so beautiful!" gasps Doreen. "But shouldn't you find one that fits your ring finger. You know, for the full symbolic impact?"

"No," I say, shaking my head. "This is exactly right. In Jewish weddings, the ring is placed on the woman's right index finger during the ceremony—I think it has to do with being closer to the heart or something. Or maybe it has to do with reading the Torah with a pointer that looks like the right index finger. The seat of wisdom maybe? Anyway, it feels right to keep it exactly where it is."

"Then that's all that matters." Kara puts her arm around me and gives a tight squeeze. It is the just-right end to a just-right day.

But on the car ride back from Rockport, I become consumed with sadness—not because of Liz—but because the reality that I have only four weeks left in Boston finally hits me.

"What day are you moving, again?" asks Kara, glancing at me in the rearview mirror, sensing something.

"June 7th. It's a Sunday. My classes end next week, and I finish up my externship at the counseling center the last week of May. I thought I'd give myself a week to spend some time with Zayde, pack up, all that. I was actually going to leave a few days earlier, but Zayde just told me that he arranged to host the luncheon that Saturday at our synagogue in honor of my move."

"That's so nice!" says Doreen.

I think about my three years living with Zayde. I will miss him, and Rabbi Stein, and the experience of being a part of the Beth El community. "I think so, too."

The next weeks are all about termination. I say goodbye to my clients, transferring those who need to stay in treatment to the new trainees who will be starting in August. I say goodbye to the teens at The Neighborhood. I have only met with them for ten sessions but I am seriously attached to several kids and feel jealous of the volunteer (a twenty-something gay man who'd been joining me as co-leader for the last several meetings) who will spend his future Wednesday evenings with them. I say goodbye to Dr. Vargas and to Kevin, crying through those last meetings. It is said in psychology circles that every loss brings up every former loss. My last months in Boston are so full of goodbyes that I can't even tease out what I am feeling in each instance. Saying goodbye to Kevin is saying goodbye to Dr. Vargas is saying goodbye to my clients is saying goodbye to Liz. It is all a tangle of endings.

I am the star of the Shabbat luncheon. During services, the rabbi calls me up to the Torah for an alliyah. She puts her arm around me, the way she'd done to Liz that first time I saw her, and offers me a blessing. At the luncheon, the congregants I've come to know over the past three years come up to me for hugs and congratulatory pats on the back. Murray Goldblatt pinches my cheek. I am relieved to notice that Pearl Zimmerman isn't among the congregants this morning and wonder if she noticed the luncheon in my honor listed in the monthly bulletin and decided to stay home.

Zayde, Bess, and I are among the last to exit the building, having lingered over our fruit salad and cinnamon rugelach. When we get up to leave, Zayde excuses himself to the men's room, while I accompany Bess to the little coat room where, despite the warm, June day, she has hung her long trench coat.

I am helping her on with it when she turns to me and almost whispers, "Rachel, I've been looking for a moment alone with you. I think I owe you an apology."

"What could you possibly need to apologize for, Bess?" I ask, leaning toward her in a similarly hushed tone, though I don't know why.

"I didn't realize dear, back when I had that conversation with Lew, oh it was months ago now, that he didn't know about your relationship with the Abraham girl. If I'd realized he didn't know, I never would have—"

The coat room begins spinning around us. I find myself hearing her voice but as if from some faraway place, over a speaker, echoing and muffled. My mouth goes dry.

"Wait," I say. "Bess, I don't know what you're talking about."

"When I came to the house that day to talk to him about coming back to shul? It occurred to me that maybe he was making a stink over your lifestyle and that it wasn't just about the rabbi and her progressive ways. I asked him straight out. 'Lew' I said, 'if this is about Rachel and that Elizabeth Abraham being lesbians, I think you need to get past it.' Well, he just about took my head off with that bark of his. 'Oh shut up, Bess,'" she imitates. "'I don't know what you're talking about!' Rachel, dear, I never would have said anything if I thought he didn't know. I just hope he hasn't been impossible to live with, that's all."

I cross my arms, tucking in my hands to hide the shaking, sweat blooming out of every pore. "No, Bess. He hasn't been impossible to live with . . ." And then he is there, in the doorway of the little coat room, his keys to the Mercury jingling in his big hand.

"I wondered where you ladies were hiding!" he says.

As we follow him down the steps to the side parking lot, I hold on tight to the banister and to the fact that I am leaving in the morning.

After we drop Bess off and park the car on Sandal Street, I thank Zayde again for the luncheon and say that I need to do a few errands in Harvard Square. I run into the house and change into sneakers, yoga pants, and a T-shirt. I want—I need—to walk. Like the middle-aged women in sweat suits powerwalking in the mall before the stores open, I am purposeful and fast. I don't know where I am going but the urge to put distance between myself and the house drives me onward.

When had Bess come to the house? Was it November? Has Zayde known about Liz and me since November? Did he not believe her? Did he not hear her correctly?

I don't know what to believe but I do know that I have to talk to someone about it. I could call Doreen and Kara or call Zeke, but I am already in Harvard Square, descending the stairs to the T. I am going to Central Square to find Liz.

ↅ

I ring the buzzer four times before accepting that Liz isn't home. I rest my forehead against the frame of her front door, feeling the jagged curls of peeling paint press into my hairline. I'm not sure why I am here, but the fact that she isn't makes me feel alone and angry. I am holding a bucket brimming with words and imagine heaving them in her face, drenching her with them, though I am only just starting to parse out what they are. *What does this mean about Zayde and me? Why am I going to California tomorrow? Why wasn't I enough?*

The coffee shop across Mass Ave from Liz's has put tables and chairs outside on the sidewalk as they always do at this time of year. I cross at the corner and run in to order an iced coffee. If I sit at one of those tables, I can watch for her to come home.

I wait for almost an hour, all the while deliberating about whether or not I should just go. *I don't need her. I don't.* And yet.

And then I see them. Laughing, walking toward Liz's block from the exit of the T. There is no question that they are together, the way they walk without any space between them, their shoulders pressing. I don't realize right away that I know her, this woman in my spot. Then I place her—on the ladder, at The Neighborhood, that first day fixing the light. The day I wore the skirt and the ballet sweater and wished I hadn't.

I am grateful to be sitting. It is as if everything inside me—physical things: organs, blood vessels—are falling and falling and falling. It feels like a sink hole has opened up in the sidewalk beneath my chair and everything about me—my body and soul both—are plummeting.

I wait until they go inside before standing too quickly. Instantly, I hear ringing in my ears and feel a wave a nausea that lands me back in the chair. A middle-aged man at the next table asks if I am all right.

"Fine," I lie, pretending to tie my sneaker so that I can bend over and get the blood back into my head. When I stand again, it is slow and deliberate. I put one foot in front of the other, begging my feet to take me far away from what I've just seen. *Just one, then the other, one, then the other . . .* all the way back to Sandal Street.

Chapter 29

As I edge Essie between an SUV and a convertible on a side street near Santa Cruz's Pacific Garden Mall, I don't even notice how good I've become at parallel parking. My years on Sandal Street have made me quite the city parker, and Essie and I, after traveling across the country together, are like the dearest of old friends. My mother, pointing out her rust spots and twice-repaired cassette player, calls her "that hunk of junk," but I swear I'll drive her until the day she dies.

I am surprised to see that the Pacific Garden Mall is not a mall at all, but a lush, outdoor shopping plaza where I hope to buy some warmer clothes, not having expected Santa Cruz to be so chilly at night in the summer. I visit a café first though, and sit at a little iron table outside, people-watching and eating a Panini with thick avocado slices. An older woman wearing a thin wrap around her shoulders sits alone at the table next to me. She reminds me a little of Bess and I smile at her.

"Beautiful day," she says, smiling back with perfect teeth, which seem a little too big for her mouth. I think they might be dentures.

"It is. This is my first week in town and it's lovely. We don't have malls like this on the East Coast."

"Ain't that the truth! I grew up in New Hampshire, and it was just too cold most of the year for sitting outside like this. I moved to Santa Cruz when I was thirty and never looked back. It's a special place, this town. We've come a long way since we got clobbered in '89."

"Clobbered?"

"Yes—you do know about the earthquake, don't you?" Her eyes widen and she leans in a bit.

"Oh, yes—I know," I lie. I don't know. "Um, it was bad, wasn't it?"

"Oh, this whole area was very badly damaged—buildings torn apart, businesses ruined. But each year, there's more rebuilding—"

"Janet?" A middle-aged woman walking by in pink scrubs interrupts us. She stops at my new friend's table.

"Oh, Ellie! Hello. I was just talking to this lovely young woman who's just moved to town. What is your name, dear?"

"Oh, Rachel Levine." I shake Janet's hand and then Ellie's.

"I'm Janet and this is Ellie—she used to be my physical therapist after my hip replacement."

We all chat briefly and then I excuse myself to go shop. It is true what they say about people being more friendly out West; I can tell already. As I stroll Pacific Garden, I see it everywhere—store owners chatting with customers they seem to know well, people dropping dollar bills into the coffee cans of musicians busking on the sidewalk. Though I hadn't been to Santa Cruz before that devastating earthquake, I wonder if the people here are more united in the years since, more familial to one another, the way people often are after coming through a crisis together. Downtown Santa Cruz feels like a colony of survivors, and, though I certainly haven't survived anything remotely as tragic, I feel as if I belong here, as if I might rightfully be counted among them.

The university, with its turnover in population, feels less identified with the earthquake and more with its progressive politics. I get to know it on little solo visits, exploring campus with a map I picked up at the University Center, trying not to look like my dad navigating his way out of Penn Station so many years ago. Despite the fact that students won't be back for several weeks, there are a smattering of fliers and handmade posters, perhaps leftover from the spring semester, hanging on campus bulletin boards announcing events and meetings. Black Sistas United and the Black Men's Alliance are co-sponsoring a lecture. The Latin Dance Troupe is holding auditions. I feel at home—like at a sister school of my beloved Wesleyan. I realize that, despite the Santa Cruz counseling center being my second choice for internship, it is where I am supposed to be.

The two other pre-doctoral interns and I are able to sublet a beautiful three-bedroom house from a faculty member who is on sabbatical and spending the year abroad with her family. The house is just off campus, on a pretty street called Limestone Lane where a lot of faculty live. We three, all women in our twenties, immediately fall in love with the house, which is decorated in a southwest motif and has an unusual number of throw pillows and blankets. We spend our evenings wrapped up in them on the back deck, eating the experimental meals we've stir-fried from the food we've picked up at the farmer's market.

I don't go back East at all that year, somewhat daring myself to make it on my own for the whole eleven months. I do, however, have lots of visitors including four wonderful days with just Zeke during his December break. I love showing off my almost-doctor baby brother to my new friends and colleagues. We drive up and down the coast, eat at Upper Crust Pizza on Mission Street, and build a killer sand castle at the beach like the ones we used to make at the Jersey Shore when we were little. On the last day of his visit, I take Zeke to my favorite walking trail in the State Park just north of campus.

"Can you believe this is just ten minutes from my house?" I say, still giddy with all of the newness of my temporary California home.

"I just can't believe I've never seen trees this tall!" says Zeke, looking up with his mouth slightly open like a thrilled little boy. "These are amazing!" He runs then, almost skips, and I chase him.

We come to an especially tall redwood with a huge, hollow trunk, and watch as giggling kids come tumbling out of it like clowns from a small car, first three, then a fourth, then a fifth. The two sets of parents who belong to them sit at a nearby picnic table watching, bemused.

"I want to go in there," whispers Zeke.

"You'll have to wait your turn," I whisper back with the exaggerated expression of one speaking to an eager toddler.

When the parents gather their squealing kids and move on, Zeke grabs my hand. "Come on!" He pulls me over to the wide, gaping trunk. We dive in. It is dark like a cave; I can't see my hand in front of my face.

"Let's sit here," I suggest, turning back to the opening in the great bark and sitting half in, my legs sticking out into the daylight. I pat the ground next to me for Zeke, and he takes his place by my side. With the families gone, the woods have become quiet and still. We sit, feeling the tree over and around us like the most primal of shelters. I think of Zayde's big hand surrounding my little fist from so many years ago.

"Zeke, tell me more about your trip to Somerville this fall." He and my parents had gone up to spend Rosh Hashanah with Zayde; it was the first year I hadn't.

"Everyone at Beth El was asking about you. I was like 'chopped liva' to them," he says with thick New York, Yiddish emphasis.

"I'm sure you weren't chopped liver."

"Seriously, that woman Zayde's friends with, Bess? She wanted to know all about how you were and where you were spending the holidays. The rabbi asked about you, too."

I smile. He doesn't mention whether he met Liz at Beth El. I don't ask. "How did Zayde seem to you? Sometimes when I call him on Fridays, he seems a little confused."

"He was okay. A little slower, maybe. And, he sleeps late now. I stayed at his place instead of with Mom and Dad at the hotel, and I was up before him both mornings. I even made breakfast! I think Mom has been toying with the idea of asking him to move down closer to her and Dad."

"I'm not surprised. I'm sure it's really hard for him to be living on his own."

"You know, he did do one really bizarre thing while I was there."

"What's that?" I ask, holding my breath, fearing what Zayde might have said about me.

"Both mornings, you know how I said I was downstairs before him? When he came down the steps, he stopped just before the bottom and called out, 'Good morning, Rachel!' It was like he thought you were still there or something. I didn't say anything about it but it was weird, you know?"

"Huh," is all I say.

As we sit and listen to the sounds of the forest a few minutes longer, I press the palms of my hands into the pine-needled ground beneath us. I think of the violent shaking, the shifting and sliding that earthquake had surely brought to these woods on that long-ago October day, imagining the jarring jolt of branches, the crashing down of limbs.

I hear myself say, "I wonder how a tree this old and tall survives an earthquake."

"You know, the whole intertwining of roots," says Zeke, a little matter-of-factly.

"What?" I had thought it was a rhetorical question.

"I saw it on the Discovery Channel. There was this whole documentary about redwood forests. They have really shallow root systems, but when they're next to other redwoods, they intertwine their roots with the roots from trees around them."

I look out at the trees, amazed at this hidden network of support they provide one another.

Noticing the awe in my face, Zeke nudges me with his shoulder. When I look at him, he is smiling at me and simply says, "They hold each other up."

2019

I am on the bimah again, in a different shul in a different town, about to recite the blessing before the Torah reading. This morning's Torah portion will be chanted by my son, who is becoming a Bar Mitzvah today. I can barely look at him, my little Gabriel Lew, with his crazy curls and his still pre-pubescent baby face; I am afraid I will burst into tears and he will never forgive me for the mortification. I am swollen to bursting with the intensity of my pride in him.

So I don't look. Instead I let my eyes wander out to the congregation—to Zeke and Becca, Rose and Lindsay between them. To my parents—my dad's eyes brimming, my mom sitting up so straight nodding at Gabriel as if to say, "Yes, yes, you are doing it, my sweet grandson." To my in-laws one row over, following along in the prayer book they are sharing. To Doreen and Kara and their families. To Dr. Vargas who has become a dear friend and has traveled from Boston to be here today.

I suddenly remember the Hebrew words that were embroidered on the heavy curtain covering the arc on the bimah at Beth El. I hear Zayde's whisper in my little girl ear, *"Know before whom you stand."* I hear the crinkle of hard candy wrappers. I smell dusting powder and old upholstery. Without thought, my right fingertips brush over the nails of my left fingers; I find my bubbe's ridges there.

There is so much I can't know. *Will my father's recent test results come back negative? Will my marriage last forever? Are the souls of my grandparents in this sanctuary with us today? Is God?*

These questions live within me, but I live within something greater. As my eyes scan the room, I feel held. Held by the people that matter and the love that they give. They are my guardians, my shomrim.

And I know before whom I stand.

Acknowledgments

In the beginning, there was Rabbi Rachel Brown, who caught all of my halachic mistakes, especially that Zayde would never have bought Campbell's soup because it isn't kosher. Thank you for being my first reader and cheerleader.

I offer so much love to my friends and early readers Daniel Coplon-Newfield, Jennifer Shotkin, Kendra Smith, Mary Hufnell, Leslie Lenox, and Lisa Yost. You have accompanied me on this journey for eight years and I thank each of you. To my cousin, Susan Baer, you get the amazing proofreader award.

To my dear friend, Leah Cohen: thank you for reading, for blurbing, but most importantly for believing in me and for helping me see that I could do this.

To Rabbi Deborah Waxman, Idit Klein, and Sharon Chatkupt Lee: your early reading and words of endorsement are so appreciated. Thank you for lifting this story up.

Thank you to Ruth Greenstein of Greenline Publishing for our early meetings, for your kind advice, and for pointing me toward Julie Miesionczek, my fabulous editor. Julie, you helped me bring Rachel to life, and I will be forever grateful.

To Rabbi Jeff Sultar: thank you for the D'var Torah that explained

how Redwood trees hold one another up, and for prominently dis-
playing דע לפני מי אתה עומד on your podium.

I am eternally grateful to Elizabeth Wagenheim for teaching me
about the Earthquake of 1989, for your ongoing support, and for
introducing me to She Writes Press.

To all the amazing women of She Writes Press and the SparkPoint
Studio family, especially to my publisher Brooke Warner, my edito-
rial manager Samantha Strom, cover designer Julie Metz, proofreader
Laura Matthews, and interior designer Kiran Spees: thank you for
championing debut women writers, for your passion and vision, and
for saying yes.

To Books Forward and my dedicated publicist Jackie Karneth,
thank you for helping me get *Closer to Fine* into the hands of readers.

And last but never least, to my beautiful family, Jon, Zachary, and
Talia: you have supported me and this project for so many years.
Thank you for your encouragement and love, and for being my home.

About the Author

© Rachel Gregory Photography

Jodi Rosenfeld is a clinical psychologist specializing in anxiety and acceptance-based therapies. She holds a degree in English and Women's Studies from Tufts University and a doctorate from the Massachusetts School of Professional Psychology (now William James College). She lives with her husband and two teenaged children in the western suburbs of Philadelphia and will be starting rabbinical school in fall of 2021. *Closer to Fine* is her first novel.

SELECTED TITLES FROM SHE WRITES PRESS

She Writes Press is an independent publishing company founded to serve women writers everywhere. Visit us at www.shewritespress.com.

The Rooms Are Filled by Jessica Null Vealitzek $16.95, 978-1-938314-58-2
The coming-of-age story of two outcasts—a nine-year-old boy who just lost his father, and a closeted young woman—brought together by circumstance.

Bess and Frima by Alice Rosenthal $16.95, 978-1-63152-439-4
Bess and Frima, best friends from the Bronx, find romance at their summer jobs at Jewish vacation hotels in the Catskills—and as love mixes with war, politics, creative ambitions, and the mysteries of personality, they leave girlhood behind them.

Profound and Perfect Things by Maribel Garcia $16.95, 978-1631525414
When Isa, a closeted lesbian with conservative Mexican parents, has a one-night stand that results in an unwanted pregnancy, her sister, Cristina adopts the baby—but twelve years later, Isa, who regrets giving up her child, threatens to spill the secret of her daughter's true parentage.

How to Grow an Addict by J.A. Wright $16.95, 978-1-63152-991-7
Raised by an abusive father, a detached mother, and a loving aunt and uncle, Randall Grange is built for addiction. By twenty-three, she knows that together, pills and booze have the power to cure just about any problem she could possibly have . . . right?

Beautiful Garbage by Jill DiDonato $16.95, 978-1-938314-01-8
Talented but troubled young artist Jodi Plum leaves suburbia for the excitement of the city—and is soon swept up in the sexual politics and downtown art scene of 1980s New York.

The Fourteenth of September by Rita Dragonette $16.95, 978-1-63152-453-0
In 1969, as mounting tensions over the Vietnam War are dividing America, a young woman in college on an Army scholarship risks future and family to go undercover in the anti-war counterculture when she begins to doubt her convictions—and is ultimately forced to make a life-altering choice as fateful as that of any Lottery draftee.